playing for keeps

ANDREA MICHELLE WOOD

Playing for Keeps
Home to Heritage, Book 4

Published by Sunrise Media Group LLC
Copyright © 2025 by Sunrise Media Group LLC

Print ISBN: 978-1-966463-07-8

This book is a work of fiction. Names, characters, places, and incidents are either products of the author's imagination or used fictitiously. Any similarity to actual people, organizations, and/or events is purely coincidental.

Scripture quotations are from The ESV® Bible (The Holy Bible, English Standard Version®), © 2001 by Crossway, a publishing ministry of Good News Publishers. Used by permission. All rights reserved.

Scripture quotations are taken from the Holy Bible, New International Version®, NIV®. Copyright © 1973, 1978, 1984, 2011 by Biblica, Inc®. Used by permission of Zondervan. All rights reserved worldwide.

For more information about Andrea Michelle Wood, Tari Faris, or Susan May Warren, please access the author's website at the following address: andreamichellewood.com, tarifaris.com, or susanmaywarren.com.

Published in the United States of America.
Cover Design: Tari Faris
Editing: Barbara Curtis

To my daughters.
Always follow your dreams.

"For this light momentary affliction is preparing
for us an eternal weight of glory beyond all com-
parison, as we look not to the things that are
seen but to the things that are unseen. For the
things that are seen are transient, but the things
that are unseen are eternal."

2 CORINTHIANS 4:17-18 ESV

LOCKED OUT? THIS COULDN'T BE HAPPENING. Piper Caveneau wiggled the doorknob to the hundred-year-old Victorian rental again as if it would miraculously give way.

Nope. She should have known the antique door handle wouldn't automatically unlock when she opened it.

Now what? She'd been careful to lock every door when her new roommates left, so the back door was undoubtedly locked too. She didn't even know anyone in town except for her roommates, Jess Gable and Devin Hendrixson. Although saying she knew Jess's cousin Devin was a stretch. Piper had only met her a few hours ago when she moved in, but she seemed kind and an easy person to have as a roommate.

She and Jess, on the other hand, had been roommates through-out college and were going on their sixth year of friendship. Jess, the art teacher at Heritage High, had been the one to call Piper last Friday to tell her that the school was looking for a long-term sub for English. Piper had never been to the small, quaint Michigan town, but without a job and with bills piling up, she had jumped at it.

Piper crossed the front porch to the bay window and peered into the living room. She could just make out the cozy couch and recliner through the reflection in the glass. Pearl, the resident French bulldog, stared back at her from the couch, head tilted. Jess had warned her not to leave Pearl uncrated, but the pup seemed docile enough.

Piper reached for her phone but came up empty. Of course she'd left it inside. Looked like she'd just have to wait for one of her two roommates to get back before she could get in.

Piper walked back to the steps and sank down on the top one. She'd just run out to her car to grab the bag of hangers she'd left in the back seat. Nothing like packing her entire life and moving towns in under three days.

She rubbed her bare arms as the September sun gradually melted into the horizon, draining away the heat of the day and leaving behind a reminder that autumn had arrived. At least she'd gotten locked out in a town that could be featured in a Norman Rockwell painting rather than her former low-budget apartment in Chicago. Moving to Heritage, Michigan, had been the one good decision she'd made lately.

She leaned her head against the porch railing and stared across the street at an old one-room schoolhouse that could've been plucked from the pages of one of Laura Ingalls Wilder's books. She'd have to explore it later, but with the Sunday-evening sun low in the sky, most everything appeared closed for the day.

Over by the gazebo in the center of the square, she could just make out a large brass hippo that rested with its belly on the sidewalk. Her first Otis sighting. Since their college days, she'd heard Jess's stories of the wandering brass hippo that mysteriously moved around the town square when no one was watching.

Pearl's bark from the other side of the door pierced the peace of the evening, and Piper jumped to her feet and rushed back to the window.

Her phone, sitting on the end table by the couch, was lit up with a text as it vibrated. She squinted to see who it was from. She could see better with her glasses than with the contacts she usually wore, but even with her glasses it was too far. Pearl continued to bark at it until the vibrating stopped. Piper started to turn back toward the steps but stopped when Pearl jumped on the couch. The dog approached the phone with caution, then began nosing it. *Oh no.* Hadn't Jess said something about getting a new phone recently because of something to do with the dog?

Piper knocked on the window. "No, Pearl."

The dog stared at her a moment then got her teeth on the edge of the phone and took off.

"No!"

Waiting was no longer an option.

Piper hurried down the steps and peered up at the second-story window to her new bedroom, the glass reflecting the brilliant colors of the sunset save for the sliver where the window was cracked open. It couldn't be the *only* open window, right?

God, please help me get in—and soon.

It had been years since God had come through for her, but she'd cover all the bases anyway.

Piper circled the house, but as expected, the back door was locked as well, and she found no other open windows. Maybe she could get one open.

After forcing her way between two bushes in front of the dining room window, she stretched to her tiptoes, reaching for the sill, but came up several inches short. Sure, her five-foot-four was handy for extra leg room on flights, but top shelves and high windows, not so much. She scanned the landscaping until she spotted the hose reel. Would that hold her weight?

Piper disconnected the apparatus and heaved it over to position it under the window. Who knew an empty hose was this heavy? She wiped her brow and came away with a brown smudge on the back of her hand. Perfect. Her first order of business as the newest resident would be a shower.

She braced one foot on the reel and balanced her weight and walked her hands up the wall as she pushed up to a stand. Then, holding the wall with one hand, she stretched again for the window.

"Can I help you?" A deep voice came from behind her.

Piper flinched, and her pulse ratcheted into high gear as the spool shifted slightly. She clung to the grooves in the siding and managed to catch her balance, then carefully turned her head. Directly behind her stood a tall guy in gym shorts and a T-shirt that strained across his broad shoulders and hugged his tanned biceps. His hands rested on his hips, and his brow arched while one corner of his lips tipped up just enough to give her the impression that he was amused. His sandy-blond curls and friendly blue eyes softened his imposing physique and gave him a boy-next-door appeal. An orthopedic brace on one knee and a slightly crooked nose were the only hints of imperfection on him.

She tried to angle more toward him, but the spool rotated, taking her feet out from under her. She flapped her arms wildly, searching for a handhold to no avail. Her heart dropped as she tumbled backward into the bushes, the juniper boughs thwacking into her back and thighs, then bending and snapping at the impact that knocked the breath from her lungs.

Ouch! Her joggers and sports tank offered little protection against the prickly branches or the humiliation of her clumsy landing. And now everything was out of focus. She must have lost her glasses in the fall.

An instant later, the specimen of a man, now fuzzy, offered her his hand as he hovered over her. "You okay?"

She grasped his hand, and he pulled her up onto her feet with seemingly little effort. "Thanks."

She turned back toward the mutilated bush, scanning the blurry foliage in the waning light.

The guy stooped down and picked something up from the mulch between the bushes. "Looking for these?"

"Yes!" She took her tortoiseshell frames and slid them on, focusing her vision.

Man, he was tall. Like, more than a foot taller than her.

Piper smoothed her faded joggers, not that straightening her work clothes was going to increase her appeal. Sure, she was pretty enough if she put in a little effort, but with no makeup, her generic brown eyes and freckle-speckled face were nothing special. Even her long dark hair, usually her best feature, was hanging limp in a frayed ponytail.

"Why are you trying to break into my friend Jess's house?" He reached out and pulled a twig from her hair.

Right, she wasn't just barefaced and in her grubby clothes, she was a regular bush woman. So much for making a good impression. Not that she needed to make a good impression on a stranger. Although, if he was friends with Jess, maybe he would be worth getting to know. "I'm her new roommate."

"She didn't give you a key?" His brow raised again as if he was beginning to doubt her story.

She straightened her shoulders. "It's inside with my phone. And I can't convince Pearl to open the door."

She nodded toward the window.

He seemed to finally believe her and nodded as he extended his hand. "Welcome to Heritage."

Piper slid her hand into his, and it engulfed hers. "Piper."

"Titus." He dropped his hand and stepped back. "So, is breaking and entering a hobby of yours?"

"I'm a beginner. Clearly I need more practice."

"I'd recommend waiting until after dark and wearing all black. Also"—he pointed to the hose reel—"maybe bring a ladder."

Was it her imagination, or was he actually flirting with her? She stole a glance at his left hand. No ring, although that didn't necessarily mean he was unattached. "Noted. I'll try that next time."

He stepped between the bushes with his good leg and reached up to try the window. It didn't budge, but the flex of his triceps when he made the effort was a beautiful thing. "Unless we break the window, I don't think you're going to get in through here. How did you manage to get locked out, anyway? I'd be shocked if Jess locks her doors. No one around here does."

"Well, that should make my future as a cat burglar much easier."

Titus snorted a laugh. "You came to the right place for that profession."

Oh my. He had dimples when he smiled. *Dimples*. And a really nice smile that crinkled the corners of his eyes.

"I just moved from Chicago, so it's habit to lock all the doors when I'm home alone."

"It's customary to lock them while you're on the inside." He flashed his dimples again.

"I knew I was forgetting something." She motioned toward her twelve-year-old dark blue Buick in the driveway. "I just ran out to Ol' Blue to grab something. I didn't realize that the door doesn't automatically unlock when you open it."

"Is Chicago where you're from or were you a transplant there?"

"I've been a transplant all my life. We moved around a lot, all over the Midwest. My family lives in the Upper Peninsula now."

"You're a long way from home, then." Titus picked up the hose reel and carried it back over to the spigot. He favored the braced leg.

"Closer than Chicago." Not that she'd be making the trip anytime soon. She pointed to the brace. "You okay moving that with your knee?"

"It's fine. I had surgery a while back. I'm still trying to get it back up to full strength." His biceps strained against the T-shirt sleeves as he nestled the hose reel back into its place.

Nice, hot, and helpful? Yeah, this guy was a fantasy, and thus, way out of her league. She'd learned the hard way not to go after guys like this. Although, not every good-looking guy was dishonest, right?

He scanned the side of the house and stepped into the landscaping to check the other window. "You haven't found any open windows?"

"Just my bedroom, but it's upstairs."

"Let's check the ground floor windows first. Maybe one will be unlocked." Titus headed toward the backyard and opened the gate in the fence, motioning for her to go through first. "So, what brings you here from Chicago?"

Piper stepped through and waited as he latched the gate. "I got a job."

Even if it was temporary, it gave her a shot at a good reference, or maybe even a foot in the door for the next school year. It was sure better than biding her time waitressing and depending on tips to pay her rent until schools started hiring again in the spring.

Titus tried the window that led to the kitchen then moved on to try the next window. "This isn't the most exciting town, but there is something homey about it."

"So far, the locals sure seem friendly." She gestured to him. "This is the kind of place I think I would've liked to have grown up in. My family moved around every few years when I was a kid."

"I guess I took it for granted. I couldn't wait to get out of here and explore the world." Titus reached across the egress well under the window to Jess's craft room and ran his fingers along the windowsill. "I went to college in Ann Arbor, then worked for a few years in Kansas City. I think this one might be unlocked, but I can't get a grip on it."

"Maybe we can find something to pry it open." Piper scanned the backyard and spotted a long wooden handle propped against the garden shed. She jogged over and found a hoe, then turned to find him behind her. "Will this work?"

"Perfect." He took the tool from her and walked back toward the window.

"What brought you back to town? Did you miss it?" Piper had to speedwalk to keep up with his long strides.

"I'm not back to stay. I was between jobs, and an old friend asked me to come back and help him out for a few months." He lifted the hoe so the long handle protruded up against the side of the house and slid the blade into the narrow crack between the window and the sill.

She didn't miss his evasive half answer. Then again, she wasn't anxious to divulge the drama that led her here either. "Do you still have family around?"

"My mom is here along with my youngest sister. My two brothers are both in college." Titus pulled back on the handle, and the window shifted upward slightly, then stuck. "Can you get something to hold it open?"

She searched the ground and spotted a short fragment of a broken branch. She grabbed it and stretched over the trench to jam it into the crack under the window. "Big family. My brother and I didn't have any other siblings."

He set the hoe down and rested it against the house, then focused on her. "Are you close in age?"

His gaze sent a shiver down Piper's spine. Those deep blue eyes, flecked with green in the center, actually seemed invested in what she had to say. "I'd say. They call us Irish twins because he's only eleven months younger than me. It was nice to have a built-in friend when we were always the new kids in school."

"You and your brother must be close, huh?" He wedged his fingers under the window, but it didn't budge.

She rubbed at the gooseflesh on her arms when a cool gust bit at the residual warmth. "Yeah. We've lived far apart the last few years, but we still talk on the phone almost every day."

Titus leaned across the window well and braced one arm on the sill, then shoved up with the other hand. It finally gave way and opened several more inches.

Piper scanned the landscaping and spotted a large garden gnome. She heaved it up. What was this thing made out of? Cement? She tried to lift it to the window, but she couldn't hold the thing with one hand and couldn't lean far enough over the window well with both hands extended.

Titus chuckled. He grabbed the gnome with one of his giant hands and easily fit it under the window to prop it open.

"Looks like I need to add a grappling hook and climbing harness to my heist tool kit." Piper surveyed the trench under the window. At this point, her second-floor bedroom might be easier. At least the roof of the porch was below it to climb on.

Titus braced his hands on the corrugated metal lip and fluidly jumped thigh deep into the well. He winced when he landed, but covered it quickly. He linked his fingers together to create a stirrup. "I'll give you a boost."

"This is a hundred and twenty pounds of awkward klutz." She motioned to her body. "You've already seen my finesse in action. Are you sure you want to risk it?"

His eyes twinkled with mirth as he smiled up at her. "I bench twice that much without breaking a sweat. I think I'll be okay."

If he hadn't already noticed how terribly her ratty old pink slippers clashed with her teal joggers, he would now. She was never leaving the house looking like she'd just rolled out of bed again. She stepped one slippered foot into his hands and leaned forward, trusting him with her weight to grab the windowsill.

"Okay, now step on my shoulder with your other foot." He

moved her foot in his hands against his chest so her calf was supported against him.

Piper gripped the windowsill with all her might and boosted her weight up off the lip of the window well and up onto his shoulder.

Please don't fall. Please don't fall.

She dove through the opening so her weight was resting on her stomach on the windowsill. As soon as her feet lost contact with Titus, she realized her mistake. With nothing close by to grab on to in Jess's craft room, she couldn't propel her bottom half through. And now her rear end was hanging out the window while she flopped helplessly like she was trying—and failing—to do the "worm." How many more ways could she find to embarrass herself in front of this guy?

"Hold on. I've got you." He gripped her shins just below the knees and boosted her up so she was kneeling on his large hands, lifting her weight up off the windowsill.

She braced her hands on the wall and launched herself forward, tumbling through the opening and almost losing her joggers in the process. She jerked around toward the window as she hiked them back up, but he wasn't there. She secured her pants with a tighter knot on the drawstring just as his head came above the windowsill. He must have stepped out of the trench.

Now she could get back to unpacking, but that meant Titus would leave, and she was not even going to analyze why that made her gut twist. She stepped back to the window. "I can't thank you enough."

"I'll put this back." He reached for the gnome.

Piper lifted the window off the figure's pointed hat. "Thanks. Come around to the front. I'll open the door."

He took the gnome, and Piper lowered the window, then opened the craft room door leading into the living room.

What in the world?

Bits of white fluff covered every surface from the dining room table in the next room to the top of the bookshelf. One of Jess's, or maybe Devin's, couch pillows had been shredded to ribbons. Stuffing was even trailing up the wooden staircase across from the entryway. It must have been a violent assault.

"Pearl!" Piper yelled.

Jess hadn't been kidding around when she'd warned Piper not to leave the dog alone. Where was Pearl? And where was her phone?

There was a slight tap at the door. Right, Titus. She'd have to investigate later. She ran to the front door and unlocked it, testing the outside knob to be sure it was unlocked.

Titus stepped back as she stepped out. "Do you want to come in? I can put on a pot of coffee or something."

He glanced over his shoulder at the last splash of color painting the western horizon. "I'd better finish my walk before it gets too dark."

"Okay." She did her best to hide her disappointment, but she was pretty sure she failed.

"Maybe coffee another time?" Did he actually look nervous? She didn't imagine he was the kind of guy to ever get nervous. His smile lifted on one side, revealing one of his dimples. "Or maybe give me a call if you need someone to show you around town. Or if you need a partner in crime on your next heist."

Piper bit her lip but couldn't keep a serious face. "I might have to take you up on that. I mean, I have to case out my next target, right?"

"Exactly." He chuckled and hesitated, then reached up and pulled another twig from her hair. "So, can I get your number?"

"You're pretty brave asking for a girl's number when she's a hot mess. You never know what you're going to get when you see her next."

"I'll take my chances." He tapped on his watch, then held out his wrist. "Just type it in here. I'll text you so you have mine too."

"I have to warn you, Pearl took off with my phone, and I have no idea what she did with it, so it might be out of commission." Piper cupped his wrist in her left hand, the points of contact sending a zing of warmth through her fingers. She tapped her number into the keypad with her other hand, then clicked the check mark.

He glanced at the road, then back at her. "I guess I'd better get going."

Titus offered her a nod, then hurried down the steps and out toward the road. Heritage was definitely the right move.

Piper slipped inside and shut the door and leaned against it, letting her head drop back. She had always been cautious when it came to relationships, especially after Drake, but that was a long time ago. Titus seemed genuine, and she couldn't help hoping he'd actually call. And after her clumsy, disheveled showing tonight, he probably figured she had nowhere to go but up.

But first things first. He couldn't call if she didn't find her phone. Not to mention, she had a blizzard of stuffing to clean up. She surveyed the scattered fluff again. How could all this come out of one pillow? She took a step toward the couch and froze. Not one pillow. Pearl must have shredded at least three. How could one dog cause so much chaos in such a short time?

Well, Heritage might be growing on Piper, but Jess just might regret inviting her to live with her after this.

As if being relegated to teaching PE and coaching high school class B football at his alma mater wasn't humbling enough, moving back to his old bedroom at his mom's house completed the indignity. But Titus Ford didn't want to dump his savings into a house in Heritage when he had no intention of staying, and after he'd paid off his mom's mortgage a few years ago, she wouldn't hear of him renting.

Titus dropped a couple slices of bread into the toaster and

stepped around his sixteen-year-old sister, Kristen, still in pajamas, as she packed her lunch box on his way to fill his favorite travel mug with coffee from his mom's old drip brewer. He'd need it this morning. Everyone complained about Mondays, but Tuesdays were Titus's worst morning. This thing was ancient and somehow always managed to spit grounds into the pot every time. Maybe he'd buy his mom a new one.

Titus glanced out the window over the old farmhouse sink. The sunrise painted the sky with splashes of orange and gold over the maple grove that abutted the backyard. His mom's dormant maple syrup boiler was framed inside a three-sided shack on the tree line. In a few weeks, that green canopy of leaves would be ablaze with color even more brilliant than the sky. He loved fall in Michigan, but with football, he hadn't been home for the season since high school.

The old toaster dinged, and the toast popped up. Titus turned on his bad leg, and a stab of pain speared through his knee. He paused to flex the joint. How long would it take to get this knee stable again?

Before Titus could grab the toast, Kristen snatched one of the slices and shot him a cheeky grin. "Thanks."

"Make your own, princess." He grabbed the toast from her and took a bite.

Kristen's blue eyes sparkled as she tucked her blonde curls behind her ear. Her grin carved dimples into her cheeks. There was no denying that they were siblings. She was a feminine version of his reflection. "Careful. I make your lunch every day. Share, or tomorrow it will be goulash."

"Eww." He wrinkled his nose and raised his hands in surrender. "You can have the toast."

She plucked the other slice from the toaster.

Yeah, spending the year back home in Heritage was not his first choice. How different his life would be right now if he hadn't blown out his knee. He'd still be playing for the Chiefs, earning a six-figure salary. Sure, his contract as an undrafted free agent hadn't begun to compare to his drafted teammates' seven figures, but it was still four times what he was making at Heritage High School. If he'd known those paychecks would be temporary, he would have devoted more to savings and investments. At least the NFL covered his medical bills, so that was one less expense he had to worry about.

In truth, if he couldn't be playing anyway, he didn't mind being home for a little while. He'd been away too long, and his visits had always been too short.

And not everything about returning to Heritage had been so bad. Jess's friend Piper, who he'd met on his walk a couple nights ago, had sure brightened his outlook. Her oval face with big exotic brown eyes in her cute glasses, freckles dotted across her nose and cheeks, and those full lips had occupied his thoughts more than he'd like to admit in the last two days. Was it still too soon to call? He'd never been good at playing it cool.

"Good morning." His mom rounded the corner into the kitchen. She opened the bread box and pulled out a plate of muffins. "I made maple pecan muffins last night if you need some breakfast."

Those looked way better than the dry toast. Titus grabbed one. Baked goods were a definite bright side of being back.

His mom wrapped her arm around his waist and gave him a squeeze, then looped her other arm around Kristen and pulled her close.

"Mom, I love you, but I've got to get ready." Kristen shrugged out of the embrace and headed out of the kitchen toward the stairs.

"It's so good to have you home." She released Titus and grabbed a mug from a hook under the cabinets where her favorite mugs were lined up.

"Don't get used to it. I couldn't say no to Coach Hutchens when he begged me to come, but I'm only here for one year." The retired coach still served on the school board, and his request came when Titus needed a buffer anyway. "I do appreciate you letting me stay while I'm in town, though."

Hopefully by the end of the year he could prove himself medically fit and get back on the Chiefs' roster, if not a full-out trade. Sure, he hadn't gotten a whole lot of game time playing second string to one of the best quarterbacks in the league, but his stats were impressive. He hadn't become a fan favorite for nothing.

And he didn't mind playing on the practice squad for a while if it kept him in the game. He'd worked his way up from there before. He could do it again. Because the alternative meant . . .

Well, it meant living life on the sidelines or worse, being stuck in Heritage for the rest of his life.

No, thank you.

"Of course you'll stay here. You paid off the mortgage when I still had fifteen years of payments to make. It's your house too."

Titus shook his head. "It's your house, Mom. When my contract ends next June, I'll be moving on."

"But you're so good at coaching. You've only been here a few weeks and already we're winning games. I heard from the other moms that the guys love you. I don't think the team has ever been this strong." She filled the mug with coffee. "Well, since your high school state championship wins."

"Those were golden years, Mom, under a coach who loved high school football. We're two and one. Not exactly state-winning stats. And yes, we're winning, but that's because we're playing out-of-conference teams from schools smaller than ours. And the only reason they like me is because I played in the NFL. But don't get excited. I never saw myself as a high school gym teacher, shouting plays from the sidelines, trying to keep kids out of trouble."

"But you could do so much good here. Don't you remember your high school team? You boys were closer than brothers."

"Mom." He gentled his voice. "This is a temporary gig. I'm not interested in getting attached."

Although a certain pretty brunette might make biding his time here much more appealing. There was something about Piper that captured his attention completely. Sure, he'd taken notice of her slim curves and long dark ponytail, but her wit and confidence were what kept her at the forefront of his mind. She laughed at herself and seemed to embrace her perceived flaws unapologetically. It was refreshing to meet a woman who could be fully herself without the masks and costumes women tended to use to try to impress him.

Too much time in the NFL had probably made him jaded.

"I believe God brought you here for a reason, and I'll be praying for that purpose, whether you're ready to embrace it or not." She added a splash of cream to her mug, then put the jug back in the fridge.

"Leave God out of it. This is a favor to Coach Hutchens. That's it." Titus checked his messenger bag for his laptop, then slung the strap over his shoulder. When he looked up at his mom, her bright eyes had dimmed a bit. He paused to pull her into a quick, one-arm hug. "It is good to be home for a little while, though. I did miss you."

She pushed up on her tiptoes and kissed his cheek. "I've got to run. Can Kristen ride to school with you today?"

"Yeah." He glanced at his watch then turned toward the stairs and raised his voice. "Kristen, it's time to go."

Footsteps slapped the stair treads a moment before Kristen appeared, dressed in jeans and a T-shirt, with her backpack dangling from one hand.

"You're with me today, kid." Titus grabbed his coffee and muffin from the counter and followed his sister out.

"Can I drive?" She held out her hand for the keys.

"In your dreams." He opened the passenger door of his restored classic Ford truck and gestured for her to get in.

"Please. I only need a few more hours behind the wheel before I can take the test. I'm a really good driver." Kristen gave him a pleading look.

Titus looked from his sister's puppy-dog eyes to the truck and back again. His truck was one of the few things he'd managed to salvage from his short-lived NFL career. But chasing that dream meant he'd missed the last seven years of his sister's life. He sighed. "Don't make me regret this."

Kristen's eyes lit up as he dropped the keys into her palm. "You're the best!"

She rounded the hood to hop in the driver's seat as he slid into the passenger side. As she navigated the truck out of the long gravel driveway and onto the road toward town, he had to give her credit. She was a decent driver.

Satisfied that she wasn't going to put his baby in the ditch, Titus pulled out his phone and opened his school email.

At least a dozen new automatically generated messages from the school's digital administrative platform popped up. What? All contained the same email subject: Notice of ineligibility.

Oh no. He opened the first email and read it through.

Effective immediately, Brett Michaels is ineligible to play football due to a failing grade in English III under teacher Mrs. MacDonald. This notification was automatically generated. Do not reply. Contact instructor with questions.

The next couple emails were exactly the same, only listing different players. Almost all of his starting offensive lineup. Titus's heart sank. This couldn't be right. Why would she have done this? "Mrs. MacDonald just failed half my team. I remember her being an easy teacher. What happened?"

"Mrs. MacDonald went on maternity leave. The sub, Miss Caveneau, started yesterday."

"I thought Mrs. MacDonald wasn't due for another couple months."

"I guess she had to go on bed rest, and they had to scramble to get a long-term sub last minute." She turned into the Heritage High School staff parking lot and pulled into a spot.

"Two days in and she already decimated my offense. We have a game on Friday. We'll have to forfeit if I can't fix this."

"Fix it? The grades are in. What can you do about it now?" Kristen pulled a small zippered bag out of her backpack and rifled through what looked to be makeup. She flipped down the vanity mirror and brushed a coat of mascara on her lashes.

"I don't know, but I'm going to find out." He scrolled down the list of notifications. Exactly how many of his players had she benched?

"Good luck. Miss Caveneau seems pretty tough. Word in school is that she didn't let the rowdy boys get away with anything." She swiped some gloss across her lips.

Figures. She was probably an old battle-ax type with thin gray hair pulled back into a too-tight knot on the top of her head like Mrs. Minson, who should have retired long before he'd suffered through her freshman world history class in high school. She'd knocked a few of his teammates off the roster for a game or two back then.

Titus glanced up at Kristen. With the makeup, she suddenly looked too grown up. When he'd left for college seven years ago, she'd been nine. He was still having a hard time reconciling this teenage version of her in his mind. "What do you need all that stuff for? Who are you trying to impress?"

Kristen dropped the tube back into her makeup bag and swatted his shoulder. "My lashes are even blonder than my hair, so without 'that stuff,' I look twelve. Besides, if I was trying to impress someone, it would be none of your business."

"I prefer it when you look twelve." He tugged on one of her

curls, and when he released it, it sprang back up into its coil. "You're going to have to get used to having your big brother watching your back."

"If 'watching my back' is code for scaring off my prospects, you're doing a bang-up job." She narrowed her eyes and shook her head with a look of exasperation. Then she shoved the makeup bag back into her backpack and hopped out. "The guys at this school won't even look me in the eye now."

Titus smiled to himself as he climbed out of the truck with his muffin balanced on top of his coffee cup and grabbed his bag. He honestly hadn't been trying to intimidate anyone, but if his presence here kept the hormonal teen boys at bay, he wouldn't complain. He waved as Kristen darted off toward the student door.

He had to go find this Miss Caveneau right away. Maybe he could talk her into giving his boys a little grace.

His phone dinged, and he glanced at the message on his watch.

Principal Franklin

Stop by my office when you arrive.

He groaned. The battle-ax would have to wait.

two

RETURNING FAILING PAPERS TO NEARLY HALF the students was not exactly how Piper wanted to end her English III class on her second day of teaching. But the entire lot of them needed a wake-up call.

It was still early in the quarter, so only a few assignments had been entered in the digital grading software, and for too many of the students, one failed paper was enough to drop their course grade to an F. With a little effort, they could get back on track before midterms.

Now, Piper closed the copy of Shakespeare's *A Midsummer Night's Dream* she'd just finished reading aloud and looked up at the twenty-some students who occupied the decades-old desks with attached chairs.

"This play is one of my favorites, and normally I would spend these last few minutes of class discussing the scene we just read. But today, we need to talk about the papers I graded last night."

Several students cringed or slumped in their seats. Apparently they knew they didn't do well on the assignment, or in some cases, didn't do it at all.

"You graded them?" A guy in the back who was too tall to be folded into the old desk groaned.

Piper arched a brow. Why would it be a surprise that a teacher would grade their homework? "I'm a little concerned and confused. I'm wondering if you were given different instructions than what Mrs. MacDonald outlined in the lesson plans."

"She never grades these. She just gives credit if we turned it in." A stocky guy in the left row explained it, as if his failing grade was just a big misunderstanding.

"Well, I will always grade your assignments." How were they supposed to learn if their teacher didn't check their work and give them feedback? She schooled her expression. These kids didn't need to know what she thought about their teacher cutting corners. But no wonder they were failing.

She grabbed the seating chart Mrs. MacDonald had left and passed out the stack of papers she'd graded last night.

"Do you feel that you gave your best effort on these?" She riffled through the papers to find the next student on the seating chart.

Several of the kids hung or shook their heads.

"I'm not going to assign you busy work that's a waste of your time, but I am going to expect your best effort so I can see what skills you have and what we really need to work on."

One boy sitting near the front, wearing cowboy boots and a flannel shirt, huffed when his failing paper landed on his desk. "It's not our fault that we didn't know you would grade them."

Piper sighed and dropped the last of the papers onto students' desks before returning to the front with the seating chart. "Believe it or not, I don't want to see anyone fail. But English isn't the only thing I want you to learn in this class. I also want you to learn integrity."

"I don't even know what that means." The cowboy picked at the edge of a stray piece of tape stuck to the desk.

Piper looked past the dejected faces to survey the classroom with its reading nook in the back corner, supplied with a plush sofa and armchair. She'd added one of her puzzles to the coffee table in the nook. This warm, inviting classroom should be a good place to learn, if not for their teacher who had set a precedent of not grading their work.

She softened. Sometimes suffering the consequences of poor choices was a necessary part of the learning process, but maybe this time there was a better way to teach a tough lesson.

"Here's what we are going to do. If you are not satisfied with your current grade, I'm going to give you one chance to change it. Write a five-paragraph essay on integrity by class time tomorrow. I want to see that you understand essay structure, good use of grammar, and the meaning of integrity. If you turn it in, I will grade it in place of this assignment. Does that sound fair?"

Most of the kids nodded, and a girl in the front row nearly melted with relief. "Thank you, Miss Caveneau!"

Piper smiled and nodded at the girl . . . Julia, maybe? She really needed to study the seating charts so she could learn all their names. The bell rang, signaling the end of the class period. As the kids scrambled to gather their things, Piper turned to review the lesson plans and schedule on the podium. What was next? Oh, this would be her planning period. She was still getting this schedule down. She walked to her desk at the back of the classroom and grabbed her coffee cup. Time for a refill.

As the commotion of kids making their escape died down, Piper turned toward the door.

Titus, the guy who'd helped her climb through the window the other night, stood in the doorway. Still tall, still handsome, only now he was wearing athletic pants and a blue T-shirt that strained against his biceps and turned his eyes even bluer.

Oh. My.

She remembered that he'd been attractive, but her memory hadn't done him justice.

But if she read his frown right, he seemed confused as his gaze swept over her from head to toe. At least the contacts, pencil skirt, and heels she'd been rethinking all morning proved that she wasn't always a poorly dressed slacker.

But really, what was he doing here?

He almost looked disappointed to see her. "*You* are Miss Caveneau?"

"Yes." She drew the word out and arched a brow.

Titus blew out a heavy sigh, then folded his arms. "You just made half my boys ineligible to play."

The smile fell from her face. She hadn't thought about the zeros she'd doled out affecting the kids' playing time.

Wait. His boys? Was he a parent? That couldn't be right. She'd estimated him to be in his twenties. Maybe she could be a little off, but he still couldn't be the father of *teenagers*.

"Hey, Coach Ford?" A tall boy with shaggy red hair poked his head into the room as he passed by. "I have to leave right after school, so I'm going to miss practice today."

Coach? Oh no. That would explain why he was at the school. Worse, she'd guess he coached *football* from his stature. A football coach that thought his players deserved special treatment. Of course. Ugh.

"Practice is mandatory, Brett. What's going on to keep you from it?" Titus asked the kid.

"I know. Sorry, Coach. It's a family thing. I can't get out of it." Brett shoved his hands into his pockets and looked at the floor.

"Okay, but don't make a habit of it."

Brett gave a nod, then disappeared out the door.

Titus pushed the door closed behind him, then strode toward

Piper and pulled out a sheet of blue paper from his back pocket. He held it out to her. "Care to explain?"

It was only her second day, and she already had to defend her standards. Not again. "I didn't know the scores would make anyone ineligible, but I gave everyone the grade they deserved."

"They were doing just fine before you got here, and overnight, nine players are failing." His lips pressed into a hard line as he displayed the paper, pointing to a list of names.

Where was the nice, helpful guy she'd met the other night? Maybe he was more like her ex than she thought. "Those boys didn't even do their assignments. They deserved a zero. I already talked to them and gave—"

He threw his free hand in the air. "Not according to the digital logs. They all completed their assignments. Seems to me like *you* are the problem."

She'd been about to tell him that she'd already given them a chance to make it up, but after this, she almost wished she hadn't. Then again, she wouldn't punish the kids for the coach's behavior.

"Well, the assignment was to write an essay about their summer reading." She pointed to the first name on the list. "This one wrote a manifesto about how much he hates his sister's cat. These six all turned in the exact same paper, word for word except for the name at the top. This one repeated the introduction paragraph twelve times, and that was all he wrote. And this one used a paper written by ChatGPT. Where I come from, we call that cheating."

"Yeah, well, the assignment wasn't even supposed to be graded." He tossed the paper onto a desk.

Was he still trying to justify? What had she seen in this guy? He was less and less attractive every time he opened his mouth.

Piper plopped her hands on her hips and straightened her posture. "Mrs. MacDonald graded on completion, but that still requires them to *complete* the assignment. Besides, she's not here. I am. And I am committed to grading every assignment."

Titus raked both hands through his hair and turned away from her. He took a deep breath and blew it out slowly, then turned back to face her. The fight seemed to have drained out of him. "You're right. They shouldn't be cutting corners on their homework. I will talk to them about it and make sure it doesn't happen again. But would you please consider giving them a chance to make it right?"

She glared at him for a long moment. Man, she hated to give in, but in all fairness, their teacher was not doing her job. It didn't excuse the students' dishonesty, but if she didn't give them a chance to learn from this and rise to the occasion, she would be failing them too. "Don't think you can just come in here and make a scene and get your way. I'm not in the habit of giving second chances, so if they want a passing grade, they are going to put in the effort."

"Come on, Piper. Please don't punish the kids for their teacher's bad habits."

She crossed her arms over her chest and lifted her chin defiantly. "I already gave them an alternate assignment."

He looked ready to argue back but pressed his lips together and headed for the door. When he reached the doorway, he looked back at her. "Why didn't you start with that?"

"Why did you come in here yelling without even asking?"

He paused and seemed to be drawing a calming breath. "Could you just do me the courtesy of letting me know ahead of time if you're going to bench my boys from now on? You *do* have my number."

"I guess it will be the only reason I am using it."

"Then we're agreed." His eyes hardened a second before he strode out the door.

Between a teacher who didn't hold them accountable and a coach who contested their failing grades, how were these kids supposed to learn English, let alone responsibility and integrity? They would need those skills to grow into successful adults. She would not fail them. And maybe if she could help them raise their grades, she'd have a shot at a permanent position at the school when Mrs. MacDonald came back.

Titus surveyed the meager selection of protein powder on the shelf at JJ's Food Mart. Even an hour in the high school's weight room after practice hadn't been enough to relax the knot of tension his argument with Piper had planted between his shoulder blades this morning.

Titus pinched the stifling T-shirt in the center of his chest and fanned it away from his sticky skin several times.

His phone rang and he glanced at his watch. Jeff Dodger. His old position coach from his college days had been far more than just a coach. He'd been more of a father figure than his own dad had ever been. Dodger had called regularly to check in since he'd graduated. Titus pulled his phone out of his pocket and answered the call. "Hey, Coach."

"You've been out of my locker room long enough. Call me Jeff. How's the knee?" Coach Dodger's signature techno music workout playlist blasted in the background. He must be at the gym with the team.

"Still a long way from playing, but getting better little by little." Titus chose a plastic container and dropped it into his cart. He'd prefer to shop local, but he might have to order his favorite protein powder online from now on.

"Playing? Grapevine chatter says the doc gave a no-go on a comeback. Isn't that why the Chiefs dropped you?" The familiar rhythmic chinking of weight bars clapping together clanged in the background.

Titus pictured Jeff circling the weight room, noting the progress of his players. Nope, he couldn't call him Jeff. It didn't feel right to even think of his former coach so casually. "I'm coming back, Coach. You'll see. I'm still training, still lifting."

No one had to know that his strength and stability didn't seem to be rebounding. But he refused to believe the doc could be right.

"Maybe you should come back to Ann Arbor and train with the team. Our quarterback could use some guidance from his predecessor."

With the workout playlist and clinking weights in the background, Titus could almost smell the rubber mingled with the sweat of the weight room he'd spent so much time in through his college days. "As much fun as that sounds, I'm back in my hometown coaching high school this year."

From the other side of the aisle, a child's piercing shriek drowned out the classical music playing through the grocery store speakers.

"Coaching, huh? How's it going?"

The kid's scream morphed into a cry. Somebody's toddler was not having a good day. Titus could relate to the kid. "When I agreed to coach, I didn't realize I would also have to play tutor and run interference against a stubborn, idealistic teacher."

Worse, even her pigheaded temper had not eradicated his annoying attraction to her.

He'd thought she looked good in her glasses and joggers, but, man, she was a downright traffic stopper when she was all done up. Her dark eyes and thick lashes, curtain of silky dark hair, not to mention her curves on display in her skirt and top, all combined to make such a striking image that he'd nearly forgotten why he'd stormed into her classroom in the first place. And somehow she'd seemed just as sure of herself standing off against him in her heels and mascara as she had making fun of herself with a bare face and workout clothes.

"Ineligibility issues?" The music volume through the phone died down a little, as if Dodger had moved across the room from its source.

"She benched nine of my guys. *Nine.*" Titus steered his cart in the opposite direction of the wailing.

"Ouch. Is she willing to work with them?"

"She did give them a chance to write an essay in place of the paper they all failed. I made them stay after practice to finish it before I let them go home this afternoon." Except Brett, who'd skipped practice today. Hopefully he got it done on his own. "Now the question is, will she give them passing grades on the new essay?"

"Sounds like she's being reasonable enough if she gave them a second chance."

Titus blew out a breath, willing away the tension in his shoulders. Maybe he was being too harsh on Piper. "Let's hope."

"Aside from the eligibility issues, what do you think of coaching?"

"I like it more than I thought I would, and the team has a lot of potential."

"That's a perfect first step for you. I've always thought you'd make a great coach."

"I don't know about that. I don't think I want to spend the rest of my life on the sidelines." The thought bruised. All he'd ever wanted to do was play. He couldn't imagine spending his life watching others do what he could not. Titus hadn't accepted this job to begin building a coaching career.

A deeper clanging sound indicated that Dodger had moved nearer to a new machine, no doubt counting some unsuspecting player's reps. "I get that, but at least you'd still have a career in the game. I know you. Football is too much a part of you to leave it behind."

Maybe Coach Dodger was right. He couldn't imagine his life without football either. Maybe he needed the win as badly as the kids did. "I guess being a coach would be better than spectator."

"Give it a chance. Focus on developing that team and get a winning season under your belt this year, and you'll be a great candidate for a bigger school next year. Soon you could be on the coaching staff at a university, and who knows where you could go from there."

Kinda felt like giving up. Titus pivoted to steer the cart around a platform in the aisle displaying several apple varieties. The movement caused his knee to collapse. He caught his weight on the cart and righted himself.

Old Ms. McCreary, who lived next door to his high school best friend, raised her brows and left her cart by the fresh tomatoes, concerned eyes scanning him until he forced a smile and waved her back to her shopping.

No doubt the story would be recounted at the retired ladies' cribbage night this week, and from there, everyone in town would hear that his knee was still not stable.

On second thought, having a backup plan wouldn't hurt. Anything would be better than staying in this fishbowl of a town where everyone knew everyone else's business.

The boys really did have what it would take to make a great team, maybe even better than his team that had won the high school state championship three years in a row. How hard could a winning season be? "They do have untapped potential."

"I'll have to keep an eye on the team this year. I'm looking forward to seeing you transform those kids."

Titus rounded the corner of an aisle and nearly collided with a cart containing a mountain of groceries—and the offending toddler. Titus jerked to a stop, sending the scant contents of his own cart sliding. The near crash triggered another shrill cry from the little strawberry-blond boy wearing mismatched clothes.

"Sorry." Titus glanced up at the cart's driver. A tall, muscular high schooler, with a shock of red hair, wearing a Heritage High sweatshirt and stress in his green eyes.

Brett? The kid was his team's up-and-coming quarterback. The junior had an arm that could launch the ball like a rocket. Maybe if the previous coach had given him more playing time, the team wouldn't be on a seven-year losing streak. No wonder they were elated over their weak victories. At least their loss was non-conference, so it wouldn't count against their record.

"Hey, Coach." Brett lifted the little boy from the child seat of the cart and let out a weary sigh. "Shh, Trevor. I know you're hungry, but we have to buy the Cheerios first."

Wasn't he supposed to be doing some family thing tonight? And why was a sixteen-year-old kid grocery shopping with a toddler? Seemed like an odd chore for a teenage boy. Titus reached over to ruffle the child's hair. "Who's this?"

"My brother. I think he must have missed his nap at daycare today." He hugged the kid to his chest, and the little boy's cry waned to a shuddering whimper as he wrapped his chubby little arms around Brett's neck.

"Looks like your hands are full. Are you headed up to the checkout?" Titus nodded down the corridor at the front of the aisles toward the checkout lanes.

"Yeah." Brett patted the little boy's back. "Hear that, Trevor? Almost done."

Titus hooked his fingers through the basket of Brett's cart and dragged it behind him toward the registers.

"Thanks, Coach. Sorry about the paper we all failed. I know I should have finished it, but Mrs. MacDonald never graded them anyway, so I thought she wouldn't notice if I just repeated my first paragraph just this once."

"Did Miss Caveneau give you a hard time about it?" Titus glanced back at Brett patting the child's back as he trailed along behind the cart.

"Well, she didn't let us off the hook, but it was cool of her to give us another chance. I was freaking out when I realized the grade was going to keep me from playing on Friday. Right now, football is the only thing in my life worth waking up for. I don't know what I'd do if I couldn't play."

Huh. But the words settled into him. "I know how you feel. I've been playing football for a long time, and I'd still rather be on the field than anywhere else."

The comment threw Titus back to his high school days when he lived for football. He'd had a chip on his shoulder, and he'd been determined to replace this town's association with his last name from his parents' messy divorce to a legacy of victory. Coach Hutchens had invested in him, and his teammates had been closer than brothers. That's why he'd agreed to come back for the year. Even now, despite his years of near misses and bitter disappointments, punctuated by a media-driven scandal that'd cost him the draft and, after working his way up from the practice team, an injury that he refused to believe had killed his last chance to play professional ball, the game still thrilled him. These boys deserved the same. His annoyance over the ineligibility situation eased a little bit more. Yes, there would be challenges with coaching teenagers, but if he could help give these boys a team like the one he had in high school, it would be worth it.

Brett reclaimed his cart. "You go ahead, Coach. I just realized I forgot something."

"See you at practice tomorrow." Titus turned his cart toward the checkout lane but spotted a display of his mom's maple syrup on the end cap of an aisle and redirected his path to take a look.

He lifted a bottle and smiled at the familiar red-and-gold maple leaf logo on the label. Titus had been ten when his dad took off and his mom decided to tap the trees in their backyard and make maple syrup as a side gig to help make ends meet. Though it had been fun to help her collect the buckets of sap every spring when he was little, it'd become a chore as he'd gotten older. It had been years since he'd been home for his mom's Maple Fest. He wouldn't be avoiding it this year.

"I expect you to fumble on the field, but I never thought your biggest fumble of the year would be in English class." The unfamiliar voice came from the other side of the checkout aisle.

Titus glanced around the shelf blocking his view of the checkout lane to see Owen Baltic working the register, but Titus didn't recognize the bag boy who was taunting him.

"Nobody did that stupid paper. Mrs. MacDonald wouldn't have even noticed. If this new teacher wasn't such a hardnose, we all would've gotten away with it," Owen said.

"Yeah, she's a pain in the neck, but at least she's hot." The other kid brushed his shaggy hair out of his eyes.

Not exactly the most respectful words for a teacher, but frankly, Titus had to agree. He returned to the syrup display and replaced the bottle. His mom had plenty at home.

"Doesn't matter how hot she is if she sabotages the football season." Owen's voice held an edge of frustration.

"You can't use her as an excuse. Our football team is a joke. You guys haven't had a winning season in years."

Titus flinched. The Heritage Panthers jersey represented a proud tradition of state championships in his playing days, but the football program had gone downhill since then. Coach Hutchens had retired the year Titus graduated, and the coaching staff had been a revolving door ever since. That's why Hutchens had asked him to come. He couldn't stand to see the program die.

"I think this could be our year to turn it around. We've won more than we've lost so far this season. You should see Brett play."

Owen was right about that, but Brett wasn't the only up-and-comer. Several of the boys, including Owen, had loads of talent and potential. True, they were young and inexperienced. Nobody had been here to really invest in these boys, but they had already come a long way in the weeks Titus had been working with them. Coaching high school football may not have been his dream job when they offered it to him, but he owed it to these boys to coach them well and show them what success felt like.

"Whatever. I wouldn't bet on that team. Even if your new coach is a washed-up big shot."

Ouch. Maybe it was time to quit eavesdropping. He steered the cart into the checkout lane. The bag boy's eyes got wide as Titus rounded the corner. "Washed-up big shot, huh? Well, maybe you're right about me, but you're wrong about the team. I'd bet on them."

The abrasive kid's bravado withered. Intimidation was a sometimes-inconvenient natural reaction to his six-foot-five-inch height and two hundred and eighty pounds of muscle. Although, Piper hadn't backed down, despite her petite stature. As a matter of fact, she didn't seem to be afraid of anything.

"I'd bet on them too."

Titus turned from unloading the cart onto the belt to find Coach Hutchens carrying a gallon of milk into the lane behind him.

Coach Hutchens offered the kid a challenging look. "The team is looking great this year, and Heritage is lucky to have a coach who has more experience on the field than anyone else I know. Titus Ford might not be playing anymore, but he's shaping up to be one heck of a coach."

One heck of a coach? What would give him that idea? He really couldn't claim that title. He hadn't been pouring into these boys the way his coaches had poured into him. Coach Hutchens in high school, but especially Coach Dodger. Titus looked over at Owen across the register. These boys really did deserve to have someone show them they were worth the effort, the way those great men had invested in him. Did he have what it would take to pour out when his own life was empty and floundering? He was committed to being here for the year, and he had to at least try.

Coach Hutchens nodded. "As a school board member, I can't actually bet, so maybe we'll call it incentive."

Brett maneuvered his cart up behind the former coach one-handed. His brother was sound asleep on his shoulder, his little arm dangled limp against Brett's chest. "What incentive?"

Hutchens set the milk on the belt, then grabbed a divider to separate it from Titus's groceries. He smiled a knowing smile. "I've been lobbying to the school board for the past couple years for new jerseys. This year I got them to agree that if your team can make it to playoffs, they will buy new jerseys."

Owen paused his progress scanning Titus's purchases, and his brows shot up. "Home or away?"

Hutchens nodded. "Go to state and we will get both."

"No more grass stains." Brett's eyes were shining, and the weariness Titus had seen weighing him down a few minutes ago evaporated.

"Or blood stains." Owen smirked as he scanned the protein powder.

"You sure about this?" The total popped up on the screen and Titus swiped his card.

Hutchens nodded. "It's already approved. I just haven't had a chance to talk to you about it yet."

Leave it to Coach Hutchens to be a champion. The uniforms had definitely seen better days. The white ones were more like a dull gray now. Yeah, these boys needed a winning season. And a coach that cared. "Thank you."

Owen scanned Hutchens's gallon of milk, and the former coach handed over a bill.

"Have a good night, you guys." Titus waved to the boys, then lifted the milk from the counter. "I'll walk you out."

The retired coach moved a little slower and hunched a little lower than his younger self who'd guided Titus through high school. But Hutchens still captured the perfect balance of warmth and unyielding firmness that had made him such a great coach.

"I'm serious about those uniforms. I'd be glad to come talk to the team and try to rally them to work for it."

"That sounds great. Thank you." Titus pushed open the door to the parking lot and held it for Hutchens.

He shuffled through. "This team is blessed to have you as a coach."

Titus scoffed. "I don't know about that."

Hutchens cocked his head and leveled a serious look at Titus. "Even when you were one of the younger boys on the team, you were always the leader, motivating the rest of them to keep up. You have a gift. Not just for playing, but also for inspiring others. With you as their coach, these boys can't help but get better."

"I can't guarantee they will win, but I can do my best to be the coach they need."

"That's all I'm asking for." He patted Titus's arm then pointed his key fob toward a Toyota. The lights blinked and the horn blipped. "It's going to be a good year."

Titus handed his former coach the gallon of milk and waved his goodbye.

Yeah, he had more reasons than one to get this team in shape. His high school team had launched him on a promising path. Just because he had crash-landed short of his goal didn't mean these boys didn't deserve the same chance he'd been given.

He wasn't about to give up on the dream of playing again. But if a winning season could give him a backup plan, maybe this year wouldn't be a waste after all.

three

AFTER THE CONFRONTATION WITH TITUS TWO days ago, the last thing Piper wanted to do was tell him that Brett Michaels was failing, along with two of the other players who were right on the edge of becoming ineligible. Many of Piper's students had risen to the occasion with their integrity essays, but of course it was a couple of the football players who were not cutting it.

Coffee first. She'd need it for the inevitable confrontation. She refused to compromise, no matter how pushy the pigheaded coach tried to be, but she'd have to find a way to be diplomatic. She needed this job, and picking a fight with the town's golden boy wasn't going to win her friends at this school.

She balanced the stack of new worksheets she needed to copy in one hand and shifted her mug to hold it against her body with her arm so she could pull open the teachers' lounge door. When she stepped in, Titus was already inside. She cringed. She'd managed to avoid him for the past couple of days, and now, today of all days, he was here to ambush her coffee break.

He glanced over at her and paused in unscrewing the lid of his travel mug. "Hi."

At least she could get this over with. Now was as good a time as any to tell him that Brett wouldn't be playing this week. "I'm glad I bumped into you."

His brows arched speculatively. "Really?"

Piper set her coffee cup down on the counter and took her papers over to the copier in the corner. "You asked me to let you know if any of your boys would become ineligible, and I'm afraid I wasn't very gracious."

"I guess that wasn't my finest moment either." He lifted the coffeepot and began filling his mug.

She pulled the creamer out of the fridge and poured a generous splash into her cup. "I'm entering grades again today, and I'm afraid one of your players is still ineligible."

"Only one this time?" He slid the empty coffeepot back onto the warmer and screwed the lid on his mug. An almost teasing smile softened the note of sarcasm in voice.

"For now. Two more are close. I'll work with them if they will come in for tutoring." She looked from him to the empty coffeepot then at her unfilled cup.

"Who's ineligible now?" He dropped into one of the chairs by the table.

Apparently he wasn't going to make a new pot. "Brett Michaels."

Titus's good humor vanished, and he squeezed his eyes shut. "Not Brett. Anyone but Brett."

She cringed. "Brett had a rough couple days. He missed one day and fell asleep in class the other. He turned in his integrity paper, but the Shakespeare quiz made it painfully clear that he did not read the book. I know it's inconvenient, but—"

"No. Inconvenient is when the team manager forgets the ice and we all have to drink lukewarm Gatorade." He set down his travel cup and scrubbed his face with his hands. "This is a disaster. We've got a conference game tomorrow night. We need to win, which means I need my team at full strength. *With* their starting QB."

Piper jerked the filter basket from the coffee maker and dumped the used filter and grounds in the trash. This guy seriously needed a little perspective. Maybe his life had been consumed by football for too long. "You do realize that football is just a game. Academics are what is going to prepare Brett for his future. I would think that, as his coach, you would care enough about him to put his future before *using* him to win yourself a rivalry game."

"Using him? Somehow I doubt that Shakespeare is going to be vitally important to his future, but football affords players like Brett opportunities—scholarships he can't win if he's not playing." He pushed up from the chair and pinned her with an imploring look in his ocean-blue eyes that had probably hypnotized many women before her.

That look was *so* not going to work on her. She added a scoop of grounds to a new filter and replaced the basket. "If he reads a different Shakespeare play and writes an acceptable paper, I'll grade it, but right now he has not met the standards to receive a passing grade in this class. Standards are put in place for a reason."

He raked his fingers roughly through his honey-blond curls. "How is he supposed to improve his grade by repeating the same assignment that he didn't understand the first time?"

"I've offered to help, but he has not set up a time to work with me." She rinsed the coffeepot in the sink then filled it with water.

Titus paced the small room with his long strides. "Give the kid a break—an extension, something so he can play while he works on it. This game is kind of a big deal."

Piper poured the water into the reservoir and replaced the pot under the filter basket then crossed her arms over her chest. "What kind of message does it send if I give him a pass? Either it tells him that I don't think he's capable or it gives him an excuse to be lazy. If he wasn't an athlete, we wouldn't even be having this conversation."

Titus stopped his pacing. "That's because athletics are important. The life lessons I needed to learn in high school, I learned on the football field, not in the classroom."

Piper craned her neck to look up at him. It really was unfair that he was so tall. "It's no surprise that someone who is so entitled that they can't refill the coffeepot like everyone else doesn't understand the damage of entitled athlete syndrome. But perhaps you will understand this. I will not be excusing Brett from any assignments or giving him an extension on work he turned in late as it is."

The coach huffed. "You're not even a permanent teacher. You are a glorified sub on a self-righteous power trip."

Piper gasped. Ouch. "I wouldn't expect an uncultured jock to understand—"

The teacher's lounge door swung open. Principal Franklin stood in the doorway, disapproval darkening his features as his gaze bounced between her and Titus. "Is there a reason why I can hear you arguing all the way down in the office?"

Piper's face heated as she dropped her crossed arms and shot a caustic glare at Titus. She took pride in being a controlled and reasonable person, but this jerk managed to get so far under her skin that she lost her cool. Twice. And now her new boss had witnessed her outburst. This was not going to help her chances of getting a job at Heritage High when Mrs. MacDonald returned.

Coach Ford kept his gaze focused on the principal, ignoring her completely. "I apologize. I didn't realize I was raising my voice so much. I was just trying to talk to Miss Caveneau about Brett's academic ineligibility."

Principal Franklin's brows shot up. "Brett's ineligible? I didn't see any notifications about that."

"I just graded the paper this morning. Coach Ford asked me to tell him before I submitted the grade."

A groove deepened between Principal Franklin's brows. "For a student like Brett whose grade has just temporarily dropped, we typically allow an extension with conditions to help the student get back on track without losing out on playing time. I'll sign off on that. I'd like to see Brett play tomorrow night just as much as you would."

He *had* to be kidding. She swallowed the retort. Insubordination would definitely not help her case today. "What kind of conditions?" Piper tried to keep the indignation off her face and out of her voice.

Principal Franklin leveled a warning look at her, proving she'd failed. "Brett will need to schedule a time to meet with you for tutoring and complete a passing assignment within a week."

Piper nodded. "And if he doesn't meet the conditions?"

"He will." Titus narrowed his eyes at Piper then turned a smile to his boss. "Thank you, Principal Franklin. You won't regret this. Now I wanted to talk to you about the football equipment trailer." He grabbed his travel cup, opened the teachers' lounge door, and escorted the principal out, without giving Piper a second glance.

Not failing these kids just became a whole lot harder. How was she supposed to uphold a high standard and teach kids responsibility and integrity when the administration cut her legs out from under her? She'd have to find a way to encourage Brett and the other football boys to come to tutoring, because her integrity would not allow her to lower her standards to keep them passing.

This fiasco of a game couldn't end soon enough. It just kept getting worse and worse. Even Brett's magic spiral and mastery of trick plays were useless when the line was a fractured mess.

Titus chucked his clipboard at the dirt as the Panthers' right guard, Jay Wilkins, failed once again to stop the Spartans' monster of an inside linebacker and took out Owen, the first-string running back. The first time, it just looked like Jay stumbled and the inside linebacker danced around him to get to Owen. It happened. But three times in a row?

Owen went down behind the line of scrimmage again, and this time, the ball popped out.

"Come on! Protect your backs!" Titus shouted as the Spartans' blitzing cornerback scooped up the fumbled ball and took off through the clutter and down the field. Wyatt, the second-string tight end, took off after him, but the Spartans gained twenty yards before Wyatt brought him down.

Spartan ball.

He glanced at the scoreboard. Down by three touchdowns, with a half left to play.

What was wrong with this team today? Especially Owen and Jay. They usually worked so well together, but today something was off. He blamed the high tension in the locker room before the game. Now, no matter what play he called, someone failed to block, or catch, or run like they were supposed to, resulting in way too many turnovers. Today was not the day for failed blocks.

As the Spartans' offense took the field and huddled up, Titus sent out the defense.

The offensive line jogged off the field.

As soon as Owen crossed the sideline, he grabbed Jay Wilkins by the face mask, pulled him close, and yelled in his face. "It's *your job* to block the linebacker blitz and make a hole." He shoved the helmet away. "I'd like to see how you like getting pounded into the grass."

Jay boomeranged right back, shoving both hands into Owen's shoulders. "I'd like to see a pansy like you try to block the Spartans' line."

"Guys!" Titus tried to step around the other players who were beginning to cluster around the altercation. He had to stop this before it got out of hand. "Save it for the other team!"

Jay mumbled something to Owen that Titus couldn't make out.

Rage flared on Owen's face, and he jerked the snap of his chin strap and tore off his helmet. With a choked snarl, he charged.

Titus shoved his way between the boys and caught Owen just before he collided with Jay.

Nate Williams, the Panthers' volunteer assistant coach, broke through the cluster of boys on the other side and pulled Jay back before he could retaliate.

"Owen, you are on that side of the offensive bench. Jay, over there." Titus pointed to the opposite side of the defensive line's bench. With a firm grip on his shoulder pad collar, Titus walked Owen to the end of the bench and sat him down. Out of the corner of his eye, he saw Nate do the same on the opposite end with Jay.

Titus pulled his headset off and handed it to the special-teams volunteer coach. David Williams nodded, donned the mantle, and took Titus's place at the sideline.

Owen dropped his head in his hands.

"You want to tell me what that's all about?" Titus squatted in front of Owen, but the kid would not meet his eyes. Behind him, a whistle sounded, signaling the start of the play. "What's up between you and Jay today? What did he say to you?"

Owen covered his face with his hands, and his shoulders shuddered. Was he crying?

"Are you hurt?" Titus scanned over Owen's form, taking inventory. "Should I call the trainer?"

Owen gave a nearly indiscernible shake of his head, and his whole body began to quiver.

"This isn't about the game, is it?" Titus rested his hand on the back of Owen's head and sighed. "We *will* talk about this later."

Brett stepped up and set Owen's discarded helmet on the bench beside him.

Titus shot a pointed look at Owen and offered Brett a shrug.

Brett took a seat on the bench next to Owen. "Jay was out of line. He never should have said that about your mom."

Titus nodded his thanks to Brett and returned his attention to the game just as the Spartans put another one in the end zone.

Titus switched Jay to the defensive line to avoid allowing Jay and Owen on the field together for the remainder of the game. One by one, each of the players gravitated toward Jay's bench or Owen's as they came off the field until the team was divided. Literally. He was going to have to get to the bottom of the issue before this rift in the team became permanent.

In the last ten minutes of the game, thanks mainly to Brett, who seemed to be the only player with his head in the game, they finally managed to score a touchdown with the extra point, but it wasn't enough. Wyatt, the wide receiver, was too distracted to catch, and Owen was too stiff and angry to run.

Titus stood outside the locker room door after the game, ushering in the uncharacteristically quiet team. Assistant coach Nate followed at the end of the line of boys in mud-streaked uniforms.

Nate halted and waited until the locker room door swung shut after the team. "Those new jerseys are looking less likely by the minute."

Titus raked his fingers through his hair. "Did Jay tell you what in the world is going on? Owen wouldn't talk to me."

Nate shook his head and opened his mouth, but a shout and scuffle sounded from inside the locker room, cutting him off.

Titus and Nate barreled through the door just in time to see Jay's fist connect with Owen's jaw. His head snapped back, and the momentum sent him sprawling between the benches. "... dad was a real man, your whore of a mom wouldn't need to be hitting up my dad for—"

"Enough!" Coach David lunged to stop Jay, cutting off his words, but Jay ripped free and landed a couple of kicks to Owen's stomach.

Titus shoved his way between them. David and Nate each grabbed an arm and dragged Jay back. Jay already had blood smeared across his mouth, and his eye was nearly swollen closed and beginning to purple.

Owen grunted as he struggled to his feet, jerking toward Jay. Titus pivoted to block him, but the movement violently speared searing pain through his knee. The joint collapsed, and Titus stumbled to the side, catching himself on a locker to keep from going all the way down.

Owen took the opportunity to step around him. "Since my mom's not the first woman your dad's hooked up with—"

"Stop!" Titus pounded his fist into the locker, sending a clanging sound reverberating through the room. He tested his weight on his knee, and it held, but if the pain level was any indication, he'd just set himself back significantly. He tried to mask his limp as he pushed through the circle of players watching the action, and grabbed hold of Owen. "Both of you, to my office, *now*!"

Both the winning season and the healed injury Titus needed seemed to be as elusive as sand slipping through his fingers. As if an obstinate teacher trying to disqualify his star players wasn't enough, how were kids supposed to keep their heads in the game when their parents' bad decisions were tearing their families apart?

As soon as both of the boys were seated in the chairs in front of his desk, Titus sat on the edge of the desk to get the weight off his knee and gave each of them a hard look. "Fighting is not tolerated. You are both suspended from the team for a week."

Owen just hung his head and nodded, but Jay's head jerked up and he looked ready to argue.

He shouldn't have even let them finish the game after the scuffle on the sideline. He was still getting the hang of this coaching thing. "Not a word."

The pain radiating through Titus's leg was not helping his patience. He took a deep breath. "This behavior is unacceptable, and you will suffer the consequences if you want a spot on this team."

Jay's lips pressed into a firm line, but he held his tongue.

"Now I'm gathering you have some family issues playing out. I know how difficult that can be. I've been there. If you need to talk, I'm more than happy to meet with you. But those personal issues do not belong on the field. When I send you out there, you've got to keep your head in the game and leave your personal baggage on the sidelines. Is that clear?"

Owen met Titus's gaze with an earnest expression. "Sorry I let you down, Coach. It won't happen again."

Titus nodded to Owen. "Go hit the showers."

Both boys got up from their chairs.

"Jay, hang back a minute." Titus waited until the door closed behind Owen then turned his hard gaze back on Jay. "Three times in a row you let that inside linebacker past you."

Jay put his hands up in defense. "Coach, I—"

Titus cut him off. "Sit."

Jay's eyes took on a wary look and he backed up and dropped into the chair.

Titus leaned over to the mini-fridge beside his desk and pulled a couple of ice packs from the freezer. He handed one to Jay and motioned to his swollen eye and wrapped the other around his own knee. "You are a good guard. One of the best I've worked with. You could have stopped him, and the whole team saw you let him through. You not only sabotaged the score and cost us the win, but you're lucky Owen got up and walked away after those hits."

For the first time, Jay's expression softened, and guilt crept over his features. He pressed the packet of frozen blue gel to his eye and lowered his gaze.

"You know one hit ended my playing career. Owen was your friend yesterday. Do you want to be responsible for costing him this sport for the rest of his life? The players on this team are your brothers, and they need to know they can trust you to have their back, even when you're mad."

Jay's shoulders sagged. "I found texts and pictures on my dad's phone last night. His mom . . . they've been . . . she was begging my dad to leave my mom. His mom destroyed their family last year, and now she is trying to destroy mine."

"Do you really think your dad is innocent in all of this?"

"No. I know he's not. My dad was Owen's position coach last year. Helped him get to first string. Now I know why he was so motivated to help Owen when he can't be bothered to help his own son." Jay scrubbed the toe of his cleat into the floor and sighed. "I just couldn't focus on anything else."

Jay's dad had been a coach? No wonder the whole team seemed to be so invested in the scandal. "It's a lot to be dealing with, and I understand the anger. But if you are not in a place where you can be a team player and do your job, you shouldn't be on the field. Too much is riding on it, and I'm not just talking about a win. Your relationships with your teammates are at stake. You know the goal of the opponent's defense is to take your brothers out of the game. You are the only one who stands between them and catastrophe." He lifted the ice pack and pointed to his knee. His skin puffed up unnaturally out of the kneecap hole in his brace. That wasn't good. "You are the foundation that all of our plays rest on. Do you understand how important you are?"

Jay nodded, defeat dragging down his features. "I'm so sorry, Coach. I never thought about it like that."

"Okay, then you will understand why I'm gonna have to move you to third-string defensive line. You're going to have to prove yourself to earn your spot back."

Jay's brows knitted together and his mouth sagged open, but he didn't argue.

"Tomorrow's a new day. We'll start working on earning that trust back in practice, okay? Now go hit the showers."

Jay nodded and pushed up from his chair. "Yes, sir."

Titus had to find a way to get this team to bond, because until they started supporting each other off the field, they were not going to be able to work as a unit on the field. The problem was Titus had no idea how to do that.

four

PIPER WANTED HER STUDENTS—ESPECIALLY Brett—to succeed but they had to do their part. She checked the neat stacks of papers spread across the living room coffee table for a third time. Despite Titus's confidence that Brett would get his Shakespeare paper in on time, it just wasn't here. And with an away game just a few days away, she was not anxious to deliver that news.

"Did you know you left a stack of papers on the table?" Devin stood in the cherry wood archway, holding out a small stack of papers. Her long light-auburn hair had a slight wave to it and hung past her shoulders. She wore an oversized sweatshirt and pajama pants with a Hello Kitty print. And with the novel tucked under her arm, Piper guessed she had a quiet night of reading ahead of her.

Why had she become a teacher again? Right, the kids—especially for kids like Brett. Piper got to her feet and reached for the stack. "Thank you." Piper thumbed through the top right corners, searching the names. Nope. She thumbed through it a second time and paused on a no name and pulled it out. It was a hand-drawn

Wanted–style poster with her head on an exaggerated figure with a mermaid tail. "Beware of Siren: Caveneau might look like a fun teacher but watch your back. She will drown you in homework and kill your GPA" was written in perfect penmanship across the paper.

Whoever made the poster had a fair amount of talent. They had captured the slant of her dark eyes, freckles, and full lips perfectly. One of her hands held a dagger coated in red, and the other displayed a paper with a big red dripping *F*.

She tossed the paper onto the coffee table and sighed.

Devin, who had taken up the recliner by the window, looked up from her book. "Everything okay?"

When Piper just pointed at the sign, Devin stuck her thumb in her book and lifted the poster. "Where did this come from?"

"Someone turned it in with the assignments." Piper had been well on her way to becoming the school's least popular teacher, and making Brett Michaels ineligible for the next game would cinch it.

The door opened, sending Pearl into a round of barking as Jess slipped in and quickly shut it behind her, nearly trapping her long blond hair in the process. She kicked off her heels that heightened her already tall frame. Having two tall, slim roommates just accentuated Piper's short stature and curves. Her roommates tried to make it sound positive by calling her figure hourglass. All she saw was that she couldn't borrow any of their clothes without them being too long or too tight. Jess hung her purse on one of the coat hooks before stooping to greet the dog. "What did I miss?"

Devin turned the paper toward Jess. "Piper is a Siren."

Piper flopped her head back on the couch. "They hate me, especially the football team."

"That's not true." Jess claimed the other end of the couch, Pearl immediately jumping up and settling next to her. "You're just new. And different from what they were used to."

"Before I got to school this morning, someone had broken into my classroom and written 'Come back Mrs. MacDonald' on my whiteboard. It wasn't even grammatically correct. Then there were timers and alarm clocks hidden all over my classroom with alarms set to go off every fifteen minutes during all my classes. Every time a new one went off, I had to hunt for it before I could turn it off. And now *this*"—she gestured to the poster—"tucked into the papers they turned in. Worst of all, someone stole a piece from my puzzle, so it's just sitting there with a gaping hole."

"It's going to take some time for them to warm up to you." Jess scratched her pup under the chin. "Like Pearl here."

"You do know your dog hates me too, right?" Her phone had chew marks on the corners of the case to prove it. At least it had still been functional when she'd discovered it buried under the blanket in Pearl's kennel. "I even bought her those stinky bacon treats, but she refuses to come in my room to get one."

"Patience. It can take a while to warm up to new people. Just meet them where they're at. When they see you're a safe person, they're loveable and loyal."

"Dogs or high schoolers?"

"Both. And if you consider the way they will eat anything, they aren't that different." Jess laughed and scratched Pearl again. "All they can see right now is that they used to have an easy English class, and now it's really hard."

Devin cocked her head and examined the poster again. "You 'look like a fun teacher' . . . I think you should actually take this as a compliment."

Piper made a face at her. "Oh yes, I've always wanted to be compared to a creature of the deep."

Devin lowered the poster and focused her gaze on Piper. "The truth is you can't help someone who doesn't want to be helped. I run into the same problem working with families involved with foster care and adoption at the nonprofit. Until they're ready to accept help, nothing will change. But just because you don't see it doesn't mean change isn't happening. There are kids who have struggled all their lives believing that no one cares, and when they realize that you really do care, you're going to make a difference. You have to trust God to soften their hearts."

If she had to trust God to make this work, it probably never would. She'd always had more success making things happen on her own.

"So how do I convince them that I care?" Piper dropped the rest of her stack of papers and her red pen on the coffee table.

"That's the part that takes time. You have to be persistent and show them you aren't giving up on them." Jess kicked off her shoes and nudged them under the coffee table.

"Just like God doesn't give up on us." Devin set the poster on top of the papers.

Piper might not be convinced, but she had to respect someone who stood for what they believed in like Devin and Jess did.

Jess scooted to the edge of the couch and stretched, disrupting Pearl, who hopped down and trotted toward the dining room. "Anyone want to watch a movie tonight?"

"I have to finish these papers." Piper motioned to the stack in front of her.

"Sorry, I'm not doing anything until I finish this book." Devin lifted the hardcover of her dark blue book boasting the words *The Keeper* above the metallic name Victor Holt. The fantasy adventure by the previously unknown author had taken the world by storm over the past year. She hadn't seen this type of book craze since *Twilight*. Only, instead of a primarily female audience, Victor Holt was being read by everyone. If only she had the luxury of downtime to read these days.

"I told you." Jess sent Devin a knowing look. "Just wait until you get to book two, *The Fighter*."

"There's another one?" Devin's eyes went wide. "I'll never get anything done."

Jess scooted to the edge of the couch and stretched. "And a third coming out on January third. *The Defender*. And I think there's supposed to be a fourth, but the release date is unknown. There are rumors that movies are being discussed but nothing confirmed yet. How far are you?"

"Bastian and Ellia just—"

"No!" Piper held up her hands. "I want to read the series too. No spoilers."

Piper's phone vibrated on the side table, and she scooped it up to glance at the screen. The goofy picture of her brother, Cam, made her smile every time he called. "It's Cam. I'll take this up in my room, and you two can discuss Bastian and Ahleah."

"Ellia," they both said in unison.

Piper tapped the screen to accept the call on speaker as she headed up the polished cherry wood staircase toward her bedroom. "Hey, loser."

"Is that any way to talk to your big brother?" Cam's voice echoed through the speaker.

"Big brother? I'm eleven months older." Piper pushed open the door to her bedroom, where blank white walls greeted her. She really needed to hang a picture or something. At least the pile of boxes that had yet to be unpacked in the corner was getting smaller.

"Yeah, but I'm eight inches taller, so there's that." From the wind noise and blasting radio in the background, Piper imagined his shaggy dark hair ruffling in the breeze through his car's open windows, his muscled forearm resting across the sill as the northern Michigan landscape flew by.

"So unfair. Are you on your way home from work?" Piper straightened the skin care products and makeup in the organizer on her dresser.

Cam sighed. "Yeah. I really hate working at the truck stop. I think I'm going to quit."

"You just got this job."

"But this one is worse than the last. I don't even know what to look for anymore."

"Just don't quit until you have something lined up." She turned and sank down on the edge of the bed.

"Yeah, I know." The music in the background shifted mid-song, picking up garbled snippets of music and voices before landing on a song Piper knew her brother loved. She could almost see his brown head of hair bobbing to the beat.

"Have you been going to your meetings?"

Cam hesitated. "I don't like that AA group."

"Going to the meetings is an important part of recovery." She pulled at a loose thread on her comforter.

"I know, but I don't connect with anyone there. It's awkward. Besides, my new work schedule doesn't work with their meeting schedule."

"Maybe there's a different organization in your area that offers meetings. Would you try a different program?" She'd have to look up some options and send them to him.

"Yeah, maybe. Do you like Heritage?" He changed the subject.

"Yeah. It's been great . . . mostly. School has been a little rough some days, but the majority of the people here are really wonderful. My first night—" She cut herself off. She couldn't very well tell him about the nice guy who'd helped her when she'd been locked out after he'd turned out to be a jerk.

"What about your first night?"

"Never mind. Just going to say the locals have been helpful and nice."

"But the sub job's been rough?"

She snorted. "It's been horrible. This teacher didn't even grade most of the work she assigned, so the kids have had no account-ability. Now that I assign grade-level appropriate work and actually grade their papers, a bunch of them are struggling, especially the football players. I'm going to have to make one of them ineligible.

You can imagine how the football team and coach feel about me. The principal isn't my biggest fan either."

"What did you do?" The wind noise died down, so Cam must have slowed the car. He was probably just getting back into Escanaba from the truck stop five miles north of town.

She shoved up from the bed and wandered over to her window that overlooked the square. In the waning light, Otis was no longer by the gazebo where she'd last seen him. She'd intended to go get a closer look while he was close by. Too late. Now she'd have to track him down. "He caught me and the football coach yelling at each other last week. It was embarrassing."

"Glad to hear you're making friends."

"Oh yeah, we're besties." She turned back to the door and caught Pearl peeking around the corner. She took a step toward her, but the dog bolted. *Meet them where they're at.*

"Tell me about this coach. Is he some old paunchy guy stuck in his ways?"

"Worse. Ex-NFL player who thinks he knows everything." She walked over to her desk, where the dog treats now had a designated spot in her drawer organizer, and pulled out the bag.

"NFL?" Cam's interest lifted his tone. "What's his name?"

"Titus Ford."

"Wait. *The* Titus Ford?" His radio clicked off.

"Have you heard of him?" Pearl's nose peeked around the door again. Piper sat on the bed and set the treat next to her. Then patted the mattress. But the dog just bolted again.

"Um, yeah. I'm pretty sure everyone in Michigan but you has heard of Titus Ford. He was a big deal at U of M. He was even considered for the Heisman, but he got caught up in some sort of scandal. People think that's why he didn't get drafted. But he signed on with the Chiefs as an undrafted free agent and worked his way up from their practice team and finally got some game time last season when the QB was out for an injury." His voice sped up as he rattled off the facts. "He became a fan favorite practically overnight. After playing for five consecutive games, he earned some of the best stats in the league. Then he blew out his knee. Last I heard, the Chiefs released him. Rumors were that doctors told him he'd never play again. Man, I can't believe Titus Ford is at your little school. I'm coming to a game."

"Well, your golden boy is a pain in my neck." Never mind that his blue eyes, broad shoulders, and dimples haunted her dreams. "He thinks his players are entitled to special treatment. He went over my head and got the principal to give this kid an extension so he could play last Friday. Can you believe that? The kid needs help—time to get some tutoring, not a free pass."

"An extension isn't exactly a free pass. Is he getting his work done?"

Out of the corner of her eye, she saw Pearl peek back in for a third time. Piper picked up the bacon treat and held it out. Pearl seemed to be waiting for her to toss it. Not a chance. She only purchased these overpriced treats to make Pearl like her, so she'd come close enough for Piper to pet her. That wasn't going to happen if she tossed it for Pearl to take and run. "He hasn't turned it in yet, and the deadline is tomorrow. Now I'm going to look like the bad guy when I have to make him ineligible."

"I know you. When you think you're seeking justice, you're like a bulldozer. That can be a great quality, but you can also steamroll some of the very people you're trying to help."

"I'm not pushy." Okay, maybe she was a little pushy occasionally, but only when she was fighting for what was right.

Cam groaned. "Figure out what they need, then meet them partway. Earn their trust."

She stared at the treat, then the dog, who peeked at her again from the hall. She broke the treat into pieces and made a trail from the middle of her room to right inside the door. Pearl stared at the treat closest to her, then up at Piper.

Cam continued. "I know, you're just passionate. Once people get to know you, they can understand the heart behind it. But when you come on strong to someone who doesn't know your heart, your passion comes across as harsh and inflexible."

She paced across the room. "I don't come across—"

Her brother cleared his throat.

"Okay, maybe I can come across a tad harsh, but not in—"

"Try again."

She sighed and sank down onto the bed. "Fine."

"So, what are you going to do?"

A whimper caught her attention, and she glanced down. The trail of treats was gone, and Pearl was next to the bed, staring up at her with wide eyes. She pulled a treat from the bag and held it in her palm. The dog snatched it, then took off. Progress.

Maybe her brother and Jess had a point about meeting the kids where they were at.

"I guess I'll just have to find another way to help these kids. Maybe I can offer tutoring after practice or before school so they wouldn't have to miss football."

"That's a good start." Cam's music restarted in the background.

Only now she needed to find the right way to connect with the kids.

She doubted bacon treats would work.

If Titus had ever needed to work off his frustration in the gym, today was the day. His knee had not improved since reinjuring it when he broke up the fight almost a week ago. He'd had it checked out yesterday. The orthopedic specialist who had originally given him a twenty-percent chance of a full recovery said the new injury cut his chances to less than ten percent. But it still wasn't zero. He could still beat the odds.

"Now you see why I've been trying to get you to come to the arena with me." Nate Williams, the team's volunteer assistant coach and local pastor, turned to the next obstacle at the Thunder Arena's ninja course.

"It is a good way to blow off some steam." Titus wiped the sweat from his brow and guzzled a couple large gulps from his water bottle before following Nate.

The embarrassment that was last Friday's game shone a glaring light on the team's disunity. And if that wasn't enough, Brett missed his deadline to redo Piper's assignment. Without him, Jay, and Owen in tomorrow's game, he didn't expect it to go any better than last week's disaster. Titus needed to get the boys to work together, or they could toss any hope of a winning season out the window.

They paused at the start of the Rope Junction to watch Seth Warner, "The Storm" to *Ninja Warrior* fans, dominate the obstacle. He swung across the six ropes that hung down at varying lengths, making it look easy. From Titus's previous failed attempt, he knew that was not the case.

"I thought I was in pretty good shape, but you put me to shame," Titus called to Seth when he'd safely landed on the opposite platform. How could the confident and skilled hard-bodied Seth of today be the same skinny stoner he'd known in high school? Sure, they hadn't exactly been friends, but everyone knew everyone at Heritage High.

"You're recovering from knee surgery." Nate slapped his shoulder. "Maybe you should cut yourself some slack."

Titus glanced down at the still-puckered scar and puffy skin peeking through the kneecap opening on his brace. "I'll have to take it easy on the knee for a few weeks, but I can still keep my upper body in shape, and some of these obstacles are perfect for that."

Seth waved him over. "You're welcome to train with me. I'm here every day."

Titus attempted the course and managed the part that required arm strength but couldn't get his bad knee to cooperate on the landing, and he ended up in the foam pit below.

Seth offered him a hand up onto the low platform. "You'll get there."

Nate swung across the ropes and landed on the platform nearly as effortlessly as Seth.

Yeah, Titus definitely needed more practice if he was going to keep up with these two. He scooped up his bottle and drained it.

Seth lifted his bottle, then pointed at Titus's. "Want me to fill it?"

"I've got it." Titus stepped down gingerly from the low platform. "The knee could use a little walk."

"Rough game last week. Looked like there was a little scuffle on the sidelines." Seth tossed the words over his shoulder to Titus as he stuck his bottle under the stream of water.

"That was nothing." Titus rubbed his temple with his free hand. "There was an all-out brawl in the locker room after the game."

"What happened?" Seth replaced the lid, then stepped aside to give Titus room.

"A couple of the boys were working through some family issues, and it spilled out onto the field." Nate joined them as he drained the last of his bottle.

"The whole team seems to have fractured. I had to suspend the two who were fighting for the next game." Titus stepped back from the bottle filler to give Nate space to use it.

"And we just lost another player to ineligibility." Nate pulled the lid off his bottle.

"Principal Franklin even gave him an extension and let him play for an extra week, but he still didn't meet the conditions. I just don't get it." Titus ran his hand roughly through his damp hair.

"My team in high school was my lifeline. My teammates were there for me when life was just too much. I want to foster that kind of brotherhood in this team, but it doesn't seem to be happening naturally. Wish I knew how my coach did it."

"Is he still around? Maybe you could ask him." Seth wet his hands, then pressed them to his face.

"I'll have to give him a call one of these days." Hutchens was probably rethinking the wisdom of asking him to come right about now. Maybe Titus didn't want to call when he was sure to hear disappointment in his former coach's voice.

"Well, I wasn't an athlete in high school, but I know Grant helped turn my attitude around on the ranch by getting me into weights, although God had a lot to do with it too." Seth grabbed a towel from the shelf beside the fountain and dried his face, then slung the cloth around his neck.

"God? I'm not so sure these boys take an interest in stuff like that." Titus walked over to the bench where he'd abandoned his bag. He wasn't in the mood to talk about God.

But Nate wasn't done. He'd slipped into pastor mode. He dropped into step beside Titus. "He cares about you, and He cares about those boys."

Maybe God cared about the boys, but him? No, if what his dad did to his mom and the family years ago wasn't evidence enough of God's indifference toward him, God letting a linebacker take out his knee had sealed the deal.

Some of his doubt must have telegraphed on his face, because both Seth and Nate grew more serious.

"I'm guessing that injury"—Nate pointed to Titus's knee—"then landing you here as a high school teacher and coach were curveballs you weren't expecting. But He has you here for a reason."

Doubtful.

Titus reached his bag and dropped his full bottle inside, then finally looked at Nate. "Maybe." But that wouldn't get the pastor off his back.

Nate clasped his shoulder. "He's not finished with you yet. It's hard to trust that God is working when you're slogging through challenges, but He always has a plan to bring you through the storm."

"Guess I'll have to take your word for it." Titus's eyes trailed to the wall above the bench that displayed a number of photographs. One of a group of teens in front of an old barn caught his attention. This was the Seth he remembered from high school. Skinny, dark stringy hair, hundred percent attitude. Titus didn't recognize anyone else, but they all had a rough edge to them, without one smile among them. Except for the big blond guy on the end of the group of kids. "Is this the ranch?"

Seth nodded and pointed to the guy with the smile. "That's Grant."

"What did he do to turn your attitude around?"

"We did activities that forced us to rely on each other instead of competing against each other. The team wins or the team loses. That encouraged us to help each other train so we could succeed together."

Something about Seth's one-eighty from addict and delinquent to successful athlete and business owner whispered a breath of hope. Titus might just be able to rebuild some semblance of a life, even if it wasn't the life he'd planned. "What kind of activities did he have you do?"

"He tried different things, challenges that played to different strengths. For me it was weightlifting and strength training. We all had our individual goals, but he always gave us incentives if everyone reached their goals, so we won as a team or lost as a team. That's how I first got into training and competing for *Ninja Warrior*."

"I'll have to brainstorm on that." Titus zipped up his bag and slung it over his shoulder. "They already have to lift. I need something more team focused."

"Why don't you bring them here?" Seth drew a long gulp from his bottle.

"That is a great idea." Nate scanned the room, the wheels obviously turning. "They could all try the course, then we could have them strategize as a team to decide who should do which obstacle. It would help them see each other's strengths."

The plan began to take shape as Titus jumped on the idea. "We let them train together for a few weeks, then offer an incentive if the whole team can finish in a certain amount of time."

"Like a free pass to the arena for a month or something." Nate looked back at him, then seemed to see the bag on his shoulder. "What are you doing? We aren't done."

"I don't think my knee can take more."

"This is all upper body." Seth motioned him toward the salmon ladder on the side wall.

"Yeah, okay." His urgency to leave had been more about the preaching than his knee anyway. Titus dropped his bag and followed. "Now we just need to fix the ineligibility problem."

"Who lost eligibility?" Seth dusted his hands with chalk from a bucket near the salmon ladder.

"Brett, the quarterback." Nate began a shoulder stretch, pulling his left arm across his chest and cradling it with his right arm.

"There's a new English teacher at the school who is determined to turn every athlete into an honor student." Titus estimated the distance to the start. At least with his height he wouldn't have to jump much.

Nate paused his stretch and eyed Titus. "Sounds like she's getting under your skin."

"Yeah, like a sliver." He shook off the memory of her fearlessly craning her neck to glare up at him with her dark chocolate eyes.

So what if she was braver and more determined than any football player he'd ever met? "She's so unbelievably irritating."

"I wonder if I've met her." Seth dusted off the excess chalk, then jumped for the metal cross bar. He worked the salmon ladder up four rungs then back down before dropping to the floor. "What does she look like?"

"Tiny." Titus leveled his hand in front of his chest to measure her height. "She has long brown hair, dark eyes, and freckles. She always wears skirts with tall, spiked heels to teach in. Who does that? They make her look all pretentious." And smokin' hot. "But don't let her appearance fool you. At home she's this down-home-joggers-and-glasses-funny-confident enigma. She's a force to be reckoned with."

"At home—huh. Sounds like you must be getting to know her pretty well." Nate lifted one brow in question, but Titus ignored him. "Maybe the *funny, confident enigma* of a teacher could help you come up with a team-building academic activity."

Titus dug his hands into the chalk bucket then dusted them off and reached for the bar. "We aren't exactly on friendly terms."

"Grace and I weren't on friendly terms at first either." Seth exchanged a look with Nate.

"Wipe that look off your faces. That's not what is happening between Piper and me." Titus worked the salmon ladder up two rungs but then had to drop. This was harder than it looked. "What I need to focus on is the team bonding and Brett's grade. Any chance you're good with Shakespeare?"

Seth let out a deep laugh. "You're asking the guy who barely graduated high school. Sorry, man. But I can help you here with the team. We just need a game plan to get them to work together."

Seth walked toward his office, and Titus and Nate followed. This had to work, because he was out of ideas.

five

PIPER WAS DETERMINED TO HELP THESE KIDS even if it killed her, and at this rate, it just might. She stood battling a classroom of blank stares. Either they were all still half asleep, or refusing to interact was their new sabotage tactic. At least it was Friday.

"Can someone tell me the difference between mood and tone in literature?" She looked over the stony-faced students, waiting for an answer.

Crickets. But were they silent because not a single one of them was listening to her explanation yesterday or because they refused to participate?

"Since I'm not getting any participation with the discussion, maybe we should break into groups. I'm going to give each group a script, and each group will perform a skit for the class to demonstrate mood or tone."

A collective groan accompanied their dirty looks.

"Okay, if you can show me you know the material without another object lesson, you can skip the skit. Tell me the difference between mood and tone in literature."

One of the girls, Kristen, tentatively put her hand up. "Tone is the way something is said. It's determined by the author or speaker."

"Good." She offered the student a bright smile. "I'm glad at least one person was listening yesterday. Now, can someone else tell me how mood is different?"

"Mood is the way the reader or listener feels about what is said." Beau spoke up without raising his hand. "Kinda like how, when we have to listen to you, we all feel—"

Piper shot him a warning look. "Do you really want to finish that sentence?"

The defiance in his expression dulled. He pulled his cowboy-boot-shod legs down from Aaron's empty chair in front of him and sat up a little straighter.

Where was Aaron today?

"You are correct about mood." Maybe her idealism would get the better of her this time. She'd been determined to find a way to stay in Heritage, but what kind of teacher was she if she couldn't win over a bunch of teenagers?

The bell rang, thank goodness, and the students began gathering their things.

"Brett, can I talk to you a minute before you head out, please?" Piper moved over to her desk and pulled up attendance on her computer.

The log listed Aaron out for in-school suspension. A whisper of compassion stirred in her spirit. The kid was generally surly and uninterested, but every once in a while, he'd spout off a one-liner that made her laugh out loud, and although he rarely participated in class, his written work showed glimmers of potential. His grammar was atrocious, but his insight proved he actually read and understood the literature. He'd be a decent writer if he put some effort into it.

She glanced up as a sullen Brett approached her desk with his bag slung over his shoulder. "Hey, Brett. How's your paper coming?"

He shrugged. "I don't really get Shakespeare."

"I'm happy to help, but I haven't seen you for tutoring this week."

"I can't stay after school. I have football practice. I'm ineligible for games, but I still have to go to practice if I want to stay on the team." He looked down at the floor and scuffed his toe into the industrial linoleum.

"I don't mind staying late or coming early. What time *would* work for you?"

"Students aren't allowed in the building after four."

"I know football is important to you, and I would really like to help you get that paper completed so you can get back to it. If I can find a different place for us to meet up, would you come?"

Brett's gaze jerked up to meet her eyes. "You would do that?"

"Of course. I'll work on it." The school really did need to have tutoring options that didn't exclude the athletes. She'd have to ask Principal Franklin if there was an after-hours space she could use.

When the last of the students had vacated her classroom, Piper gathered up the reading selections and worksheet Aaron had missed, along with a package of M&M'S she had tucked away in her desk, and headed down to the office.

She found Aaron in the office conference room slouching low in his chair and spinning a coin like a top on the table. "Hey, Aaron. I missed you in class today."

The kid rolled his eyes. "Yeah, right."

Piper pulled out the next chair and turned it to face him, then sat down and looked him in the eye. "I actually did miss having you in class. And I'm going to keep telling you that until you believe me."

He eyed her warily. "None of the teachers *like* having me in class."

"Well, if that's true, it's their loss. I enjoy your sense of humor. I wish you'd share your thoughts during class discussions because I think you have a really valuable perspective to add."

"Why?" He broke eye contact and looked down at his hands in his lap.

"Your book report on *Lord of the Flies* was very astute. Not everyone in your class can look past the overt and understand the symbolic message of a story. Anyway, I brought you the work you missed today." She pushed over the stack of papers with the M&M'S on top. "And a little treat to lift your spirits."

He looked up at the candy then back at her, brows scrunched. "Why are you doing this?"

"I know what it's like to have a bad day. Something told me you might be having one today." She pushed up from the chair and rested her hand on his hoodie-clad shoulder for a moment. "Hang in there. I'll be looking forward to having you back in my classroom soon."

She headed for the door.

"Miss . . . um, Miss Caveneau?" His voice had lost its harsh edge.

She paused in the doorway and turned back toward him. "Yes?"

He offered her a slight smile and squirmed in his seat. "Thanks."

That might have been the first time she'd seen him smile. She returned the smile and gave him a nod. "My door is always open if you ever need anything."

Maybe she did have hope of getting through to this one. And if she could make a difference for even one, this struggle would be worth it. *Meet them where they're at.* Maybe treats were the ticket for teenagers too.

Piper aimed for Principal Franklin's office with the door slightly ajar. Hopefully she could catch him. She peeked into his office and caught a glimpse of him behind his desk. She knocked a couple raps on the doorframe.

"Ah, Miss Caveneau. I'm glad you stopped by." The principal looked up over his wire-rimmed reading glasses from behind his big mahogany desk. "Did Mrs. MacDonald put anything in her sub plans about the homecoming parade float?"

"I haven't seen anything about it." What did that have to do with English class?

"Each teacher is assigned to the committee for one of our school's events. Mrs. MacDonald was assigned the homecoming parade, which means we will need you to help decorate the float next week. I think the committee reserved the school garage next Tuesday after school. Your friend Jess is helping with it too, so she can give you the details."

Piper wasn't having much success connecting with students in the classroom. Maybe getting involved in a fun school event would help her get to know them away from the stress of expectations and homework. "I'll be there."

"I'd like to put you on the list of chaperones for the dance as well, if you're available." He ran his finger down the desk calendar in front of him and pushed his glasses up higher on his nose as he scanned the dates. "It's two weeks from Saturday."

"I don't think I have any conflict. I'm happy to help." Did she have anything to wear to a dance? How much did the chaperones dress up? She'd have to ask Jess. "I actually stopped by because I'm trying to schedule a time to tutor Brett. I know he and everyone else around here are anxious for him to get back on the field after he missed the extension deadline you gave him and he became ineligible. But the building closes before practice ends, so none of the athletes can get tutoring. Is there any other space available so I can work with kids after school hours?"

Principal Franklin folded his hands on the desk and cocked his head to the side, sizing her up for a long moment. "You know we can't pay you overtime if you stay late to tutor kids, right?"

Piper shifted her weight back onto her heels. Is that what he thought of her—that she was just trying to get a bigger paycheck? "I'm not asking for money."

Franklin eyed her, then gestured to the chair on the opposite side of his desk. "Come in and have a seat."

Piper stepped in and sat in the straight-backed wooden chair. "These kids, all of them, even the athletes, deserve academic support. If that means I need to put in a few extra hours, I'm happy to do it."

"I agree that it would be a great option, but we don't have the staff or the funding to develop a more functional tutoring program right now. These things take time. The school board would have to be involved, and they aren't fast-moving. Even if we start now, it will probably be a year before we can get traction to start a new program."

"I get that, but I'm not asking for staff or funding. I'm just asking for space. If there is interest for more than I can offer on my own, we can go through the proper channels to build on it when the time comes."

He considered her a moment longer, then opened his desk drawer and pulled out a key ring. "A few years ago, C wing flooded, and we had to bring in a modular classroom. We don't allow students in the main building after four, but since this trailer is not connected to the school, I think we could allow it for the time being."

Piper smiled. Now she would just need to set up a little tutoring space. She reached for the key.

The principal withdrew his hand, keeping the key out of her reach. "Hold on, now. It's out back by the football field and is being used for equipment storage by the football program. But there is probably enough space in there for both. You and Coach

Ford will have to work out a compromise on how to use the space. Can I trust you to do that without causing a scene?"

That dampened her enthusiasm like a bucket of cold water to the face. She wanted to sink through the carpet. Her screaming match with the coach was not her finest hour. "Yes, sir."

She was doing this to help Brett and the other football players. With that as a common goal, surely she and Titus could come to an agreement.

Finally, he extended the key. "I appreciate your commitment to working with the kids."

"Thank you." Fighting for a long-term job in Heritage hadn't been her motivation for today's plea, but if this helped her repair her image in his mind, she'd take it. She got to her feet and hurried out to the rear of the school toward the football field. She still had half an hour before her next class. That ought to be enough time to check out her new tutoring space.

Five minutes later, Piper had to shove on the door. When it finally gave way, a pile of heavy-duty blocking pads toppled, tumbling into the three-foot square the door needed to swing inward, the only open floor space in the entire modular classroom. Then the smell hit her. The odor, a combination of weight room rubber and rank armpit permeated the place.

This was not exactly what she had in mind. The place was packed, not to mention a cluttered mess. How was she supposed to even fit a desk in here? She pushed up on her tiptoes in the doorway to look above the stacks and piles. On the opposite side of the trailer, the larger pieces of equipment were parked next to a garage-style roll-up door.

"What are you doing here?" Titus's voice reverberated directly behind her.

Piper jumped and spun to face him—well, face the whistle hanging around his neck, swinging over the blue Henley T-shirt that covered his broad chest. After tracing a path up his chest and corded neck, her gaze landed on his face. The ball cap he wore over his blond curls left his eyes in shadow, but the sun reflected on the stubble shadowing his strong jawline. The last time he'd been this close, he'd just pulled her from the bush, all smiles.

Now, not so much.

She took a step back to put some space between them, but she backed against the doorjamb, trapping her a mere two feet from him on the small landing. "Principal Franklin gave me a key so I can use this place to tutor after hours. He said we have to share the space."

He snorted a sardonic laugh. "You can't have my equipment trailer."

"I'm not trying to kick you out. I just need a little space—"

"No. I need this space, and you'll mess it all up." He stepped past her to restack the toppled pads.

"Mess it up? Have you seen this place? How can you find anything in here?"

His brows lowered, darkening his gaze. "Organization isn't my strong suit, but I know where things are. Mostly."

She lifted her chin defiantly and ignored his refusal. "I'll take this side. Since you will probably need the big door to get your stuff in and out."

"Maybe you didn't hear me. I said *no*. I'm not sharing this place with you. There is barely enough room to keep all the equipment in here as it is." He placed the last pad on the top of the stack and let go cautiously. The stack swayed but stayed upright.

"If we organize it better, I'll be able to fit a desk or two in here. Or you will just have to store some of it somewhere else." Piper checked her volume and worked to modulate her voice. She could not allow this oaf to shatter her control again. She took a deep breath. "I'm doing this so *your players* can get tutoring after practice. Would you prefer that I just let them fail? Three more of them are on the verge of becoming ineligible."

Titus swiped the cap off his head, leaving his wild curls sticking up every which way. "Three more?" He let out a sound that was more growl than groan. "You're killin' me, Piper. I know you couldn't care less about football, but I cannot afford to lose three more players. It will crush any chance of making it to state. We leave for an away game in forty-five minutes. I can't focus on this right now."

Her eyes locked onto his blue ones. Although *blue* didn't really do them justice. They were more like turquoise with little green and gold flecks. And right now, they were shooting daggers at her. "Do you think I want to spend my evenings in this smelly equipment locker? I'm doing it to help them stay on the field or get back on the roster as soon as possible, but this is the only place that I can tutor after practice."

"You can tutor anywhere. My equipment has to be by the field." He punctuated the statement with a jab in the air toward the football field.

Clearly *he* had not promised Principal Franklin he would not cause a scene.

"I can't tutor in the school after four and *you* won't let the boys miss practice to come get help before then."

"The school isn't the only building in town. Tutor somewhere else."

"Compromising is a two-way street. Work with me here!" She could feel her control slipping as her voice rose again. In the distance, the school bell sounded. "I have to get to class, but this isn't over."

She stormed toward the school. So much for hoping they were on the same page. Right now, it seemed to be less about the kids and more about Piper versus Titus. She needed to stay focused, because she refused to let him keep her from doing what she came here to do.

Titus stood outside the door of the arena and sent the players in to find Seth and Nate as they arrived. Despite the tension still plaguing the team, they'd managed to squeak out a win last Friday, but it was certainly not a result of their teamwork. Hopefully, the weekend had cooled their conflict enough that they could make progress on team unity today. Although, with Brett still ineligible, and others also on the verge of failing, he had to find a way to help them with their homework as well. He'd start by talking to Brett today. Titus needed to catch him before he went in.

Last week he'd planned to ask Piper to help him brainstorm how to support them. But now he couldn't even *think* about her ridiculous demand that he find a new place to store the football equipment so she could use the space for tutoring. And suddenly Principal Franklin was on her side. He'd love to know how she managed to manipulate that turnaround.

Across the street, Brett's car pulled up to the curb.

Titus waved to get his attention as Brett jogged over. "Hey, Brett, you promised to get that paper to Miss Caveneau over a week ago. What happened?"

"I'm sorry, Coach." Brett hung his head. "I'm working on it."

Titus couldn't pinpoint why, but something in Brett's tone triggered concern. "Is something else going on?"

Brett hesitated, refusing to meet Titus's eyes. "I just can't make sense of that book."

Whatever it was, he clearly wasn't ready to divulge the details. "Which one are you reading this time?"

"It's called *The Taming of the Shrew*. The title doesn't even make sense."

Another car pulled up to the curb and a couple more boys piled out, and Titus waved them toward the door. Why was Beau bringing his guitar to the arena? The kid carried that thing everywhere.

Titus refocused his attention on Brett.

"Have you looked for an audiobook version? I'm sure Miss Caveneau wants you to actually read the words, but maybe you could listen and follow along. Hearing the inflections and pronunciations might help. Also, there was a modern remake a while ago now, but my sister loved it. I think Heath Ledger was in it. Ask Miss Caveneau. It might help you at least have a reference point for the storyline."

"That's a good idea. Thanks, Coach."

Titus glanced at his watch. "We'd better get in there. We need to get started."

Titus led the way into the arena. Inside the warehouse-style building with its high lofted ceiling, obstacles—complete with colorful tilting platforms, swinging ropes, bars, and rotating wheels—were arranged in a circuit with thick red and blue mats under the aerial stations.

The rest of the team was already gathered by the first obstacle, the Ring Jump, with Seth and Nate.

Seth blasted a quick whistle with two fingers in his mouth, and the noise of thirty-some players talking died out. "Your coach brought you here for a challenge, and I'm looking forward to seeing how you all do. I'm going to run the course, and I want you to watch so you know how to tackle each one."

Titus stepped up as Seth moved onto the starting line. "Seth will make this look easy, but trust me, it's not. Each obstacle uses a unique set of skills. Get out your playbooks and use the blank pages at the back to note the skills in each obstacle. You'll need that list later, so leave room for extra notes between each one."

After Seth ran the circuit and gave a quick safety brief, Titus jumped up to the starting platform. "Starting here, you will each try the course in turn."

At the base of the platform, Nate spoke up. "Pay attention to your own strengths and also watch your teammates and recognize their strengths."

"I don't want to hear a single negative comment." Titus scanned the group, making eye contact with the most critical boys as a silent warning.

Seth wiped his brow with a small towel. "I'm offering an incentive for the team. If everyone attempts every obstacle in the course today, you all get a free pass to the arena for a month."

An excited murmur traveled through the team as the boys looked at each other and grinned.

"And don't forget," Nate added, "the school board offered us an incentive too. New jerseys. But to earn them, we need to work together. So, if we hear so much as a single word of criticism or if you laugh at your teammates' struggles, you'll lose your pass and you'll be spending tomorrow's practice doing running drills." Nate waved a clipboard with the team's roster, indicating he would be keeping track.

Titus stepped down from the platform, favoring his bad knee. "Anderson, you're up first. There is no failure today. There is only opportunity to improve."

As the boys each attempted the course, enthusiasm grew. When an underestimated player managed to complete an obstacle the stronger players couldn't finish, his teammates exploded in cheers.

Nate nudged Titus with his elbow. "I think this is going well."

"This is a great start." Titus turned to Seth, standing on his opposite side. "Thanks for lending the arena and for all your help."

"This is what I was hoping for when I built this place." Seth stood with his arms across his chest, his eyes tracking the movement of the kid on the course. "I think I saw your teacher friend outside that house on the other side of the block."

"She lives with Jess and Devin on the corner across from the library." Nate pointed his thumb in the direction of the house.

"Friend? Hardly." Titus groaned. "She's on this kick to start tutoring after hours, and she pretty much demanded that I clear out my equipment trailer so she can use the space. Where does she think I'm going to put all that stuff?"

Nate laughed. "I can't wait to meet this woman. She sounds like a boss."

Titus shot him a resigned look. "It's less funny when she thinks she's your boss."

"Why can't she tutor in her classroom like all the other teachers?" Nate jotted a note on the side of the roster as Noah attempted the course.

"Apparently the only time the school allows students to be in the building for tutoring is during practice, so the boys on the team can't go."

"So, this teacher you're always complaining about is going out of her way to try to help the team?" Nate quirked a brow at Titus.

When he said it like that, it sounded like she was doing him a favor. Maybe he'd been a little too quick to judge her motives for wanting to take over his trailer.

"If you help her find a different place, she could help the boys without taking over your space." Seth leaned forward when Beau dropped into the foam pit halfway across the Rope Junction, watching carefully until he appeared at the ladder to climb out.

"That's an idea. Any chance you know of any place around town that would donate space for a tutoring center?"

"You could talk to my cousin Jon. His company owns several properties around town, including this one." He gestured to the gym.

"I'll bet Thomas and Janie would reserve a table for her at Donny's." Nate clapped and whooped along with the rest of the team as Nelson, a skinny freshman, managed to scale the wall that had stopped everyone else. "Probably wouldn't be ideal, but maybe she could tutor there for now."

"Thanks. I'll make some calls." Titus returned his attention to the course as Owen attempted the Gauntlet.

Titus glanced over when he heard a sharp intake of breath beside Nate. Jay tensed as Owen dodged the pendulums while balanced on a narrow beam. When he made it to the end of the beam without getting knocked off, Jay relaxed and hollered along with his teammates.

If the only result of this experiment was reminding Jay that he and Owen were friends, he'd count this exercise a success.

As the last player finished the course, the team was laughing and carrying on.

"Can we try again?" Noah piped up. "I want Nelson to show me how he got up that wall."

Several players echoed the sentiment. Nelson, who was usually overlooked by the other players, stood a little taller.

"I have a kids' class coming in soon, but you have all earned an arena pass." Seth pulled a stack of cards out and began distributing them. "The QR code on these will link you to the app and set your account up with a free month once you create a profile. After that, you just need your phone to check in."

Nate motioned to Seth with his clipboard. "Seth has agreed to let us train here as a team once a week this month."

"You can come on your own with your passes anytime open gym is on the schedule, if you'd like. Did everyone get one?" Seth glanced around as the players nodded.

"At the end of the month, you are going to run this again as a relay." Titus pointed to the course. "After training together, you will decide which players run each obstacle."

"If all thirty-seven of you can collectively complete the course in under forty-five minutes, you will earn another incentive." Nate put the clipboard into his bag.

"I don't want to go home. Anybody want to hang out until open gym starts later?" Owen took a swig from his water bottle.

"Yeah, where can we go?" Xavier mopped his brow.

"We can go to my place." Titus scooped up his gym bag and shoved in his water bottle. "We can have a bonfire. I think I've got s'mores and hot dogs." The place wasn't really his to offer, but in his years as a player, his mom had never minded hosting the team. She still kept the pantry stocked with graham crackers, marshmallows, and chocolate bars. He'd better send a text to verify the hot dog situation. After all, these boys could eat.

If he intended on staying, he should probably find his own place.

Wait . . . if?

Nope. Not the plan.

Besides, his current salary made his rent or mortgage budget pretty small.

"You coming?" Jeremy slapped Nelson on the back.

A hopeful look lit Nelson's eyes. "Yeah."

"I'll come." Beau tucked his pencil inside his playbook like a bookmark and closed it.

"Maybe you should skip it and go do your homework. We don't need anyone else to become ineligible." Noah gave him a stern look, then directed his glare to the other players who were struggling.

"Give them a break. We need team time too. Let's all go." Wyatt finished tying his shoe and rose to his feet.

Jay flashed a rare smile. "Sounds like a plan."

Several other boys echoed Jay's acceptance, but Owen cut his gaze to Jay then back to the playbook he was loading into his bag. "If he's going, I think I'll pass."

Brett turned an uncharacteristic look of disdain on Owen. "You know he's not the one you should be mad at, right? Get over it already. At least you *have* both your parents, even if they do separate."

Brett was usually the one who brought the team together and helped make peace. Titus had never heard such bitterness from him before. That was strange. Apparently the others thought so too, as they all fell into an uncomfortable silence.

Owen stared at him, stunned, for a moment, then his expression hardened. "Maybe I don't want to be there if *you* are going either."

Titus needed to shut this down before another brawl broke out. "Enough of this! Brett's right. Jay is your teammate, and this team *will* work together and play together. If you want to be part of this team, then you need to be part of it. I suggest you adjust your attitude toward your teammates."

Titus would have to think fast if Owen did dig his heels in, because he didn't really have a plan for how to enforce an attitude adjustment.

Owen deflated as he returned his gaze to Jay, who was observing him with tense shoulders and wary eyes, as the rest of the players watched. "Fine. I'll go, but I'm not sitting by him."

These boys needed to quit seeing each other as the enemy. "Actually, you *will* sit with him." Titus pointed from Owen to Jay and back. The comment had been offhanded, but Titus formed a plan quickly. Hopefully this would work to make an example of them and repair their damaged friendship at the same time. "You two will be paired up for every activity I can think of from now until you become a shining example of teamwork. If Jay is late to practice and has to run ladder sprints, you will run them with him."

Jay smirked, and Titus could see his plan to be late on purpose written all over his face.

Titus turned to Jay. "If Owen gets cleanup duty, you'll be sanitizing the equipment with him." Titus turned back to Owen. "You will share a locker, be partners for warm-ups, and sit together on the bus for away games. Do you understand?"

Titus turned in a slow circle, making eye contact with each player. Some looked ready to protest, while others awkwardly tried to avert their eyes.

"That's harsh, Coach," one of the braver players spoke up. "Don't you know what's going on?"

"I do know. And while neither of these guys are at fault for their personal situation, right now, your course of action"—he pointed to Owen and Jay—"is disrupting this team and affecting everyone around you."

Nate stepped up, backing Titus up. "We don't get to choose our circumstances, but we do choose how we react. You cannot allow someone else's choices to dictate your actions. You *have* to have people you can trust. And for you right now, you need to trust and depend on your teammates."

Titus nodded. "We are down a player with a couple more right on the edge. It's more important than ever that we work together. Between academic challenges and personal circumstances, this team is wounded. But instead of supporting each other, you're kicking your teammates while they are down. That ends today. If you want any chance of a winning season, you have to band together and unite against a common enemy instead of making each other the enemy."

"Are you ready to behave like a team?" Nate issued the call to action, then stared down the boys until they began to nod and voice their agreement.

"Good. Because we are Panthers and Panthers fight! Just not with each other. Huddle up and say it with me now." Titus motioned for them to gather.

The boys gathered and put their hands into the center of the circle.

Team captain, Brett, gave the count. "One, two, three . . ."

"We are Panthers and Panthers fight!" the team chanted in unison.

Titus clapped his hands together. "Now, let's go. Hot dogs are waiting."

"Sorry, guys." Brett glanced at the door. "I've got to run."

"Come on, Brett." Ben sighed. "Why are you always ditching us?"

Brett boosted his book bag onto his back. "I've got homework. I'll never get my eligibility back if I can't get through that dumb book."

"Why can't Miss Caveneau just pass you guys? Mrs. MacDonald would have." Owen shook his head.

"I'll get back on the field soon. I promise. I'll see you at school tomorrow." Brett waved and headed for the doors.

Beau watched Brett go. "Why did the school have to hire a hardnose like Caveneau as the sub? She might cost us our whole season. I barely passed my paper last week, and I know MacDonald would have given me a B."

Several others echoed the grumbles.

Titus hadn't intended for them to make Piper into their public enemy number one. He expected them to lay aside their differences for the sake of unity, and he needed to do the same with Piper. Time to call a truce and show the boys that she was trying to help. "Hey, guys, you don't have to like your teachers, but you do have to show them respect. All right. Time's up. Thank Seth and get packed up. We've got to get out of here."

On the bright side, all the boys were finally agreeing on something. That was half the battle. Now Titus just had to find a way to get them to agree on something positive.

six

PIPER HAD BEEN SO FOCUSED ON GRADING papers and rewriting lesson plans since she'd moved to Heritage that she'd forgotten to relax and have fun. Piper glanced at Jess as she pulled into the school parking lot on Monday night after grabbing a quick dinner at Donny's. With Jess in charge of building the homecoming float, it could be just the break from her routine she needed. Jess had a way of making everything fun, and if Piper could make connections with some of her students, that could only help her in the classroom too.

"I swear, the weather in Michigan is bipolar in the fall, beautiful one day and bitter the next." Jess parked and looked out the windshield of her car at the turning leaves whipping helplessly in the wind. "Race you to the garage."

Before Piper could protest, Jess threw open the car door, letting in the cold breath of autumn, and sprinted across the parking lot.

Piper pulled her jacket tight around her and ran for the garage, but Jess beat her there. "That's so not fair. Your legs are twice as long as mine."

When they tried the door, it was locked. Jess pounded on it, dislodging a few flakes of chipping paint from the metal.

Piper's teeth chattered, and she pulled her hands inside her sleeves as the wind nipped at her ears and nose. She didn't expect mid-September to be too warm, but this was frigid. Time to pull out her winter coat.

A moment later, someone from inside pulled the door open. Before it was fully opened, Piper pushed into the warmth of the garage, nearly plowing into Titus.

"Whoa." He dodged her charge.

Seriously? Principal Franklin had conveniently left out the very important detail that Titus would be here too. "Oh good. It's you."

The instant the words left her mouth, she wished she could pull them back in. Why was she like this? Antagonizing him would definitely not work in her favor if she wanted to get him to work with her for study space.

"I see sarcasm is one of your many talents." He flashed his dimples at her, seemingly unfazed by her attitude.

At least he didn't seem ready for another fight. His smile even seemed genuine. She hadn't seen those dimples since the night they'd first met.

"Okay, you two, play nice." Jess closed the door behind her.

Time to turn off the snark and make peace. She offered Titus a sheepish smile. "Sorry. I guess being mean to you is just a knee-jerk reaction. I need to work on that."

He offered her his hand. "Truce?"

She pulled back and eyed him suspiciously. Why was he being nice? It was weird.

"I mean it. I even have a peace offering for you. I talked to Thomas and Janie at Donny's Diner, and they own the empty space next door. They planned on making it a bakery years ago, but the diner has kept them pretty busy. It isn't ideal since there is a large counter and just small café tables, but they said it would be quiet and that you could use it for tutoring for a while. They're thinking about doing something with it over the holidays, but it's available until December first."

Piper's jaw fell open, and she made an effort to snap it shut. He made arrangements for her to tutor at the diner—or rather, next to the diner? That was way better than that smelly equipment trailer. "Are you serious?"

He nodded and lifted his extended hand a little higher. "What do you say? Friends?"

"I can't believe you did that." She clasped his warm hand and met his gaze. Maybe there was some good in him after all. Then again, she was tutoring his players, so he wasn't just helping her out of the goodness of his heart. Making his team whole again was a powerful motivator. But she'd take it. Friends might be a stretch, but she could be friendly.

Like now. Why was she still holding his hand? She dropped it and turned her attention to the garage, willing her cheeks not to warm.

A flatbed trailer with a football goal post constructed from large PVC pipes secured to one end was parked in the large garage.

In one corner of the garage, Holly and Ashley, two seniors, were untangling strings of lights, and a couple other students were milling around, in need of instruction.

Jess pointed to a green tarp folded up in another corner. "That needs to be painted with yard lines. I want the two of you"—she looked from Piper to Titus—"to work on that."

Piper jerked her gaze to Jess and shot her friend a look. Seriously? Jess had to pair her with Titus? So much for connecting with her students.

Jess smirked at Piper unapologetically, then grabbed a pair of paint brushes and a quart of paint and handed them to her. "He knows what a football field should look like, and you are the only one here meticulous enough to get the lines straight and even."

Titus led the way to the tarp. "Come on, cat burglar. I won't bite."

"Time will tell." She followed Titus.

Titus shook out the tarp. "So, besides tutoring and planning heists, what do you like to do for fun?"

Memories from the day they'd met surfaced, and an echo of her initial attraction to him tickled the pit of her stomach. She needed to shut that down. "You would definitely think I'm a dork if I told you that."

He stared at her a moment and seemed to be fighting a smile. "What can I say? I've got a soft spot for dorks."

Piper averted her gaze. The flirting was too much. This one-eighty was throwing her off-balance. "You first. Do you have any hobbies besides football?"

"Uh, I can't really think of anything." Titus glanced around, then jogged over to the workbench against the wall and picked up a notebook and pen.

"I suppose football is a kind of hobby, but don't you need a break from it once in a while?" She tightened the lid on the paint, then shook the container.

"I can't get enough of football. I miss playing so much."

He'd tried to cover it, but Piper hadn't missed the shadow of pain in Titus's eyes. A whisper of compassion stirred her soul.

"I do get a break in the offseason, though." He flipped open the notebook as he walked over to Piper's side and sketched out the lines of the football field. "We need twenty-one evenly spaced white lines."

"Do you suppose there's one of those things that makes straight lines with a string and chalk around here?" Piper glanced around the garage.

"A chalk reel?" Titus searched the pegboard covered in tools. "I don't see one."

Titus tossed the notebook aside and scanned the garage. "If I need a hobby, maybe you should share yours with me."

"Fine." It wasn't like her hobby was a secret. Piper spotted a two-by-four against the garage wall. She walked over and picked it up. "I love puzzles."

"Puzzles?" He chuckled, his expression saying it all.

"I warned you." She tried to lift one end of the board up as she swung around but didn't get it high enough, and Titus had to duck to avoid getting hit. Oops! At the look on his face, she burst out laughing.

"Now I know what happens when I get on your bad side." He chuckled along with her, then tried to put on a serious expression but couldn't quite pull it off with the twinkle in his eye. "You're escalating from breaking and entering to assault."

"If you know what's good for you, you'll watch your back." She laid the board across the tarp and scooped up a brush. "I have a paint brush and I'm not afraid to use it."

"I will exercise extreme caution." He held up his hands in sur-render, then grabbed a tape measure off the tool bench. "Why puzzles?"

"It's a long story." She unscrewed the lid from the paint and set it near the two-by-four.

Titus looked down at the tarp, then back at her. "Looks like we've got time. If I'm going to take up this hobby, I'm going to need some convincing."

How was she supposed to put that feeling into words? "There's just something calming and satisfying about it."

"I'm going to need more than that to become a puzzler." He spooled out the tape measure alongside the tarp. "What got you started?"

Piper grabbed the end of the tape and held it even with the end of the tarp. He didn't know what he was asking for. "My grandpa gave me a puzzle after some things had happened that made me feel like my life was falling apart."

"What happened?" Titus snagged the pen he'd been using earlier on the diagram and used it to make marks down one side of the tarp, wincing as he squatted on his good leg and extended the injured one out in front of him.

She couldn't even think about that night without reliving the fear and betrayal. This was so not the time for that story. And he hadn't earned the right to know it.

"Hey, Piper," Jess called out.

Piper turned and spotted her friend approaching. *Perfect timing, Jess.* "Yeah?"

"My brother's car broke down, and I've got to go pick him up. I don't know when I'll be able to make it back here to pick you up. Do you want me to just take you home now?"

Something in Piper deflated. Yeah, she'd wanted a change of subject, but she didn't want to go home and spend the evening alone.

Wait. Was she actually enjoying Titus's company?

Before she could answer, Titus spoke up. "I'll take her home when we're done."

Piper jerked her gaze up to meet his. Maybe she wasn't the only one who wasn't ready for their conversation to end.

"If that's okay with you." He spoke the words to Piper this time.

She nodded. "Yeah, sure. Thanks."

Piper turned back to Jess and read a whole interrogation in her friend's knowing gaze. Jess had always been able to read her too well.

"If you get home before I do, can you please let Pearl out?" Jess asked.

"Sure."

As Jess headed for the door, Titus moved his end of the tape measure to the other side of the tarp. "Aside from puzzles, do you have any other hobbies?"

Piper blew out a breath, expelling the tension her memories always coiled in her chest. He wasn't going to press her for the story. Hobbies. She could redirect with that.

"Does organizing count?" Piper moved her end along with him.

"No. That's work." He marked the other side of the tarp.

"I think I like it for the same reason I like puzzles. It's so satisfying when everything is sorted and labeled and in its place. I swear, it actually melts away stress." Piper lifted her side of the board as Titus moved the other side to bridge the gap between the first set of marks.

"My equipment trailer must have driven you crazy." Titus grabbed the can of paint and set it in the middle between them before dipping his brush.

Yeah, it was a disaster that had her itching for her label maker. But she chose her words carefully. "It's a perfect before picture."

"It needs to be organized so badly, but I don't even know where to start. Feel free to get your organization fix in there anytime. Not sure I'll ever get on board with that hobby, but I think I'm going to have to try a puzzle. Maybe I can work on one with you sometime?" He ran his brush carefully along the edge of the board.

Her heart rate increased at the thought of working on a puzzle with him. "I hate to say it, but I don't think you are ever going to convince me to want to play football. How old were you when you started to play?"

An hour ago, spending time with him didn't hold any appeal. But now that off-balance feeling was back. She had been so frustrated with his attitude these past weeks, then today he'd shown up all helpful—and even arranged a place for her to tutor. What was up with that? Not that she was complaining.

"I can't remember a time when I didn't play." A shadow of pain stole some of the light from his eyes. "My dad loved the game."

"I'll bet he's proud of all you've accomplished." She moved the paint down over the lines they'd painted and sat crisscross at the end of the tarp, then dipped her brush.

"I wouldn't know. He left when I was eleven." A little bit of bitterness came through in his tone as he dropped down beside her, brush in hand.

The pain he tried to mask mirrored a bruise on Piper's own heart. She was no stranger to daddy issues. She reached across the paint canister between them to cover his hand with hers. "I'm sorry. I didn't know."

As if startled by her touch, his gaze shot over to meet hers. "It was a long time ago."

"If my experience is any indication, wounds inflicted by parents never fully heal."

"He was a good football player, but he wasn't a good guy. When I was old enough to realize that he was just as rough with my mom as he was on the field, I didn't want to play anymore. I didn't want to be like him." Titus broke eye contact and swallowed hard.

Maybe standing up for his players' grades was more about being their protector than it was about getting them off the hook. He must have felt so helpless when he couldn't protect his mother. Her heart ached for him, and she squeezed his hand. That glimpse past his tough exterior just made her want to know him better. "What made you decide to stick with it?"

A couple of girls rounded the side of the trailer, carrying a gallon of yellow paint and a couple brushes. Piper pulled her hand away from his. Holding his hand at a school function in front of students was probably not the best idea.

Titus cleared his throat and busied himself with painting a line along the edge of the two-by-four. When the girls had moved out of earshot, he continued, seeming more in control of his emotions. "Football is the only thing I've ever been good at. I've had great coaches who were good men. They gave me someone to emulate and taught me to love the game."

Piper ran her brush along the board to finish the line. "Which coaches had the biggest impact?"

"Coach Hutchens in high school gave me a sense of brotherhood with my teammates. He did a great job of helping us bond as a team. But it was my college position coach, Jeff Dodger, who really took me under his wing. He helped me brush the chip off my shoulder and showed me how to be a decent human being." He got to his feet, favoring his bad knee, and picked up one end of the board, while Piper grabbed the other. They moved it to the next set of marks.

The line was pretty straight and even. They made a good team. Piper almost didn't believe it herself. "Now you have a chance to do that for the boys on your team. Your experience will make you a great coach."

Titus shook his head. "I don't know about that. I definitely never gave my coaches enough credit. It's harder than I ever thought it would be."

"Teaching is like that too. But you are proof that it's possible to make a difference. That's why I keep teaching even when it seems like I'm not getting through to anyone." Piper moved the paint container to the other side of the board so they wouldn't have to lean over the line they had already painted.

"Maybe these kids will be thinking about us a decade from now." Titus dropped down beside her on the tarp. "We're going to have this done in no time."

In his truck well after nine p.m., Piper was no more anxious for the night to be over now than she had been when Jess left. Titus had surprised her today. Between his peace offering of setting her up with a spot for tutoring, his good-natured banter, and that glimpse of vulnerability, he was shaping up to be far more than the entitled jerk she'd judged him to be. Maybe friends wasn't such a stretch after all.

As Titus pulled his truck around the corner toward Jess's house, the streetlight illuminated a yellow Jeep parked diagonally across the driveway, the hood partially hidden behind the corner of the house. She leaned forward to get a better look. "Who's at our house?"

"That looks like Beau's Jeep."

Before Piper could reply, a small white projectile flew toward the side of the house from the driver's side of the Jeep. "What was that?"

"Oh no. I think it was an—" The Jeep tore out of the driveway in reverse, chirped the tires while coming to an abrupt stop, then squealed rubber when it sped past them.

Beau was in the driver's seat, and Piper recognized a couple of football players in the car too. "Did your players just egg my house?"

Titus pulled the truck up to the curb, and she threw open the door to a blast of icy wind. She ignored the cold and hopped down, then ran to the place where she'd seen the white orb fly. Sure enough, at least a dozen slimy yellow splatters dripped down the otherwise pristine white siding. The remnants of shattered shells littered the landscaping under the slimed wall.

She pulled her jacket tighter around her shoulders, but the wind still bit at her exposed skin. Could eggs damage paint? She swallowed hard against a stone that had suddenly lodged itself in her throat. Pranks at school were one thing, but attacking her home? That was crossing a line. She turned toward the street, half expecting Titus and his truck to be long gone, but instead she found him striding across the lawn just a few paces away. She blinked away the moisture collecting in the corners of her eyes.

"I know they're all anxious to get rid of me, but this"—she

jerked both hands toward the mess—"is taking it a little too far, don't you think?"

"They shouldn't have done this." He walked over to the hose reel, turned on the faucet, and pulled the end of the hose toward the wall.

"Shouldn't a good coach be able to keep his players in line?" Piper's teeth chattered in the wind.

"I'm doing the best I can. I'm new to this." He aimed the stream of water at the mess and used his thumb to block the end of the hose and pressurize the flow. He sprayed at the egg with the higher pressure. Some of it washed away, but smears of yellow slime remained. "Do you have a scrub brush?"

"Maybe you should make sure they aren't vandalizing other teachers."

"I doubt they'd do that. They like . . . they just wouldn't do that."

She gestured to the remaining smears. "I am well aware of their disdain for me. They probably picked it up from you."

"You think I put them up to this?" His face reddened as his brows pinched. "I would never—"

"Not directly, but there is no doubt they picked up how much you dislike me." Piper clenched her teeth and returned her attention to the wall. "Maybe you should just go."

She needed to get this cleaned up before the egg dried and became impossible to wash off, but most of the splats were out of her reach. Another gust of frigid wind whipped her hair and penetrated her layers. Why did they have to do this on the coldest day of the year so far?

She glanced back as Titus walked toward his truck. Probably for the best anyway. First order of business, cleaning supplies and something sturdier than the hose reel to stand on. She opened the gate, ran around to the back door, and tried the knob.

Locked.

Piper's heart plummeted. Her purse with her phone and keys

was on the floor of Titus's truck. Locked out again. The lump was back, and this time she couldn't blink away the tears. She sank onto the step and dropped her head into her hands.

Why did everyone always assume the worst of him? Titus heaved a ladder out of the bed of his truck and headed back through Piper's lawn. Luckily he'd loaded the ladder up last week to help his mom pull some broken branches trapped in a couple of maples on the far side of the grove and hadn't gotten around to returning it to the garage yet.

Really, he should be making the boys clean up the egg. But by the time he hunted them down and got them back here, it would probably be dried on, and he didn't want to risk any damage to the house. He would find another way for them to make it up to Piper.

He *had* encouraged them to band together against a common enemy. He'd just hoped that common enemy would be the opposing team.

When he rounded the corner of the house, just out of view from where he'd parked his truck on the curb, Piper was gone. Where did she go? He leaned the ladder against the side of the house and caught sight of the open gate. As he approached, he heard a sniffle. He stepped through the gate and found Piper crumpled on the stoop at the back door. Her face was buried in her crossed arms, propped over her knees. Her shoulders shivered, whether with sobs or the cold, he wasn't sure. Probably both. The broken sound and defeated posture contradicted everything he knew about this stubbornly persistent and brave woman. "Piper? Are you okay?"

She jerked up, and her startled, watery eyes latched onto him. Her mascara had left dark streaks down her cheeks, and her nose was red. She sniffled again. "I thought you left."

"I just went to get a ladder from my truck." She really did think the worst of him if she thought he would just leave, no matter what she had said to him. That pricked at his conscience.

"My purse is in your truck." She swiped at her cheeks, further smearing her makeup. "I'm locked out."

No wonder she was upset. This was not the night to get locked out. Maybe humor would lighten her mood. "Want to grab your keys from my truck, or try another window?"

She cracked a smile through her tears.

He offered her his hand. When she took it, he pulled her to her feet and gave in to an impulsive urge to gather her into his arms. He'd only meant it as a quick, friendly gesture to comfort an upset friend. But the moment she curled closer into his chest, everything shifted. Suddenly he was aware of every place they touched, the scent of vanilla in her hair, and the way the tension melted from her shoulders.

He could get used to this.

After a long moment, she pulled away and offered him a quick glance, then motioned toward his truck. "I'd better grab my keys."

Right. Apparently, he was the only one caught up in the moment. Head in the game.

He ushered her through the gate and pointed to the remaining egg mess. "If you can get me a bucket of soapy water and a sponge, I'll take care of this."

Piper's gaze bounced from him to the ladder to the slimy mess on the wall and back to him. "You don't have to do that."

He got the impression that although she was eager to offer her help to the kids or, he suspected, anyone else who needed it, she didn't like the idea of needing help herself. "It won't take long."

He clamped his jaw shut to keep his teeth from chattering, then jogged out to his truck, grabbed her purse, and met her at the foot of the front steps to hand it off.

Piper took her purse and dug her keys out. "Come in for a minute. You can warm up too while we find a bucket."

"Thanks." He followed her up the steps.

She unlocked the door and stepped inside, holding the door for him.

Titus pushed it closed behind him and stepped into the warmth of the house. His fingers and ears began to thaw. "Are you settling in here?"

Titus spotted a small table, tucked into a corner just to the left of the stairs, covered in puzzle pieces.

Piper veered to the right through a large wood-framed opening that led into the dining room and kitchen. "Yeah. I like Heritage, and I'd like to stay. But if I can't get the kids to warm up to me, I doubt I'll be getting any offers from the school. At this point, I'll be lucky to even get a decent reference."

"I doubt the situation is as dire as you think. You've got Principal Franklin on your side." Titus leaned on the kitchen island while Piper pulled open the pantry door.

Instead of random packaging from the store on the pantry shelves, everything was in clear containers of graduating sizes neatly stacked and color coded, so the pantry looked like a cascading rainbow. He'd seen her puzzle table. This was clearly evidence of her organization hobby.

"And you've won me over."

She turned from the pantry, bucket in hand, with her brows raised.

"Was it my stubborn temper or my unyielding high standards that drew you in?" There was a matter-of-fact tone to her sarcasm.

Titus got the impression that she was covering a tender spot with humor.

She lifted the bucket into the sink, flipped on the water, then grabbed a bottle of dish soap from under the sink and added a squirt.

"I think those qualities are the result of your determination and idealism." Not to mention compassion. When he'd mentioned his dad, she'd immediately shifted into compassion mode. She'd taken his hand, and any lingering resistance toward her had faded away. But suddenly friendship didn't seem to be enough. Honestly, he'd wanted to ask her out from the moment he'd helped her out of that bush. The only thing that had derailed it was how differently they viewed the kids.

He stepped up by the fridge and eyed a photo of her and some guy who was dressed for graduation. He was positioning his graduation cap on her head while making a face at her.

The water shut off. "That's my brother Cam. He said I should wear his hat because I was the only reason he graduated. We both struggled in school when we were kids. Then when I was in the fourth grade, we went to a new school. My teacher that year was amazing. She worked with me and took the time to understand my challenges and learning style. She spent the year showing me how to overcome my struggles. The next year, Cam was assigned to a different fourth-grade class. His teacher was a nice lady, but she didn't push him. After that, school came easy for me, but he continued to flounder. He played football, and teachers would just excuse him from missing assignments and grade him extra leniently so he could keep playing. I would try to help him with his homework and tell him he's smarter than everyone gave him credit for, but with his teachers letting him squeak by, he never had the motivation to try harder."

"So that's why you're determined not to let my boys slide by?"

She nodded. "When it came time for college, he had never learned the value of hard work. He ended up dropping out in his first semester with a .98 GPA. It completely crushed his confidence and made him believe he would never be competent."

"That had to have been hard to watch."

"He really is smart and capable and full of potential, but no matter how hard I try, I can't convince him of that, because too many people were eager to give him a break in high school."

Maybe her number one goal had always been to help kids succeed. That was what he was trying to do as a coach too, just in a different area. Maybe they weren't so different after all. "And that's why you teach and you're going to spend your evenings tutoring?"

She pulled a sponge and scrub brush out from under the sink and dropped them in the bucket. "Well, probably not *all* my evenings, but helping kids who struggle is why I pursued teaching in the first place. I might have been in the same boat as Cam if my fourth-grade teacher hadn't cared enough to push me. She changed the course of my life. I hope someone can say that about me someday. I love seeing students discover they are capable of more than they thought possible."

Yeah, both he and the kids had misjudged her. He knew too well what it felt like to be misunderstood. The media had made him out to be a monster, and he'd never fully recovered. He'd have to work on correcting the kids' opinion of her.

Titus walked over and lifted the steaming bucket from the sink. He met her eyes, still red rimmed with smeared makeup. "They'll see it eventually. Give them time."

He'd need to give her time too. He couldn't very well go from cold to hot overnight. But maybe he could speed the process up if he could spend a little more time with her.

"The old shop beside Donny's hasn't been used in years. Janie said it's going to need some cleaning up. I could meet you there tomorrow evening and introduce you to Thomas and Janie then help you get it set up."

"Really?" Her eyes lit up.

Yeah, he'd spend the evening cleaning to earn that look. "Sure. Practice should be done by five. Meet you there."

He knew she was there for the right reasons. Now he'd prove to her that he was too.

seven

PIPER HADN'T KNOWN WHAT TO EXPECT WHEN Titus had told her about the shop yesterday, but he'd come through for her in a big way. Piper stood on the top step of the empty unit next to Donny's Diner and stared through one of the double doors. Janie and Thomas, who owned the diner, also owned this but had yet to do something with it. They said it'd been a candy store twenty years ago but had sat empty ever since.

"Do you think it'll work for tutoring?" Titus's words ruffled her hair as he looked at the space over her shoulder from a step below her.

Piper sucked in a breath as the warmth of his breath on her ear sent a jolt of heat through her bloodstream. No. No. No. This was not how she was supposed to react to him. Just friends. That's what he'd offered. And that's all she could ever allow him to be. He was a football player, after all, and she knew firsthand how singular their focus could be. She couldn't play second fiddle to a game for the rest of her life.

Piper stepped in and set down the bucket of cleaning products and a mop and broom. Aside from a thick coat of dust covering every surface in the vacant old candy shop, the space could work. The furniture, not so much.

Titus followed her in and closed the door behind him.

She turned in a circle, taking in the whole space. A large L-shaped glass-front display case occupied the bulk of the left wall. A door on the right wall presumably connected the space to Donny's Diner.

"It's a whole lot better than that smelly equipment trailer." She ran her finger across the glass of the display case, leaving a clear line in the thick dust.

"I still can't believe Principal Franklin thought we could share that space."

She turned to him. "How do you feel about the chaos in there? Does it bother you?"

"The equipment trailer? Drives me crazy. Especially since it's a black hole where things disappear. I put my extra playbooks and my autographed football from college in there. And now they probably live with the other half of my mismatched socks and all the things I put *someplace safe*. But I don't have to live in there, so it's fine."

"I imagine the clutter is a hazard for your knee too. I'd be afraid to step wrong and injure it again." She'd have to find a way to help him out and return the favor for finding her this place.

"Yeah, I already reinjured it a couple weeks ago. I can't afford to do that again." He leaned over to rub his knee through the brace.

She turned back to the shop.

"Why did Thomas say they weren't using the space?" She glanced back at Titus, who was wiping a swath through the dust on the front display case.

"Janie wants to eventually make it a bakery. It just has never been the right time. But they aren't ready to sell it or get rid of any of this either. And they said we can't move the display cases."

Too bad. The big display cases that doubled as a counter only left room for a few tiny café tables in front and a row of them down the right side. The area behind the display case housed a prep counter against the left wall and a walkway only wide enough for a couple of people to stand. That area would not work for tutoring. But the front and right side would accommodate a desk or two. "Can we at least move the bistro tables and chairs somewhere?"

"You don't think they'll work?" His arm brushed her shoulder as he reached to dust off the metal mesh top of the nearest table.

Piper didn't know how to act around Titus now. It was like last night had been a visit to an alternate reality, and here in the real world, she didn't know where they stood. In truth, nothing had happened between them yesterday. But the visceral moment in his arms hadn't felt like nothing. Exactly where was the boundary between friendship and . . . more?

They had a job to do. She couldn't lose focus. Besides, her logic-challenged heart had a track record of getting her into trouble. "With any pressure, a pencil would poke straight through the paper and into the gaps. It would be much better to bring in some desks."

"I can ask Thomas about it, but I doubt it'll be a problem as long as we're careful. We might be able to tuck these into the back." He pulled out his phone and tapped at the screen for a few seconds, then dropped it back into his pocket. "Do you have desks?"

"No. I'd planned on tutoring at school so I could use school resources." Maybe she hadn't thought this tutoring thing all the way through. Here, she would need to provide everything herself. Her meager savings wouldn't go very far, and if she used that money now, she'd have no cushion to hold her over while she looked for a new job when this sub contract ended. Maybe this wouldn't work so well after all. "Maybe I could find some used furniture cheap."

"Have you considered doing a fundraiser?" He lifted the bucket of cleaning products onto one of the dusty tables and began fishing through it. "I told my team they owe you for yesterday. Also, Beau and his friends had detention today. Anyway, what can they help with?"

He was holding them accountable. Nice. She'd take all the help she could get.

"I don't even know what people around here would show up for. What do you think? I can't quite imagine your boys baking for a bake sale. Maybe a silent auction?"

"When I was in high school, we always had good luck with a car wash. There isn't a car wash in town, so the whole town showed up. Don't set a price, just ask for donations, and people get pretty generous for a worthy cause." He unloaded bottles of cleaner, sponges, and wash cloths from the bucket.

"I'm afraid it's too late in the year for a car wash. It's freezing out there." Piper snagged the dusting mitt as Titus set it aside on the table.

Titus pulled out his phone again. "Looks like this cold snap will be over by the weekend. Saturday is supposed to be beautiful. Should we put it on the calendar?"

"This Saturday? I guess so. But can I justify asking the town for funding when I don't know how long I'll be here?" She wiped the first section of the display case glass.

"How long do you plan to be here?" He set the empty bucket down in the corner and set the mop inside, then propped it against the wall.

"Just today, I got an email from the school board asking me to extend my contract because apparently Mrs. MacDonald is having some complications. I'll have a job through February now and maybe longer, depending on her recovery." Two extra months to connect with these kids. The image of egg dripping down the side of her house, stony faces refusing to participate in class, and the poster depicting her as a Siren played through her mind. She had to find a way to get through to them, and maybe tutoring was the way to do that.

"Well, you could always have the fundraiser and donate the desks and materials to the school when you're done with them. What do you say?"

Yeah, that could work. "Okay. That would be amazing!"

Piper had a feeling the boys would not share her enthusiasm, but hopefully, they could make it a fun day.

Titus's phone chimed, and he glanced at his watch. "Thomas says it's fine to move the tables. Where do you want them?"

Piper scanned the space. "At the back and behind the counter if they fit, but I would like to have a path free to the sink."

He pulled the chairs out from around one of the tables and lifted the table effortlessly.

Wasn't that thing heavy? Must be nice being made of muscle. It was certainly nice to watch his T-shirt strain against his biceps and broad shoulders.

He made the chairs look featherlight, but he still limped just a little when he walked. That knee must really hurt, but he never complained.

"At my last job, I didn't get to stick around long enough to make a difference. I have even less time here. I wish I could speed up the process of getting these kids to trust me so I can do some good here." She clapped the dust off the mitt, sending a cloud into the air, and sneezed. She'd have to do that outside next time.

"You didn't get to stick around? Why not?" He set the table down against the back wall.

Maybe she shouldn't be quite so candid, but clamming up now that she'd already said too much would just raise suspicion. If these last two days were any indication, she should be able to trust him not to use it against her. "My contract got canceled because the administration told me to change a particular student's failing grades, and I refused. I wanted him to earn it. I tried to help him raise his grade, offered him special tutoring and extra credit, but he told me he didn't have to do any of that because his dad would buy his grades anyway."

"Talk about entitled." He lifted another table, inverted it, and stacked it on top of the first one he'd moved.

She dropped the dust mitt with the other cleaning supplies and grabbed a bottle of window cleaner and a rag and began wiping the big front window. "When I talked to the principal about it, he said the kid's dad was the school's biggest donor and he'd threatened to pull his funding if his son failed. He said they'd already changed his grades behind my back, and when I protested, I lost my job for insubordination."

"So when I asked you to give my players grace, it struck a nerve."

She bit her lip and peeked over her shoulder at him. He stood with a bistro chair under each arm, and his eyes were on her. It almost looked like he was invested in what she was saying. And that attention, when he wasn't getting anything out of it, chipped away at her defenses even more. "Yeah, I guess so. I'm sure you've gathered by now that I have a tendency to jump to conclusions, but I do appreciate that you are holding the boys accountable."

"I'm trying. Has Brett come for tutoring during study hall at all?" Titus set the chairs down.

"No. I actually peeked into his study hall during my break yesterday, and he had his head down on one of the desks in the back, sound asleep." She stepped back and admired the streak-free window. Despite the overcast sky, the room looked brighter with a clean window.

Titus continued to stack the chairs next to the stacked tables, then scrubbed his face. "I really don't know what to do with him."

She set down the rag and spray bottle, then grabbed the bucket next to the mop in the corner and carried it behind the display case. She set it next to the sink and flipped on the water. Brown water poured out. Eww! "What is wrong with the water?"

Titus stepped behind the counter with a couple more chairs in hand. He stashed them under the counter and rested a hand on her shoulder as he peeked around her to look in the sink. "Nothing. Pipes have just been sitting still for a while. It'll run clear in a minute. Are these chairs okay here?"

She nodded. How could he be so casual when her heart was pounding like a jackhammer? Clearly, she was more affected than he was. Of course she was. Look at him. As she got to know him on a deeper level, that initial attraction she'd felt toward him when they'd met was coming back full force, but it went past the surface now.

"What do you think I should do about Brett?" He rounded the display case and headed toward the front of the shop and began to sweep the cleared space.

As soon as the water was clear, she tested the temperature and then stuck the bucket under the stream. "I tried reaching out to his parents, but I didn't get a response back. Will you hand me that bottle of Pine-Sol?"

He paused his sweeping and sifted through the bottles, then handed her the cleaner over the display case. "I've tried to get ahold of his parents too with no luck."

"Teenagers are forgetful and aren't always good at prioritizing, especially if they aren't getting a lot of support from their family at home. Maybe you need to sit down with him one-on-one and find out what's going on, or do a house call and see if you can catch his parents in person. I think if I can just work with him, he could have a breakthrough. We just need to find something that will motivate him to show up." If she didn't find a way to make tutoring work here, who would come alongside Brett? She poured a glug of cleaner into the bucket of hot water, sending a plume of pine scent through the air.

"I know he loves the game. I can't believe losing playing time hasn't done the trick." He carefully brushed a pile of dust into the dustpan.

She shut off the water and carried the bucket around the display case. "Brett and all these kids at the school, your players, they are bright and capable and full of potential. I don't want them to get out of high school without knowing that."

Titus stopped her with a hand on her arm and took the handle of the heavy bucket from her. "You're a good person, Piper. I'm glad I met you. And these kids are lucky to have someone who cares so much about them, even if they can't see it just yet. What will you do when your contract ends?" He carried the bucket to the front, now cleared of tables, and set it by the mop still propped against the wall.

Before, she would have said she'd just move on, but a future in Heritage was looking more and more appealing. She grabbed the broom and made quick work of sweeping the front section of the shop. "I don't know."

At a tap on the glass of the front door, Piper turned to find Jess gripping something large that was rolled up.

Titus stepped over to let her in. "Did you finish it?"

"Finish what?" Piper left her broom behind to peek around Titus.

"Titus asked me to make something for you." Jess shot a sug- gestive glance between Piper and Titus then unrolled a laminated two-foot by three-foot banner. "Missing Piece Tutoring Center" was painted over a pattern of puzzle pieces.

Tutoring center. It sounded so official and permanent.

And right.

Yes, this was more than just a temporary supplement to teach- ing. It was exactly what she was supposed to be doing. And Her- itage was exactly where she was meant to be.

If her future was here, she couldn't just wait to see what might happen. She needed to *make* it happen. The pieces clicked together, and a peace she couldn't explain settled in her spirit. It was the same feeling she got when she finished a puzzle.

She could do this. She'd be needing every penny she could raise from that fundraiser and many more like it.

The little shop was great, but it was temporary. She was going to need something permanent.

Titus had expected some pushback from the team when he'd told them they were required to sacrifice their Saturday to come help at the fundraiser, but aside from razzing Beau and his friends a bit, they actually had a pretty good attitude. Maybe that had to do with the win they'd scored against a tough team last night.

The day had dawned warm and sunny as promised, and as busy as they had been all morning and into the afternoon, they must have washed nearly every car in Heritage. Better yet, the boys were getting along. The water fight Jay had started turned into laughing and bonding that began to unwind the knots in Titus's shoulders. Beau and his friends had even offered Piper an unprompted apology. He hadn't gotten a final count from Piper before he'd left, but the cash box had looked pretty full. Yeah, it'd been a good day.

Except Brett hadn't shown up.

Now, an hour later, Titus pulled into the driveway his GPS indicated and eyed the rundown two-story house that lacked the charm of many of Heritage's houses. He checked the address against the paper that he had pulled from Brett's file. This was it all right. Children's toys littered the lawn in a jungle of grass a month past when it should have been mowed.

Titus slipped out of his truck and hurried up the three steps and tapped out a knock on the door.

A moment later, a shirtless Brett opened the door with the toddler Titus had met at the grocery store, now clad only in a diaper, on his hip and the voices of more rambunctious kids arguing in the background. In Brett's free hand, he held a war-torn copy of *The Taming of the Shrew* with his thumb propped in the center of the book.

Brett quickly pulled out his earbuds and put the toddler down.

"Trevor, I need you to go find Sarah."

The little one popped his thumb into his mouth and nodded before toddling around the corner out of the entryway.

"Hey, Coach, sorry about missing the car wash this morning. I had to babysit my siblings. I couldn't get out of it."

"Mind if we chat?" Titus took a step toward the door, but Brett blocked his path.

"Now is actually not a great time. My dad's gonna be home any minute."

"I'd actually like to meet your dad."

Brett glanced over his shoulder, then stepped out onto the stoop and closed the screen door behind him. "It would be better if you didn't."

"I'm worried about you. You've missed tutoring, you've missed practice, you even have unexcused absences from classes at school last week, and now the fundraiser. You've been ineligible for two weeks now." His happy-go-lucky demeanor had been fading as well. And he seemed withdrawn and sometimes downright surly too, but he'd leave that out for now. "What's going on? Talk to me."

An old rusty Chevy truck growled into the driveway next to his F-250.

"Please, Coach, you've got to go." Brett's eyes were pleading as he watched a middle-aged guy with a receding hairline, presumably his dad, get out of the truck.

"Who's this, Brett?" The guy approached the front door with narrowed eyes that didn't exactly lay out the welcome mat. Despite his softened middle, he looked like he might have been a football player himself when he was younger. "I've told you before, don't bring anyone to the house."

Titus wasn't about to let the guy intimidate him. He held his ground and extended his hand. "My name is Titus Ford. I'm Brett's football coach. He didn't invite me. I just stopped by to check in."

The guy ignored Titus's extended hand and shot a caustic look at Brett. "This is exactly why I told you to quit that team. Being involved with stuff like that just makes people like *him* think he has the right to stick his nose into our business." He turned to Titus. "I'm sure you've got good intentions and all that, but Brett's my issue. And his priority needs to be home and family. Football is always his excuse for not pulling his weight around here, so with all due respect, get off my property and leave my boy alone."

The crestfallen expression on Brett's face proved just how much he loved football and how hard he'd fought for his spot on the team, not only at school, but at home. "Dad, we talked about this. You said I could stay on the team if I still kept up with my chores and helped with the kids. Please." His voice broke on the final plea.

"Sir, I know football is a big commitment, but Brett is a re-markable player. He really has a good chance of getting college scholarship offers."

Brett's dad snorted his distaste. "Brett ain't getting into no fancy college. He can't even keep his grades up enough to play in high school. College is nothing but a waste of time and money anyway. He'll just give up four or five years he could be working and helping his family out, then end up back here probably workin' the line at Heritage Fruits anyway. He don't need no piece of paper slapping a title on him to do that."

The last thing Titus wanted was Brett's dad to take this as a chal-lenge or an insult. "Playing college ball can lead to pretty amazing opportunities and—"

"I never went to college, but his mother did." A touch of pain entered the man's expression. "We've been paying off those stupid student loans for sixteen years, and she never used that degree for nothing. After all that debt, she ended up working part-time as a cashier anyway. Said she would get a job in business when the kids were all in school, but now she's dying, and it was all for nothing."

Titus's gaze shot to Brett, but his head was hanging and he wouldn't meet his eyes. His mom was dying? Yeah, a little distraction and absence made perfect sense now. Why hadn't Brett told him?

Brett's father didn't pause his rant. "So, no, I don't want you filling his head with all this college talk, convincing him that it's his ticket out of here."

"I'm sorry about your wife. I didn't know. I'm sure this is a really difficult time."

"No thanks to you thinking you have the right to Brett's time at all hours. Family comes first, and his family needs him."

"You're right. Family is important. That's one of the values I try to instill in my team. So if you ever need anything, please let us know."

The guy pulled back and eyed Titus suspiciously.

"We don't need nobody's charity."

"Brett's teammates consider him a brother, and they would be here in an instant if your family needs them, and so would I. Not for charity, but because you are family, and family takes care of their own."

After a long moment, he relented, but he still looked wary. "I guess maybe it would be okay for the kid to have some guys in his corner. But practice and games are enough. Nothing extra."

Titus nodded. "I understand."

Finally, he extended his hand. "Name's Walter."

Titus shook his hand. "Would it be okay if I talked with Brett for a minute?"

Walter looked from Titus to Brett and back again. "Just for a minute." He turned back to Brett. "I'm going to need your help with dinner."

"Yes, sir."

Walter stepped past them and into the house.

Before the door swung shut, a child's voice squealed. "Daddy!"

Brett watched through the screen until his dad disappeared from sight. "Sorry about that. Dad wasn't always like this. Since Mom got sick, he's been working two jobs trying to make up for her income and keep the bills paid. The hospital bills from all the rounds of treatment they tried are a lot too."

"I think all of that might make me a bit irritable too." Titus was lucky his own medical bills from his surgery and physical therapy were covered and that he only had himself to take care of. He couldn't imagine trying to pay down the medical debt and provide for a family at the same time. All the while watching the one you loved the most suffer and fade.

"He's always stressed. Mom can't be left alone for too long, and I'm the only one old enough to help when my dad isn't here. When he's here, he's stressed about not getting the bills paid. And when he's working, he's stressed about missing her last days, and he can't be in two places at once."

"Why didn't you tell me about your mom?" What would Titus do without his own mom? He'd squandered years away, rarely visiting or even calling as much as he should have. He'd taken her for granted.

Brett shrugged. "Don't really want to talk about it. It's nice going to practice and just being free to think about something else for a while. Does that make me a terrible person?"

"No. Not at all. But you are also choosing to walk alone through something hard, and you don't have to." But Titus had made the same choice over and over, isolating himself from his family either with distance or just losing himself in practice. Maybe he was still burying himself, only now it was as a coach. Was he trying to do it alone? "How long has this been going on?"

Brett dropped down onto the step, and Titus lowered himself to sit beside him.

"She got sick about a year ago. Cancer. She and Dad are both really private people. They didn't want everyone to know, so she'd been doing treatments down in Grand Rapids. My dad's sister lives there, and Mom would stay with her during the chemo and come home between. They tried a couple different medications, radiation, and chemo, but she just kept getting worse. About a month ago, the doctors did some tests to see if the chemo was working, but they said the cancer was aggressive and not responding to treatment, so they sent her home for hospice."

"So with your dad working all the time, that leaves you to care for your mom and siblings?"

"Yeah. The neighbor, Mrs. Schabat, watches Trevor and stays with Mom while the rest of us are in school. My sister Sarah is eleven, and she walks the younger boys home and tries to take care of things so I can go to practice, but she's really too young to watch them for long. And Mom and Dad can't afford extra home health or daycare costs, so it's hard for me to get away."

"How many siblings do you have?"

"Four. I'm the oldest, and Sarah is my only sister, then there's three more boys. Benson is eight, Corbin is six, and Trevor is almost three." He looked down at the step. "Trevor and Corbin aren't even going to remember her. They aren't going to remember her amazing lasagna or her laugh or how much she loved Little Sable Lighthouse."

Titus dropped a hand on Brett's shoulder and squeezed. "You can keep those memories alive for them. Save pictures and videos, tell stories, get her recipe and learn to make her lasagna."

Brett nodded. "Yeah. I'll have to do that. Maybe Sarah can help."

"Your dad doesn't like you having people over, so I'm going to guess that includes babysitters."

Brett nodded. "Mom is immunocompromised, so he doesn't want her to get exposed to anything, and the house is a mess. We can't keep up with everything Mom used to do."

"I have three siblings that I was responsible for when I was in high school, so I know how hard it can be to balance school, football, and home. My dad left when I was eleven, and my mom worked two or three jobs to keep us afloat. My team was my lifeline back then. They would help me babysit, cover for me when I couldn't keep up with everything, and let me vent to keep me sane. Your team would do the same for you. I won't tell them if you don't want me to, but I think you should consider letting them in." Coach Hutchens had encouraged his team to become a band of brothers, and this team was making strides toward similar bonds. If Titus wanted to foster more of that, he had to teach more than plays and skills.

"I'll think about it. I've got to get back in before Dad comes looking for me." Brett got to his feet.

Titus also stood. "Say, would you mind if I share some of this with Miss Caveneau? Maybe she could find a way to make tutoring more flexible for you. I know she can be discreet."

"Yeah, that's fine. I'm sure she's about ready to give up on me at this point. It'd probably be good for her to know there's an actual reason why I keep blowing her off." Brett reached for the screen door latch.

Titus gripped Brett's shoulder. "Hang in there, and you have my number. If you need anything, just call or text and I'll be here."

Brett swallowed hard. "Thanks, Coach." His voice was thick with emotion.

Titus had set out to find out what was going on so he could help, but he couldn't fix this. Piper had said football was just a game. For the first time ever, Titus could understand the perspective. What were football games—or English papers for that matter—when Brett was facing such loss? But Brett hadn't discarded football. On the contrary, it had been clear how much his team meant to him. That was what a team should be.

Titus pulled open the door of his truck and slid into the driver's seat. He rubbed at his chest over his heart, where an ache had settled deep.

Sure, coaching was about football, but it couldn't only be about football, not if he wanted to be a good coach. Coach Hutchens in high school had brought the team together. He'd encouraged them to be there for each other, but Coach Dodger had taken the relationship a step further and become a mentor. He lived as an example. He gave of himself. That kind of investment went way beyond the football field, but then, so did his impact.

Piper hardly even knew these kids, and she was already doing all of that. She was making an investment, even when it cost her time and energy. Even when it hurt. Maybe that was why he was so drawn to her. He recognized the same qualities in her that he'd so admired in his mentor. Maybe he could learn a few things from her, because that was the kind of coach he wanted to be. And maybe that meant sticking around Heritage longer than he'd originally planned.

eight

SINCE THE MOMENT JESS HAD UNFURLED that sign three days ago, Piper had been turning over the possibilities. The tutoring center wasn't just a temporary thing anymore, so she needed a plan to make it permanent. The money this morning's fundraiser had brought in would help buy desks, but where would she put them?

She'd just posted the tutoring center hours around school, and the office had announced her services in morning announcements last week. A few kids, including Aaron, had trickled in throughout the week for tutoring, but it was nothing like today. Eleven kids showing up in the old candy shop at four o'clock on a Saturday afternoon for a study group was evidence that Heritage needed a place like this. Not to mention someplace bigger. She'd had to adjust her strategy at the last minute because there was no way she could offer one-on-one tutoring with this many kids in such a small space. Luckily, most were there for a big chemistry test on Monday, so she'd opted for a group competition.

Notes in hand, she scanned the young faces gathered into two groups on the bistro chairs that were squished into the cramped space in front of the display cases. A few of the football players had even come, despite a busy day at the car wash.

"This could be the tiebreaker. Are you ready?" Piper put on her best game show host voice and looked at Kristen, Titus's sister, and Aaron, who were up to the buzzers representing their teams.

When they both nodded, hands poised expectantly over their buttons, Piper read the question from the list she'd gotten from Mrs. Merrick, the chemistry teacher. "What are the horizontal rows on the periodic t—"

One of the buzzers went off, and Piper glanced at her computer screen to see which of the competitors had hit it first. "Team two, Kristen. Get this right and your team takes the lead, but if you're wrong, Aaron will have the chance to steal."

"Horizontal rows on the periodic table are called periods."

"Correct!" Piper added a point on the digital scoreboard on her computer screen. "Team two takes the lead."

Twenty minutes later, the kids grabbed a piece of candy from her reward bucket on their way out as Piper packed up her set of *Family Feud*–style buzzers. The door clicked shut just as she carried the box behind the display counter and grabbed her purse she'd stashed back there. When she stepped out from behind the counter, Aaron still stood by the door, his backpack slung over his shoulder as he shifted his gaze from her to the floor and back to her.

Piper set her purse on top of the display case. "Is everything okay, Aaron? How'd you do on that government paper we worked on a few days ago?"

Aaron offered her a genuine and big-enough-to-show-his-teeth smile, as if he'd been waiting for her to ask. He lifted a red folder from his bag and pulled out a paper and turned it to her. "I got an A on the paper and the test. That analogy you taught me in tutoring about the wheel with the executive branch in the center really helped."

This couldn't be the same surly kid she'd talked to during in-school suspension. Since that day, he had slowly been shedding his apathy. Even Wednesday, when he'd come in for help on his paper, he'd seemed restless and uncomfortable. But today, along with the attitude shift, his eyes, which had frequently been dilated or bloodshot when she'd first met him, were now clear and focused. "From the sounds of the review today, I'll bet you're going to ace the science test too."

"Science and math are easy. English, history, and government are the ones I don't get." He pulled his phone from his pocket and glanced at the time. "I've got work at five-thirty. I just wanted to say thanks."

He stepped through the door and down onto the sidewalk outside. Yeah, she would find a way to make this tutoring center work, and not just for a few weeks.

Today's car wash had given her some petty cash, but it wouldn't come close to what she needed. She'd spent the last few days researching grants and developing a business plan.

Piper carried her laptop over to the folding table in the corner where she'd been compiling her notes and research. A tap on the glass drew her attention back to the front of the shop. Jess waved at her through the window, and Piper motioned for her to come in.

Jess let herself in. "I saw kids leaving and thought I'd stop in and check it out. Looks good in here."

"With the place clean and a couple of small folding tables Titus borrowed from his mom, it's at least functional, but really cramped." Piper lifted the lid of her laptop and opened her business plan. "Which is why I am working on this."

Jess came up beside Piper and glanced at the screen, then scooped up a printed spreadsheet sprinkled with handwritten notes. "Didn't the car wash raise enough? I think we washed every car in the county."

"People were very generous. But I can only use this place until

December first. I'll need to look for a permanent space. I'm compiling a list of funding options that might help me buy or rent a permanent building." She clicked the mouse to flip the screen to a grant database.

"Permanent? That's amazing! So many of the kids at the school need a place like this. I just saw Aaron leaving. He was telling me yesterday about how you helped him. When I started at the school last year, I couldn't imagine him volunteering to do anything school related, but he actually smiled when he told me about going to tutoring with you."

The thought of Aaron warmed Piper's heart. Yeah, she had to do this for Aaron and all the other kids like him who needed to recognize their own potential. "I just hope all the funding and details all come together. It's a big undertaking. I simply have to find a way to make it work."

"I really think God made you for this, so you can trust Him to bring it together."

Piper couldn't fault Jess for voicing what she believed in. But God hadn't exactly proven Himself to be trustworthy for her in the past. And she was far too flawed to be the kind of person He could use anyway. They had mutually parted ways, and that was fine with Piper, because she didn't need a "higher power" bossing her around. "God and I aren't exactly on speaking terms. I think pulling this together is going to be on me."

"Well, He's already working through you in Aaron's life. That's a good indication that you and God have the same goal. And when that's true, He's working with you whether you acknowledge it or not. And I'm pretty sure God is on speaking terms with everyone. The question is if we're listening."

Okay, as much as Piper would love to be able to take sole credit for Aaron's change of attitude, her experience with Cam was evidence enough that she was not that good. Maybe God did care about Aaron. But she was pretty sure that God actually talking to people was an Old Testament thing. "I think I'd notice a burning bush."

Jess dropped the spreadsheet back onto the stack of papers. "Wouldn't we all. But sometimes His voice is a little more subtle. Even your intuition can be God's prompting."

That day Aaron was missing from class for in-school suspension, something had propelled her to go find him. Could that have been God?

Another knock rattled the door, and Piper spotted Titus through the window. She waved. "Come in."

He stepped inside and closed the door behind him.

"Hey, Piper." Titus spotted Jess and seemed to hesitate. "Hey, Jess, I didn't know you were here. I hate to interrupt . . ."

"I was just leaving." Jess gave Piper a quick hug and pointedly bobbed her brows while her back was to Titus.

Piper's cheeks heated, and a little shiver tickled down her spine. She glanced over Jess's shoulder, and her gaze connected with his. An inner alarm bell went off as she took in his pinched brows and sagging shoulders.

Jess paused by Titus, seeming to catch his mood as well. He only gave a slight shake of his head that indicated he didn't want to talk about it. Jess seemed to accept that and hurried out. What could he want to talk to her about privately?

He stepped closer to the table and looked at her computer screen. "What are you working on?"

Piper snapped her laptop shut. "Just a project."

Why had she done that? Because she felt silly saying she wanted to start a business when she had no money and barely an idea.

"You want to go for a walk?" Titus took a step backward toward the door.

"Sure." Piper gathered her papers on the table into a pile and stacked them on her laptop, then headed to the front door. She'd have to stop back here later to collect her things.

Outside, Titus turned toward the town square and led the way across the street.

Clouds had rolled in this afternoon, so it wasn't quite as warm as it had been earlier for the car wash, but it was still unseasonably beautiful for this time of year. The cold snap this week had transformed the mantle of the trees throughout Heritage into a brilliant red-orange-and-gold canopy.

Piper cast a quick glance at Titus as she tried to keep up with his long-legged strides. Even with a limp, he was fast. Whatever it was, he'd share when he was ready.

He seemed to realize he was rushing her and slowed his pace. "It's about Brett."

"What happened? Is he hurt?"

"He's okay." Titus's gaze traveled over the grassy area of the town square dusted with yellow and orange leaves, as he seemed to search for words.

Titus took her hand, and a zing tickled up her arm and settled low in her stomach. He seemed to be holding onto her for support. She stopped on the sidewalk and turned toward him.

He looked down at their linked hands and took a deep breath. "Brett's mom is dying of cancer. She went into hospice three weeks ago, the same week he missed that first assignment."

"That poor kid." A weight settled over Piper's chest.

Piper wasn't on the best terms with her mom right now, but even the thought of losing her during high school made her feel sick. And Brett had younger siblings too. Her throat thickened, and she blinked back moisture that had sprung to her eyes. He was too young to be dealing with such loss.

"His dad is working a lot, and Brett is responsible for helping his mom and taking care of his four younger siblings most of the time. The youngest is only two, so he really can't leave them alone."

"Why didn't he tell me?" Piper hung her head. "I feel terrible. I've been pushing him pretty hard."

"We all have." Titus squeezed her hand. "No one knew. I only found out because I went to his house after he didn't show up for the car wash."

"This week at school we were talking about character archetypes in fiction. I want to be the guide who helps these kids realize their potential to be a hero, but maybe I'm actually the villain."

"You are not the villain." He met her gaze. "But you do have the bar set pretty high, and it's frustrating to those who struggle, when they feel like success is out of reach."

"I don't want to be like that." Their linked hands were beginning to feel more like holding hands than offering comfort. Piper pulled hers free to climb the steps of the gazebo. "I know my expectations are higher than they're used to, and it's uncomfortable when something doesn't come easy, but that's the only way to grow."

"True, but it doesn't happen overnight." He followed her up the steps and gazed at her. "You might not see the growth from the investments you're making today for months or even years."

In the center of the gazebo, Piper shivered as his lingering stare began to heat up. Friends. Right? Just friends. She pulled her gaze away and looked up at the overhead glass fixture. It really was beautiful. She needed to stay focused on this matter at hand and stay in bounds of the friend zone. "I want to help Brett. But I don't know how. Maybe I could arrange babysitting or virtual tutoring."

"His dad won't let anyone come over, including babysitters. They also don't have internet at the house." Titus dropped down onto a bench on the edge of the structure and rubbed his knee.

"He really is battling every possible challenge to get his schoolwork caught up, isn't he? Maybe I could excuse him from a nonessential activity. I'm going to start training some students as peer tutors. One of them could work with him during my class. The problem is there isn't a good place for tutoring in the school building when the classrooms are in use."

"They could use my office. I'm usually in the gym for classes during the day."

Piper sat next to him on the bench. "I've never seen your office. Where is it? Would there be enough supervision for me to send a couple students unattended?"

"It's in the same hallway as the teachers' lounge. If they left the door open and the office knew what they were there for, I think it'd be okay. Do you have someone in mind?" He stretched his arm across the back of the bench behind her, brushing her shoulders in the process.

Another breach of the friend zone. Maybe he could keep himself in check with all the touching and flirting, but she wasn't so confident with her own ability to do that.

She met his gaze. Right, she hadn't answered his question. "So far, Kristen is the only one who has agreed to train as an English tutor. Normally I wouldn't send a boy and girl off alone together, but she and Brett seem responsible enough. Don't you think?"

A muscle twitched in Titus's jaw. "As a teacher, yes, I think that would work. As a big brother, I would like to enroll her in an all girls' school."

She swatted his shoulder, but his look was too intense when she met his eyes. Yeah, the friend zone boundaries were in serious jeopardy. She broke eye contact and shifted her attention to the square over his shoulder. Her gaze snagged on the brass hippo on the north side of the square. "Look! Otis!"

Titus followed her gaze. "Haven't you seen him before?"

"Only from a distance. I keep thinking I need to check him out, but I haven't had the chance." She bounced up from the seat and trotted down the steps. The safe distance from him left a void she didn't care to analyze.

Titus followed Piper down the northbound path toward the statue.

Piper walked a circle around Otis, then squatted beside him and examined the place where his bronze belly rested on the cement. "How does he move?"

"That's a question for the generations. No one I know has ever figured it out. When we were in high school, my whole football team tried to pick him up to look underneath, and we couldn't even get him to budge. The town passed a law after that. Anyone caught trying can get fined. And it isn't small."

"Well, Otis, I guess you're pretty good at keeping a secret." She patted him on the back.

"I suppose I should let you get back. I don't want to keep you from your . . . project."

Oh yeah, the business plan. Maybe she should just tell him. "I've been thinking about looking for a more permanent location."

"You have the old candy shop through the end of November. That should get you through football season. Do you think you'll need a place after that?"

"Yeah. The problem doesn't go away after football. When fall sports end, winter sports start up, then spring sports, and they're all going to need access to tutoring next year too."

"Does that mean you've decided to stay in Heritage even if you don't get a full-time teaching position?"

There was so much hope in his expression she had to look away. Yes, she wanted to stay. She wanted this tutoring center to have an impact. Maybe she even wanted to explore the subtext developing between them. But there were so many uncertainties still. "I'm still figuring that out."

"I, for one, like the idea of you sticking around." The husky quality of his voice added a layer of meaning to the words.

Piper shivered despite the lingering warmth as the sun sank nearer to the horizon. At this rate, this "just friends" thing they were trying out wasn't going to last long at all. "Do you think there might be any other vacant building available? Like maybe an empty building the town owns? I'll make the calls myself. I just don't know very many people around here yet, so I don't even know who to call."

"I called Mayor Jameson when I was looking for you, and he said the only place available was the old library. And trust me, that dungeon is not a viable option." Titus bent to pick up a big maple leaf that looked like a watercolor masterpiece with gold in the center, then blazing outward into orange, then brilliant red on the edges. He offered Piper the leaf. "Jon Kensington is your best bet. I was going to call him next, but Thomas and Janie offered the space, so I didn't end up talking to him."

"Who is this guy? I've heard his name a lot." Piper pinched the leaf's stem between her thumb and forefinger and slowly rotated the leaf. She'd have to find the best way to preserve it.

"He owns Heritage Fruits and has his fingers in lots of other enterprises too. He's the local philanthropist."

In her experience, rich, influential men who wore the title "philanthropist" couldn't be trusted. She'd learned that the hard way. Their generosity always seemed to come with strings attached. This was her tutoring center. She'd never give someone the power to make her compromise again.

I, for one, like the idea of you sticking around. Those words Titus had said to Piper had been rolling round in his mind, distracting him all week. Even now, more than halfway through the Friday night homecoming game, when his focus should be on the next play, those words he'd spoken without thinking kept replaying. Why would he say he wanted her to stick around when he didn't know how long *he* planned to stick around?

Only, it hadn't felt like a contradiction. In fact, it'd gotten him thinking even more about what life might look like if he did stay.

Life with Piper. He didn't know her all that well yet, but, yeah, he could see it.

Titus shifted his clipboard to his other hand and called the play to Brett, who was looking to him from the field as the offensive line gathered into a huddle. "Panther 309."

True to her word, Piper had found a way to get Brett into tutoring during the school day, getting him excused from unnecessary activities, study halls, and free time at every possible opportunity all week and scheduling tutors if she couldn't work with him herself, until he'd gotten caught up just in the nick of time to play in tonight's game. He was still far from an A, but it was enough to get him on the field.

Maybe Piper's idealism was rubbing off on Titus, because he'd started to see a vision of what this team could become, of who he could become as a coach. For the first time since the injury—no, long before that—a future on the sidelines didn't feel like a defeat. He'd even stopped looking at the team reports and hoping his agent might call.

Evidence of bonding and brotherhood showed up in the team as cohesive teamwork on the field that seemed almost unstoppable. This homecoming game could be the fresh start the team and Titus needed.

Nate sidled up next to him and motioned to the scoreboard. "Tied in the third quarter. These boys sure like to test our blood pressure."

"With Brett in there, we'll be fine." Probably.

The other team broke their huddle and found their places on the line. Beau hiked the ball to Brett with a clean snap. Tension coiled around Titus's chest as Owen took off around the line to the left. While his wideout, Wyatt, ran around on the right, Brett dropped back for a pass. Jay, who'd earned back his guard spot on the offensive line, shut down the blitz on that side. Brett was looking for Owen, but he couldn't break free of the outside linebacker.

Titus gripped the clipboard tighter with each yard as Wyatt, who had broken free into the backfield, waved his hand.

Brett spotted him, even as the defense closed in, and sent the ball airborne.

Wyatt nabbed it, right on the numbers, and took off. Forty-seven beautiful yards, and Titus ran down the sidelines as the receiver danced into the end zone, untouched.

Wyatt performed his silly victory dance for the cheering crowd as Owen and Brett jogged over with their fists raised in celebration. They grabbed each other's shoulders and knocked their helmets together.

Yeah, this team really was something special. Seeing Owen celebrate Wyatt's success made Titus proud to be their coach. And Brett—it was like being back on the field had chased away the burdens that had weighed down his shoulders and his spirit the past few weeks. Titus had never expected coaching at this level to give him this much satisfaction.

And even though Nelson, the kicker, missed the extra points, the crowd still roared, the pulse pounding in Titus's ears. Yes! That much closer to the win.

Titus scanned the bleachers for Piper again. The stands were full and the game kept him too busy for a thorough search, but if he could just catch a glimpse of her, it would make this night even better. He couldn't banish her from his thoughts, and honestly, he didn't want to. Her passion to help these kids had made him look deeper when it came to Brett. And he was glad he had. She lived with such passion, such conviction that it made him want to strive to be a better man. She woke up something inside of him that he couldn't even fully name.

Almost made a man want to stay in Heritage permanently.

"We need the kickoff unit on the field." Nate clapped his hands urgently. "Come on, boys. You know the drill."

The call Titus should have been making himself snapped his

attention back to the game. He turned a sheepish smile to his assistant coach. "Thanks."

"Is she out there?" He nodded toward the bleachers.

"Haven't found her yet."

Nelson made the kick, and the line tore across the field after the receiver.

"Seems like the hostility between you two is long gone." Nate kept his eyes on the field.

Titus stole a quick glance at Nate. "Yeah, you could say that. Did you hear what she did to get Brett back on the field?"

Nate nodded. "It's almost like she's invested in someone special around here."

She'd certainly been warming to him, but investing in a student didn't mean she considered Titus "someone special." Helping kids was what made her tick, and hearing about Brett's mom just supercharged that desire with her compassion.

Titus and Nate turned their attention back to the field as the kick went into the air, coming down about the thirty-five-yard line. A Charger reached up to grab it, but his timing was off and he only managed to tip the ball. Owen, one of his fastest players, scooped it up from a wild bounce on the thirty-yard line and took off for the Chargers' end zone.

"Yes, Owen!" Titus dropped the clipboard to cup his hands around his mouth and yelled. "Run!"

Titus held his breath as Owen dodged a couple of Chargers, leaped over another who dove in his path. He stumbled as he shook off a tackle but managed to recover and regain his footing without going down. Finally unencumbered, he closed the twenty-one remaining yards to the end zone. Titus sucked in a breath. "Attaboy!"

The crowd roared, and every player on the sideline was on his feet, whooping at the magnificent recovery.

Titus glanced over at Coach David and nodded to the special-teams players gathered around him. David herded them toward Titus. "You up for trying for two?"

Brett rubbed his hands together, and a grin lit up his face. "Heck, yeah!"

The offense went in, and a winded Owen lined up, but Brett peeled out and hit Wyatt right over the goal line for an easy two-point conversion.

Man, this game was fun. And Titus wanted to share it with Piper. He glanced at the stands again. Two strong-willed, stubborn people were bound to attract conflict. But the thrill that traveled through him at the thought of catching up with her after the game . . . Attraction had no respect for logic.

Both teams' defensive lines held until the last minute, when the Chargers managed to squeak out a field goal, but they were still twelve points short. Panthers won twenty-two to ten.

"Maybe we still have a shot at earning those jerseys after all." Nate slapped Titus's shoulder.

"It's looking better and better." Titus scanned the crowds filing out of the bleachers. Still no sign of Piper. If he could get out there quick enough, maybe he could find her. Whether it was wise or not, he had to take a shot and ask her out.

He'd barely gotten the words out when the team surrounded them on all sides, offering each other high fives and chest bumps and thrusting their fists in the air until the huddle was too tight to move.

Okay, moments like this were too rare. He needed to be present. Pursuing Piper would have to wait. Titus cheered with the team as they began to rotate back and forth, jostling Titus, Nate, and David in the center.

Brett shouted out the start of the team's chant. "We are . . ."

The other players shouted, "Panthers!"

Titus joined in as they repeated the chant. On the third time, the players thrust their helmets in the air on the word "Panthers."

When the huddle broke and the boys started gathering their things on the sidelines, Titus scooped up his own clipboard and water bottle. As he turned to head for the locker room, a woman in slacks and a peacoat shoved a mini recorder in his face.

Titus stiffened. It had been a while, but he was no stranger to persistent reporters. He set his load down on the bench and braced himself for her questions.

"Coach Ford, it must feel good to have your team whole again after a series of weeks missing key players."

Titus relaxed. This kind of press he could handle. "It sure is. As hard as it was to lose several from our starting line, it gave some of our up-and-comers a chance for some playing time, and ultimately, we're seeing a stronger team today. I'm so proud of the boys and all they've accomplished."

"Brett Michaels is back, and that arm is better than ever. I'm sure it was a blow to be without him for so long."

"With Xavier as quarterback the past few weeks, we've been strengthening our running plays. He really did rise to the occasion and deserves the credit for that."

"Speaking of running plays, Brett surprised everyone with that two-point conversion. We knew he had a great arm, but he can run too." The woman shifted her stance.

"Brett is a remarkable player, a triple threat. He can run and throw, but he's also a leader who inspires his teammates. I know the fans have missed him on the field as much as he's missed being out here himself." Titus glanced over at Brett, who was talking to a different reporter, with his helmet propped under his arm. His red shock of hair stood in stark contrast against the blue of his jersey. "I really think we're just scratching the surface of his potential. But more than that, he's coachable. He's a team player. He's driven to improve. He really is the whole package, and it's an honor to coach him."

The reporter gestured to Owen, who had Jay in a playful headlock near the table with the Gatorade cooler. "Owen Baltic really captured the crowd with his fumbled recovery touchdown. He hasn't always had the confidence for those quick plays. What influences do you think are driving his improvement?"

"He's really thrown himself into the game this season. He's had some rough moments, but he's channeled his energy into improvement, and it's really paying off for him."

"Wyatt surprised us with his speed today. Looks like he's creeping up to Owen's level."

Titus turned toward the end zone where Wyatt had brought home a touchdown. "He and Owen have been working well together. Both Wyatt and Owen have impressed me in that regard."

Titus turned back to the reporter. Her attention shifted behind him, and her brows shot up, then she smiled and took a few long steps back.

Before Titus could turn to see what was happening, a deluge of orange liquid poured over his head. He turned as Gatorade streamed down his face and into his mouth just in time to see Jay, Owen, Brett, and Wyatt lower the orange barrel cooler.

Beau tossed a couple towels at him. "Good game, Coach."

Titus mopped his face and scrubbed his hair, trying to hold back a small laugh. He failed. He chucked the most saturated towel at them. "You guys had better not use all the hot water."

But later, as he stood under the hot shower, the sticky orange torrent, and especially the gift the boys had given him settled into him.

Maybe . . . maybe he could stay. Get serious about coaching. Not as a consolation, but because it felt right. What had his mom said about God having a purpose for him being here?

He got out and dressed, and by the time he left, the locker room and school were quiet. So maybe he wouldn't be catching Piper after all, but that was okay. He'd ask her tomorrow at the dance.

And he'd show her that she was making a difference for him and for the kids too.

nine

PIPER NEEDED PRINCIPAL FRANKLIN TO BE-
lieve in her, and if the only way was by guarding the punch bowl in a gym strung with blue streamers and cardboard cutout ocean life, so be it. The decorations didn't come close to a convincing "Under the Sea" feel. But the students seemed to be enjoying the homecoming dance anyway.

The deep bass vibrated the floor while girls in dresses that barely covered the necessities gathered around the football players on the dance floor. It reminded her why she'd skipped dances in high school.

Watching the popular girls who alienated her at school flirt with her brother, who had also been on their football team, would have been torture. Even her senior year, when she'd been dating Drake, he hadn't been into dancing any more than she was, so they'd opted out of the dances.

Her gaze skipped to the girl in the corner, who was squinting into an open book in the dim light. That probably would have been her. Who was she kidding? It would be her now if she had her way. But yesterday, Piper had put in a request to present her plan for the tutoring center at the next school board meeting, and she wanted Principal Franklin backing her. Which meant she had limited time to reform his impression of her. He'd started to come around, but she surely hadn't completely erased her reputation as an argumentative troublemaker.

Across the gym, Piper's gaze connected with Titus, and he offered her a slow, crooked smile that hitched his mouth a little higher on one side and carved that dimple in his cheek. She'd never seen him dressed up before. Even at school, as the gym teacher, he could get away with wearing shorts or sweats. But he was anything but casual now. And, oh my. Just friends was not going to work for her if he kept looking at her like that.

But could she trust another football player? That awful moment when she'd surprised Drake outside his college's athletic center played through her mind. But Titus was nothing like Drake. She had to believe that.

A group of teenage girls approached the drink table Piper had been assigned to babysit, chatting as they swayed to the music. Piper pulled her attention from Titus and smiled at them.

"Hey, Miss Caveneau." Kristen filled a glass from the large ice water dispenser.

Piper lifted her blue punch in salute. "Hey, girls. You all look so beautiful this evening. Are you having fun?"

"Miss Caveneau? I almost didn't recognize you." Ali, another junior, stepped closer, looking Piper over. "You're a hottie!"

"Thanks." Piper didn't know about that, but she didn't argue as the girls walked away.

Jess and Devin had gone away for the weekend, so Piper had been on her own getting ready for the dance. She'd tried on nearly everything in her closet, and finally she settled on a sleeveless, knee-length black dress held over from her college days, with a flared skirt and a keyhole back. She'd pulled out her favorite extra high platform heels and curled her hair and piled it on top of her head.

Piper's gaze flicked back to Titus, but he was gone. She pushed up onto her tippy toes and scanned the gym. He was several inches taller than most of these people. He shouldn't be that hard to locate. Had he left?

"Who are you looking for?" Titus's voice was low and smooth in her ear.

When Piper jumped and spun toward him, he was closer than she'd anticipated. Now she was just inches from him. She drew in a slow breath as her eyes roamed his face. The song shifted, and she remembered where they were. She took a hasty step back to put an appropriate amount of space between them. He straightened and looked around as if he'd been just as taken off guard.

Man, he looked good. His navy suit had to have been tailored to fit his broad shoulders and narrow hips so perfectly. With the collar of his crisp white button-up left open, a sliver of the hollow between his collarbones was visible. Even his unruly curls were tamed and smoothed back.

"You look amazing." His voice was a little deeper than usual as he hooked his hand around the back of his neck and flashed his dimples.

"You clean up okay yourself." Understatement of the century. She took the opportunity to look him over from head to toe again.

"I was hoping to catch up with you after the game last night, but I got a Gatorade shower on the sidelines, so I had to clean up before I could get out of there."

"A Gatorade shower?" Piper gave the students on the dance floor a quick scan. She couldn't forget what she was here for. "That sounds cold and sticky. But it's supposed to be a good thing, right?"

"Yeah. Players do it after a big victory to honor their coach. It was definitely a good thing."

A shy, bookish boy from Piper's second-hour class and an outgoing and genuinely nice girl from the sixth-hour class approached the table, holding hands. They seemed like an odd match, but Piper could see it working. Tall, athletic, attractive Titus would probably seem like an odd match for her, but she was starting to think they could work too. "I heard it was a good game."

The light in Titus's eyes dimmed just a little. "Oh. I thought maybe you were there. I was looking for you in the stands."

His evident disappointment pricked at her conscience. "I haven't been to a football game since my freshman year of college."

"Why not?"

"That's a long story for another day."

"Okay." He gave her a look that said he'd be revisiting the topic later. "Well, you heard right. It was a great game because we finally had a full team, thanks to you. You're making a difference around here."

She was starting to gain a little ground with the students, but hearing him acknowledge it was its own victory. "I'm not the only reason. You're actually pretty good at this coaching thing."

"When I started here, I really thought I'd do this for a year while I figured out what to do with the rest of my life, but lately, coaching is starting to fit. And in the locker room after the game yesterday, the boys gave me something that about broke me."

"The Gatorade shower?"

"That too. Come on, I'll show you." He nodded toward the side door that led to the hallway through the athletic wing.

There was something heady about him wanting to share this with her. Share what was meaningful and important to him. And a few minutes alone with him, yes please. But . . . She looked out through the strobing lights illuminating the dance floor in the dimly lit gym. "We can't just leave."

"We'll be right back. No one is going to spike the punch in the next ten minutes." He offered her his hand.

"The doors and gates are all locked. We can't even get into the rest of the school." And this was no time to be irresponsible. She had a reputation to repair.

Titus reached into the pocket of his suit coat and jingled a set of keys. "I have a master key, and it's just in the locker room down the hall."

Piper scanned the gym, looking for the school secretary, Alice, who was in charge of the dance. She stood near the main gym doors, chatting with the tech teacher, Mr. Straley. They were guarding the door. What could happen in the next few minutes?

"Not much of a rule breaker, are you?"

He was right about that. Instigator? Occasionally. Troublemaker? Maybe. Rule breaker? No. But with his ocean-blue eyes compelling her, she'd follow him almost anywhere.

"Come on. I'll text Alice and tell her we'll be right back." Titus grinned at her.

This wasn't really a rule, right? "Text her first."

He sighed and pulled his phone out of his pocket. He tapped at the screen for a moment, then glanced across the room at Alice.

Alice paused her conversation to pop open the clasp on her clutch and pull out her phone. After looking at the screen, she raised her gaze to the drinks table. Titus waved at her. She nodded and motioned to shoo them away.

"Come on." Titus offered her his hand again.

After a quick glance around to be sure no students were watching, Piper finally took his hand. And that annoying jolt of electricity that made his touch impossible to ignore zipped through her again.

He led her out of the gym and through the dark hallway.

Piper shivered. "This place is creepy at night."

Titus laughed. "Don't worry. I'll protect you."

Even if he was teasing, it did make her feel better to have him by her side. He didn't need to know that, though. "Aren't you gallant."

"I like to think so." He turned on his phone's flashlight to unlock the locker room door when they reached it.

"You would."

Titus flipped the lights on and led the way past the benches and lockers to an office off the back of the room.

Piper stepped inside. Unlike the odor that clung to the locker room, this space was permeated with Titus's clean, masculine scent. It sent a shiver down Piper's spine. The blank walls, outdated metal desk, and mismatched chairs didn't exactly make it a cozy space, but the desk was uncluttered, save for a single framed photo. "I thought your office was by the teacher's lounge."

"That's my teaching office. This is my coaching office. The coach and PE teacher positions used to be filled by separate people. Besides, teachers' offices have to be accessible to students, and I can't very well expect my female students to traipse through the boys' locker room when they need to find me." He stepped behind the desk, pulled a small white towel out of one of the drawers, and spread it across the desk.

The Gatorade logo emblazoned the center of the towel, and a couple dozen sloppy signatures decorated the rest. In neater handwriting, someone had written: *A good coach can change a game, but a great coach can change a life. Thanks for being a great coach!*

"I think they're giving me credit for your hard work."

Piper shook her head and ran her finger reverently across the message Sharpied across the terrycloth. "This is all you."

Titus took the towel and walked around to the back side of his desk. He opened a drawer and pulled out a few pushpins, then tacked the towel to the wall.

"And you say you aren't much of a decorator." She picked up the small frame from the corner of the desk. "Now you have wall art and a personal photo."

Titus came around and perched on the edge of the desk next to where she stood. "That's Jeff Dodger."

"Your college coach you're close with." She studied the snapshot of a younger Titus with his arm around an older guy with graying temples and a mustache worthy of Tom Selleck. "I'll bet he'd be proud of your towel."

"He is. I talked to him last night. I always wondered how I would have turned out if Coach Dodger had raised me." Titus took the frame from her and his mouth curved when he glanced at the photo before replacing it on his desk.

"That's a good perspective. I always wished I would have known my biological dad, but from what I've heard, my stepdad who adopted me and raised me is a better guy for sure." She pinched the skirt of her dress and rubbed the fabric between her thumb and fingers.

"So you never knew your biological dad?"

"I was eight before I even knew my dad wasn't my biological father."

"Is that when your grandpa gave you the puzzle?" His tone held no demand, only invitation.

Piper met his gaze as the past nudged its way to the surface. His tone was so gentle she wanted to sink into the safety and comfort it offered. Finally, she nodded. "We came home from vacation and our house had been robbed."

Titus sucked in a breath. "That must have been scary."

"When the police came, I overheard my parents giving a statement that my mom's ex had just been released from prison and he had threatened to come looking for his keys."

He opened his mouth but seemed to realize she wasn't finished and snapped it closed again.

"Then my mom said she had been pregnant when he was arrested, and she never told him about me. That's when I realized that my biological father was a convicted criminal and Cam was my half brother. My parents never told me."

Titus reached for her hand and tugged her closer to him. "That's rough. What did you do?"

"I had a hard time sleeping for a while." Piper allowed herself to be drawn in until her thigh brushed his outstretched leg. "I was so mad at my parents for lying to me. I kept wondering how I could have gone my whole life without noticing. My mom, the dad that raised me, and Cam all have blue eyes, and yet mine are brown. I never even questioned it."

"You were eight."

"I know. I guess I just felt betrayed. It made me question everything they had told me. Wonder if there was anything else I didn't know."

"And that's when your grandpa brought you a puzzle?"

"He told me that my parents hadn't intended to lie to me, they were just waiting until I was older to show me the whole picture."

"And the puzzle helped." It wasn't a question. He was just stating what he knew of her.

She turned her hand to weave her fingers with his. Instead of the gutted feeling these memories usually left in their wake, there was a lightness, like he'd lifted some of the weight of that burden just by hearing her out.

She'd drifted close enough now that his face was mere inches away.

His gaze roamed her face, settling on her lips for a moment, before he closed his eyes and took a deliberate breath. Finally, he refocused his intense gaze on her. "Piper, what do you want?"

"What do you mean?" The words came out breathless.

"I know we haven't always seen eye to eye, so if you aren't feeling…whatever this is"—he gestured from her to himself and back with his free hand—"tell me now before I do something stupid."

"What do you want to do?" It was all she could manage with her lungs refusing to cooperate and her heart hammering. She drifted closer still.

His clear blue eyes were almost desperate. As if the windows were opened and she could see into his unguarded depths. His nearness consumed her every thought.

His focus dropped from her eyes to her lips, and his breath shuddered.

Heaven help her. "Kiss me."

Titus's brows shot up, and his gaze was hot when he met her eyes just before he closed the few inches between them. When his lips met hers, the room around them fell away. Their promise to return to the dance faded to a distant echo. Everything that had consumed her moments ago melted away. There was only this moment. If only she could melt into him and stay here forever.

He angled his mouth over hers and deepened the kiss. When his powerful arms around her waist tightened, pulling her tighter against his chest, her soft curves melted into the hard planes of his body.

How would she ever function in everyday life again with the memory of this kiss consuming her?

Of their own accord, her hands wove into his hair, and his curls coiled over her fingers and tickled her palms. It was even softer than she had imagined.

He broke the kiss, panting for breath, and pulled back just an inch to look into her eyes. "Wow." His eyes dropped back to her mouth, no doubt as swollen and pink as his was.

She smiled and began pulling him back to her lips when a piercing sound sliced through the dark locker room outside the office, jolting them apart.

A blinding flash blinking on and off from the blaring fire alarm on the far wall confirmed her fear.

Someone had pulled the fire alarm.

She never should have left the dance short-staffed.

Titus hadn't had a good night's sleep in three days. The echo of that wildfire kiss crowded out every coherent thought, and he couldn't focus to save his life.

That dumb fire alarm.

He couldn't erase the image of Piper shivering in the autumn night air, until he'd slipped off his jacket and draped it over her bare shoulders as they waited for the firemen to clear the building and confirm, as they suspected, that the alarm had been intentionally pulled. She had looked comically petite in his broad suit coat, but he liked seeing her swathed in his jacket. Although he would have much preferred wrapping her in his arms to keep her warm.

And now, knowing Piper was waiting for him in her classroom so they could go out on their first official date tonight was making practice take forever.

"All right, guys, bring it in," he called through his bullhorn, signaling to the boys scattered across the football field to put away the equipment and gather for the debrief in the locker room. It was a few minutes early, but he couldn't wait anymore.

Titus's phone chirped from his pocket, and he glanced at his watch. Coach Dodger. He scanned the field. The players were still clearing equipment. He had a minute.

He pulled out his phone and answered the call. "Coach, good to hear from you. I only have a minute. We're just wrapping up practice."

"I'll talk quick, then. I just want to plant a bug in your ear. I've been following your season. Taking this team to a five and two record after last year's one and eight is saying something. I'm looking to retire in the next year or two and—"

"Retire?" The announcement hit Titus like a blow to the chest. The man had been the mentor Titus had desperately needed coming into college as a freshman, and even now, he couldn't be a halfway decent coach without Dodger's voice in his head. "I can't imagine U of M football without you."

"I'm getting old, and U of M needs new blood. They've been tossing around the idea of hiring a new position coach for our quarterbacks so we can work together for a year before I start transitioning out."

Why was he telling him all this? Titus wasn't ready to think about someone else in that role.

"I'd love to work with you again. I always thought you'd make a great coach. And now that you're embracing it, you need to be at a bigger school where you can make a name for yourself in the coaching community. I can make a case to the higher-ups that, even though you only have a year under your belt, you're a good candidate and get you an interview. What do you think?"

Wait. Titus shook his head to clear away his fixation on his mentor's retirement. "Me?"

"Come on, kid. Keep up. Of course I'm talking about you."

Between Dodger's unexpected announcement and Piper still teasing at his attention, he couldn't quite wrap his mind around the idea.

Titus hadn't expected to like coaching, but the relationships he was forming with these boys were starting to remind him what made him love the sport in the first place. He was starting to see growth and development in these boys, and it stirred something in him that he thought he'd lost for good when his playing days were cut short.

But this was an opportunity to grow under one of the greatest men Titus had ever known, and it was almost ludicrous to say no.

Titus looked up at the boys laughing as a united team as they sauntered out of the equipment trailer. He glanced over at Zane and Jimmy packing up the water station. How many times had they talked about playing football for him next year? Finally, the memory of Piper in his arms blazed through him. Could he leave all of this?

A month ago, it would have been a no-brainer, but to his surprise, Heritage had recaptured him.

"Titus? Did I lose you?" Dodger's deep voice boomed again through the phone.

"No, sorry. Just surprised."

"Hey, Coach," Brett called as he jogged off the field, helmet in hand.

Titus waved Brett over. "This is a lot to think about. I've got to go. I'll call you back later?"

"Say, don't mention this to anyone just yet. It hasn't been officially announced, but when they go public, they'll want to move pretty quickly on this."

Titus ended the call and turned his attention to Brett.

"I've been thinking about what you said about talking to the team, and I was wondering if it would be okay for me to say something to them during the debrief today?"

"Sure. If you're ready, the time is yours."

"Thanks." Brett headed toward the locker rooms.

"Where have you been today?" Nate approached with a playbook under his arm.

Titus cocked an eyebrow. "I've been here."

Nate brushed his dark hair out of his eyes, flashing the tattoo on his forearm. "Your shell has been here. Your mind is far away."

"Is it that obvious?"

"You had the boys run the same warm-ups twice in a row, then forgot the name of one of our standard plays. Plus you were just staring into space with a goofy smile on your face before you took that phone call."

He'd been thinking that Piper kissed like she argued—passionate, determined, confident, and unapologetic. There was nothing tentative about her. And it was intoxicating. But he couldn't say any of that to Pastor Nate.

Warmth climbed up his neck. He had to get his mind off her

full lips. Though, that was a lot easier than thinking about Dodger's offer.

Nate raised his eyebrows. "Okay." He nodded his understanding. "Well, someday I would like to meet her."

"I never said it was a woman."

"You didn't have to." Nate slapped him on the shoulder and headed for the locker room. Titus looked up to where Zane and Jimmy had been. The water station was already cleaned up and loaded onto the cart, and the boys were halfway down the path leading back to the building. Titus looked around. Actually, nearly everyone had completed their cleanup duties and were headed back. He really did need to get his head out of the clouds.

"The equipment trailer looks good, Coach," Wyatt called as he jogged down the path toward the locker room.

Had the kids seen the same equipment trailer Titus saw every day? What had he missed? He'd unlocked it today but hadn't looked inside. He'd have to stop in later. Maybe Nate had straightened it up a bit.

Titus trekked to the locker room as the last of the team trickled in. "All right, good practice today. Tomorrow we'll spend some of our practice time watching game tape. I know you're all a little nervous about the game on Friday. The Tigers are a tough team, arguably our biggest competition, but I know we can beat them if we can work together as a team."

"We're gonna kick some tail and earn those jerseys!" Xavier spouted, confidence lending volume to the words.

"It'll be a lot easier now that Brett can play." Wyatt gave Brett a nod.

"Miss Caveneau sure wasn't in a hurry to make that happen." Beau pitched his towel at the laundry basket with more force than necessary.

Titus had issued a firm warning about the pranks and disrespect toward Piper, but clearly their attitudes remained unchanged, at least for some of them. Maybe he could soften them. "Miss Cave-neau went out of her way to arrange help during the school day to get Brett back on the field. You ought to thank her."

Several of the boys leveled a doubtful look at him.

"I really do not understand what your problem is with her. She just wants to help." Titus dropped his clipboard on the bench.

"She'd be a lot more *help* if she didn't make her class impossible to pass." Owen kicked off his cleats.

"When you say she cares about us, I believe she cares about our grades, but she doesn't care about this team." Jeremy tugged his practice jersey over his head and stuffed it in his gym bag. "She's never even been to a game."

Titus was going to have to get to the bottom of why she wouldn't come to the games. Maybe he could talk to her about that tonight. He stole a glance at his watch.

"I saw you two sneaking out of the dance last weekend. It would be really awesome if our coach was sidetracked right in the middle of the season by someone who doesn't even support the game." Wyatt shot a deadpan look at Titus before depositing his helmet into the cubby above his locker.

They'd seen him and Piper slip away? That was not great.

"Is that true? This team has had enough of being betrayed by a coach over a woman." Owen's words held a lingering note of bitterness.

The kid had a point. Titus hadn't considered that the team would feel betrayed over who he might choose to date. In his mind, he and Piper were totally different than Jay's dad and Owen's mom. But maybe it was too much of a reminder of the upheaval that scandal had caused.

"I'm sure there's an explanation. Coach isn't in league with the enemy." Jay scoffed, then turned a questioning gaze to Titus. "Are you?"

"Piper is not the enemy." Titus realized his mistake too late. "I mean Miss Caveneau."

A hush fell over the boys as they stared at him with accusation in their eyes.

"Dude, this better not be a Yoko Ono kind of situation." Beau stood and narrowed his eyes at Titus. "You are our Lennon. Don't let Yoko break up the band."

"How do you even know that reference? The Beatles were before your time. They were before *my* time."

"The Beatles are cultural icons. They're timeless." The guitar Beau carried everywhere with him was starting to make more sense.

Maybe now was not the best time to tell them that he and their least favorite teacher were supposed to leave for a date in ten minutes. He needed to help them appreciate her as much as he did before they went public. Time to redirect.

"I promise you, this is nothing like the Beatles. Brett asked for some time to talk to you all, so I'll give him the floor." Titus took a seat on the nearest bench as Brett stood.

"Guys, I . . . I know I kinda fumbled life lately. I mean, I've been a jerk sometimes, and I'm MIA too much. I didn't really want anybody to know what's going on." Brett paused to look up at Titus.

Titus nodded his encouragement. *Come on, Brett. You can do this.*

"My mom . . . she has cancer." His voice broke, and he looked down at his stocking feet and paused for a beat. "She's in hospice and . . ." His chin quivered. "The nurse who comes in every day to check on her says she probably only has a couple weeks left." The words scraped out as if they were sandpaper against his raw throat.

The boys sat in stunned silence, their mouths sagging open, or some looking at their shuffling feet for a long moment before Wyatt stood and folded Brett into a brotherly hug.

When Owen looked up from his clasped hands, his eyes were

glossy. He got to his feet. "I'm so sorry, man. I get it now, what you were saying the other day."

Titus's heart swelled as one kid after another patted Brett on the shoulder, offered to help, and even cried with him. Yes, this was the team he was hoping to build. But could he pursue Piper without destroying the trust he'd built with them? He'd have to talk to her about it.

When the players had all cleared out, he headed to her classroom. Halfway there, he remembered he still needed to check and lock up the equipment trailer. He'd have to stop back out there before he left. When he walked through her door, her face lit up and she stood to greet him.

"Hi there." She crossed the room and reached for his hand. Then, seeming to rethink that, she dropped her hand and smiled at him instead. "How did practice go?"

He restrained the urge to claim her lips again. That would most definitely hijack the evening. He needed to slow this down, not speed it up. "It was good."

"Did anything out of the ordinary happen?" With her brows raised and knitted together, she looked hopeful but tentative.

She seemed to be fishing for an answer, but he had no idea what she wanted him to notice. Had she gotten a haircut or something? His ex, Amber, always used to get mad when he didn't notice her hairdos. "Brett talked to the team about his mom, and they were so good about it. I'm proud of them."

"I'm so glad they're coming together." The expectant look faded from her eyes, and she reached out again, and this time she squeezed his hand. "It's amazing to watch."

Man, she was tempting. How long would he have to wait for a repeat of Saturday night? Hopefully without the fire alarm interruption next time. Then again, if moving to Ann Arbor to work for U of M was really a possibility, maybe he had more than one reason to slow this down, and daydreaming about that kiss was not the way to rein himself in. "They're coming together, and that's why I need to talk to you about something."

She cocked her head to the side and gave him her full attention. "Sure, what's up?"

"I think we need to . . . slow this down a little bit."

She dropped his hand and drew back a step, a guarded look stealing some of the gleam from her eyes.

He sighed. Slowing down was the opposite of what he wanted to do. Maybe it was more about keeping it between the two of them for now. Maybe if he told her why, she'd understand. "I was just talking to the team, and they were giving me a hard time about the idea of me pursuing you."

Her brow furrowed. "You told the team what happened between us? Before *we* even talked about it?"

"No, no. They don't know anything is happening. But they suspected I'm interested." He blew out a breath and averted his eyes from her gaze. "One of them saw us sneak out of the dance. And now they're all upset."

"They must dislike me more than I thought if the idea of you and me getting too friendly sends them into a tailspin." The vulnerability in her eyes pricked at him.

He was making this worse instead of better. He should have known that would strike a nerve. She put on a brave face, but he'd seen glimpses of her raw, soft spot she hid away. She'd need to know why the boys had their guard up when it came to their coaches' dating habits, or she would inevitably take this too personally. "There's a lot more to it than that. Did you know that Jay Wilkins's dad and Owen Baltic's mom are both leaving their families so they can move in together?"

Her eyes widened. "Jay and Owen must be devastated."

Titus nodded. "They met and started messing around while Jay's dad was Owen's position coach last year. When it all came out, it crushed Jay and Owen. The whole team kinda fell apart. They're just starting to bond again."

"That's a testament to what a good coach you are." She rested her hand on his arm. "Between Brett and Jay and Owen, that's a lot of pain for a bunch of teenage boys to handle."

"It is a lot to handle, and they're very protective and suspicious right now. I've gotten pretty close with a lot of those guys, and the way they reacted . . . it was like I had betrayed their trust. They've suffered enough betrayal. I don't want them to feel that way about me."

The leery look in her eyes was a bit concerning. "I get that, but in my experience, honesty is always the best policy."

"Usually, yes, and I'm not going to lie to them, but I think we need some time to figure this out between us, first. I'll tell them when the time is right."

"Yeah. That makes sense. So I guess that means we aren't going to Donny's for dinner, huh?"

This was what he hated about Heritage and why he'd left the first time. He hated living in a fishbowl where everyone had an opinion on his life and thought they deserved a say in how he lived it. "I'm afraid a date at Donny's pretty much assures that the whole town will have our wedding planned by the end of the week. I'd like to keep this low-key for a little while."

"I understand. You really care about those boys and that's honorable. I have a lot of grading to do anyway. I suppose I should get back to it." She turned and walked back toward her desk.

Honorable? Yeah, he wanted to be honorable. He had to be if he wanted to be worthy of her. But he also wanted her. He let himself out of her classroom and into the dark hallway. She was agreeing to exactly what he said he wanted, but he was still walking away feeling like he'd lost. He headed through the athletic center door, keys in hand, and aimed for the equipment trailer.

Titus pushed open the door to the trailer, flipped on the light, then froze. The old modular classroom had been cleaned, deodorized, and meticulously organized. The previously underutilized shelves and bins, and rolling carts were neatly categorized and labeled. Even the playbooks he'd been missing since he'd taken over the space were lined up on a shelf, and his ball, signed by all his college teammates, was nestled on the shelf next to them like a bookend.

Piper. She must still have her key to the place. She'd seen his deficit and instead of criticizing, she'd just stepped in to help. And he'd just told her they needed to slow down because a bunch of teenage boys didn't like her.

He was an idiot. He was letting the pressures of living in a fishbowl get to him and influence his decisions.

But as much as he was starting to feel at home here in Heritage again, maybe this place was just too small for him. That U of M interview might be the opportunity he needed to get on with his life before this town held him captive for good.

ten

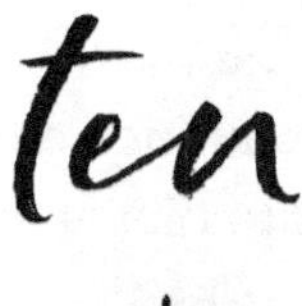

TITUS HAD BARELY SPOKEN A WORD TO PIPER since texting a profuse thank you for organizing his trailer three days ago.

But what had he meant Tuesday by slow things down? Was that a polite way of saying he wanted to call it quits? Piper stared at the text that had just come in, but that was no help.

The "miss you" seemed to indicate he was still interested. But needing to talk again? Maybe he *was* ready to call it off. Avoiding her since then had seemed a lot more like a grinding halt than tapping the brakes.

She'd overstepped when she'd recruited her roommates to help her get in without his permission to organize his space. She and Titus had interacted more when they were "just friends." For that matter, they'd talked more when they were adversaries. She wanted this to work, but was she forcing it? Like when Drake got distant and instead of her taking the hint, she showed up at his college unannounced? That had not gone well for her. Insecure. Needy. Desperate. She would never let herself be those things again.

Piper stared at the display case she'd ordered for his autographed football just after cleaning the storage closet. It hadn't cost much and seemed like a good idea at the time. The clear acrylic box had been sitting on her desk, taunting her since the mail had arrived this morning. If she gave it to him now, was it just going to make her look psycho?

Piper walked over to pull her classroom door closed to muffle the stampede in the hallway of students rushing to leave school and start their weekend.

Jess had agreed to help her prep for tomorrow's fundraiser at the Fall Festival, and Piper needed to focus on that. She opened her closet to heave out the boxes of paint she'd stashed there. She needed to get these down to Jess's classroom so they could get started. Who knew how long it would take to fill two hundred water balloons with paint?

The door cracked open, and someone rapped a quick knock. Piper glanced up.

Aaron stuck his head in. "Miss Caveneau, do you have a minute?"

She always had time for Aaron. "I'm just getting ready to carry these boxes down to Miss Gable's art room, but I've got a minute."

"I've got you, Miss C." He walked over and scooped up one of the boxes.

"Thanks." Piper lifted the other and headed toward the door. "What was it you'd like to talk about?"

Aaron balanced the box on one arm and opened the door for her. If someone told her a month ago that Aaron would be the kid volunteering to help her out, she would have scoffed, but it had been a joy to watch him test out a little confidence in her classroom.

"Well, I've been thinking . . . It might be a dumb idea, but maybe . . . I might apply for the engineering program at Michigan Tech."

Piper couldn't restrain her grin. "That's not a dumb idea at all. You would make a wonderful engineer."

Aaron's tall form parted the after-school traffic in the hall as they traveled against the flow. "The school counselor said it would be hard for me to get in with my GPA, but they might make an exception if my grades come up this year. They'll probably also want SAT scores, and the better I score, the better my chances will be."

"I one hundred percent believe you can do it." Piper shifted her box. Who knew paint was so heavy?

Aaron hung his head. "I'm not worried about the math and science sections. But I never could read very good. The words just kind of float around on the page, and I can't track from one line to the next. Then when I finally finish, I can't even remember what I read."

"Have you ever been tested for dyslexia?"

"I don't think so." His shaggy hair fell into his eyes, and he glanced over his shoulder at her.

She'd assumed that a senior in high school would have been tested by now. He'd struggled without an explanation for too long. "Well, that sounds like dyslexia to me. I'm going to refer you for an evaluation, because you may be able to get accommodations for your SAT testing."

"Really?" He stopped in the middle of the hallway and turned to her. That slight flicker of hope she'd seen in him in suspension that day three weeks ago glowed all the brighter now.

"But accommodations or not, I'll help you study, and we can work on some strategies that will make it easier to track the words on the page." Aaron already reminded her so much of Cam, but this helped her to see why. She'd never been able to get Cam motivated to overcome his struggles, but Aaron's initiative warmed her heart.

They rounded a corner toward Jess's classroom, and Piper spotted Kristen talking with Drew, a boy from her sixth-hour class. His designer clothes, Rolex, and entitled attitude were a flashback to the kid who'd caused her to lose her job at her last school.

Drew pulled his wallet out of his pocket. Nothing about his posture looked threatening, but with the wary look in Kristen's eyes, Piper slowed her steps.

Suddenly Kristen's expression shifted as she narrowed her eyes and lifted her chin. "I'm not writing that paper for you. No matter how much money you pull out of that wallet. That's not how tutoring works, Drew."

Drew's brows pinched in a scowl. "You think you're high and mighty, but I know you've helped Brett with his grades. If he isn't giving you money, what is he giving you?"

Piper stooped down, then let her box drop the last few inches to the floor behind Drew with a clap.

He spun toward the noise, his eyes widening when they met hers.

"That is bullying. You are going to have to come with me." Piper ought to investigate his previous work too. How often had he bullied others into doing his homework? Principal Franklin needed to know about this right now.

Drew clenched his teeth and narrowed his eyes at Kristen before turning his glare on Piper. He scooped up his messenger bag and tried to walk past her. "I think I'll pass."

Aaron stepped in his path and tried to nudge Drew back with the box he still held. "Don't be an idiot, Drew."

Drew sneered at Aaron. "What's a pathetic stoner like you going to do about it? When did you become teacher's pet, anyway?"

Piper straightened to her full height and pointed down the hallway toward the office. "Principal's office. Now."

Drew took a deep breath, huffed it out like her demand was a massive inconvenience, but there was no fear of punishment. He grudgingly turned toward the office.

Yeah, this jerk was reminding her more and more of Warren Crawford.

Piper zeroed in on Kristen. "Are you okay?"

She nodded and scooped up the box Piper had dropped. "Where does this need to go?"

"I'll show you." Aaron nodded down the hall toward the art room.

"Thanks, Aaron." Piper hurried to catch up with Drew.

As they approached the office, he turned back to Piper. "My mom's on the school board. I heard you're looking for funding for your tutoring center. Good luck with that."

Drew glanced past Piper, and his eyes widened.

"Drew." Titus's deep voice held a stern warning.

Shouldn't he be gone for the away game by now?

Drew took a step back and held up his hands in surrender. "All I said was good luck."

"I heard what you said." Titus was unmoved.

Piper yanked open the office door and glared at Drew. "Now."

When Drew had passed through the door, Piper turned to face Titus. She had no idea where they stood. His text said he wanted to talk, and so did she, but this wasn't the place or the time for any of that, so she just nodded. "Thanks for backing me up."

He seemed to be searching her face for an answer, but she wasn't even sure of the question. "Can we talk?"

Piper motioned over her shoulder to where Drew had dropped into one of the chairs in the reception area. "I have to deal with this."

"I know. And I have a bus waiting for me. Tomorrow? I'll be helping my mom with her maple syrup booth at the festival. Maybe we could find a chance to talk there?" Titus's hopeful gaze calmed some of Piper's worries.

Piper ignored the swirl of what-ifs that threatened insecurity. *Don't get too invested.* "Sure. If our booths aren't too busy. We'll see how the day goes."

Why was she like this? She just needed to give the man the display box. Even if they didn't have a future together, she still wanted him to have it. She could drop it on his desk tonight while he was gone for the game with a note so she wouldn't have to endure the awkwardness if it freaked him out.

Titus couldn't escape his mom's Fall Festival booth until Kristen showed up to help, but after a few days without Piper, he just wanted to go find her. He peered down the row of booths. No sign of her, but no doubt she was somewhere else on the town square getting her own booth set up.

He'd come back from last night's away game to find a gift and a note from her on his desk.

Titus,

I ordered this for your autographed ball when I was working on the equipment locker. I should have asked before I invaded your space, and I apologize. Anyway, I just want you to know what an inspiration it is to see you working so well with your team. I have never been able to master the balance between gentle and firm, but you embody both of those qualities and prove they aren't mutually exclusive. I have to agree with *the sentiment on your towel. You are a great coach.*

Yesterday, he'd taken the morning off to follow up with the orthopedic specialist after reinjuring his knee. Strength and stability had been even slower to return this round of healing than it had the first. His hope of returning to the field as a player was fading.

But with the interview pending and his fragile bond with the boys who didn't trust Piper, maybe letting his connection with her go would be the smarter play. But that wasn't what he wanted to do. He'd had a lot of first dates over the past several years, and he could attest that Piper was one of a kind. He hadn't even realized how much stress the chaotic equipment locker caused until he'd walked in to find it in order, but she knew. And her note had described him as gentle but firm. The opposite of what the press had accused him of. The opposite of his dad. Maybe she did see past the headlines.

Yeah, slowing down was a dumb idea.

"I'm so glad the town decided to do this Fall Festival again." His mom set the last of her famous maple pecan muffins in her display case next to her big pots of maple apple cider. "The syrup and goodies sold so well last year."

He rubbed his hands together to chase away the chill of the mid-October morning. At least it was warmer now than it had been an hour ago when he'd pulled his truck up to the curb of the town square to unload his mom's inventory and trade show tent. The forecast promised sunshine, and it might even get above sixty degrees this afternoon.

"What's with this town and festivals, anyway?" He'd dreaded the town events when he was in high school because he always had to help prepare and work the booth, and this week had been no different. He'd been so busy with the team and helping out his mom that he'd barely seen Piper, let alone had a chance to talk, and this was not a conversation he could have through text messages.

"Last year we were celebrating the town's one hundred fiftieth anniversary, but the city council decided to make it an annual event."

Titus had to admit that, now that he was here at the festival, it felt nostalgic, even though he'd never actually been to this one before. He peered down the row of other vendors getting their booths set up along either side of the paths that crisscrossed the square. No sign of Piper or her booth. She must be on the other side.

Where was Kristen? It wasn't like her to be late. Titus glanced at his watch. Nine twenty-seven. Oh. She'd promised to be here by nine-thirty. Maybe she wasn't late just yet.

"Hey, Coach." Jay moved into Titus's line of sight, with Owen and Beau trailing behind him.

"Hey, boys." His mom filled a few small foam cups with hot cider. "Want to try some of my maple apple cider?"

Owen, Jay, and Beau took the little cups.

"Thanks, Mrs. Ford." Owen sipped the steaming liquid. "This is amazing."

"How did the game go last night?" His mom shaded her eyes against the sun climbing the eastern sky beyond the booths on the other side of the square.

Beau adjusted his cowboy hat. "We crushed 'em."

"It was too easy. I almost felt bad." Jay finished his cider and set the small cup on the table, then pulled out his wallet. "I'll take a big cup of that."

Titus shoved his cold fingers deep into his jacket pockets. He should have brought his gloves. "Have you seen Miss Caveneau's booth?"

Jay eyed him as he exchanged a bill for a large cup with steam escaping from the drinking hole in the lid. "Not this again."

"She is not the enemy." He'd had about enough. "She's doing a fundraiser booth. I'd really appreciate it if you showed her some support. Throw some darts at paint balloons."

"Yoko. That's all I'm gonna say." Beau wrinkled his nose as he turned away from the booth to continue down the path with the other boys.

Titus resisted the urge to call after them to defend her. If they hadn't protested, he wouldn't be on shaky ground with her in the first place. He could have spent Tuesday night moving forward with Piper instead of stepping backward.

"Those boys sure are good kids. Reminds me of you in high school." His mom returned to the case of syrup and continued stocking the shelves across the back of the booth.

She was right. They were good kids. His restraint wasn't their fault. He just needed to talk to Piper. "The team is finally coming together. A few weeks ago, I didn't think that was ever going to happen."

Titus peered down the path again. Otis had parked himself in the center of the square.

"It seems to me the team might not be the only thing coming together." His mom set out stacks of tiny sample cups behind each flavor of her infused syrups on the front table. "Nice of you to encourage the boys to support Miss Caveneau's fundraiser."

Titus shot a look at her. "They don't have a very high opinion of her, which is a shame, because she is bending over backward to help them."

"A month ago, you were just as sour toward her as they are. Remember that?"

There was no hiding these things from his mom. "She's different than I thought. She's determined and fearless and hardworking. Even though she can come across a little . . . brisk, deep down she's compassionate and really cares about her job and the kids."

She pinned him with a knowing look. "I think I need to meet this girl."

After that kiss, their chemistry was undeniable, but that didn't mean she was ready to dive into a relationship with him. He'd stupidly put on the brakes before they had even defined what was happening between them. Hopefully he could get an answer to that question today. "Maybe."

"You don't have to be dating her for me to meet her. Just bring her by the booth?"

She wasn't going to let this go. "We'll see."

He spotted Kristen walking down the path with Brett. Finally.

Wait, were they holding hands? When did that happen? Brett had better be on his best behavior with his baby sister.

When Kristen found Titus watching, she dropped Brett's hand and offered Titus an innocent smile.

"It's your turn at the booth," Titus said as she approached. He turned to Brett and pinned him with a stern look. "I don't have anything to worry about here, do I?"

Brett shook his head. "No, sir."

"That's what I thought." Titus's phone vibrated in his pocket, and he glanced at his watch. The orthopedic specialist was calling. He pulled the phone from his pocket and turned back to his mom. "I've got to take this. I'm gonna take off for a bit. I'll be back."

Titus stepped away from the booth before he answered. "Hey, Doc. Working Saturday, huh?"

"Just getting caught up on some calls. I know you've been working your knee hard, hoping for full recovery, but . . ." The hesitation said it all.

"Lay it on me. I can take it."

"I'm sorry to be the bearer of bad news, but I just don't see full recovery as a realistic possibility. Your chances were slim before, but the ligaments are just not bouncing back after your new injury several weeks ago."

"I understand. Thanks for the call." Titus would never play football again. He braced for the bitter reality to crash over him, but the crushing wave of emotion he expected was more like a ripple. Sure, this was a loss, but his new dreams were shining brighter. When had his desperation to return to the field faded?

"For what it's worth, I was rooting for you to get back. I miss watching you play." The doctor ended the call.

The doctor was a fan? He'd never mentioned it before. There was something surreal about people he'd never met from across the country being invested in his career.

He headed toward the opposite end of the square. When he reached the center, he paused and looked down each corridor of booths. At the end of the west side, he spotted a large colorful canvas. That must be Piper's booth. He dodged a stroller from the family who owned JJ's Food Mart, greeted the little old lady whose lawn he used to mow when he was a kid, and nodded to Seth and Grace as he passed by them.

Growing up in Heritage, the thing he wanted to escape was how everyone knew everyone and people were always gossiping and getting into each other's business. Funny that realizing his dream of playing professionally meant he was recognized everywhere he went and the media was always in his business. He much preferred being recognized by friends and acquaintances over random strangers, and being the center of the well-intended local grapevine was way better than the media looking for a salacious story. Maybe Heritage wasn't so bad after all.

A banner of little triangular multicolored flags waved in the breeze above a table at the front of Piper's booth, and large canvases tiled the back with colorful balloons attached in a grid pattern. A couple splatters of paint showed where balloons had already been hit. Piper and Jess, both dressed in white head to toe, stood behind the table, inviting the early festival attendees to make a donation for a chance to throw darts at the balloons.

A turtleneck and leggings under a sundress didn't look warm enough. But just seeing her eased some of the tension he'd been carrying in his shoulders and neck. He refused to fumble this.

As he approached, Piper handed a young boy a couple of darts. "Which one are you aiming for?"

The kid pointed. "That orange one."

She turned to see where the child pointed, revealing a few paint splatters on her back and speckling her long dark braid. The white clothes must be meant to show off the paint splatters.

She moved to the side, out of the path of the dart. "Good luck!"

When the kid missed his three tries and moved on, Titus stepped up to the table and pulled a five from his wallet. "I'll take a shot."

Piper blinked at him, her smile wavering for a second, a little guarded. She dropped her gaze and set three darts in his hand.

His hand closed around hers before she backed away, and yeah, it was freezing. "Aren't you going to wish me luck?"

She met his gaze and seemed to search his. So much emotion in those brown eyes, but he couldn't tell if it would help or hurt his chances. Finally, she offered him another smile. "Good luck."

He let go of her hand, and she stepped to the side.

Titus took aim and pegged a green balloon in the top row a few feet over Piper's head. A few droplets of paint splattered out from the wall, landing on Piper.

"Bet you can't do that again." She raised her brows in challenge as a few passersby stopped to watch, but stepped farther to the side of the booth.

He let another dart fly, and she winced as yellow paint from the balloon next to the first one he'd hit added more speckles on her clothes and hair. The narrow booth didn't allow her to get far enough out of the way.

She bit her lip as she found his gaze again. "How about I give you your five back not to throw that one?"

"Sorry. I'm invested now." He sent the final dart into a blue balloon, three in a row.

Piper turned away but not fast enough as the paint sprinkled blue freckles on her nose and cheeks.

She turned back toward him with playful fire in her eyes as she wiped a bit of paint from her cheek. "Remember what they say about payback."

"I look forward to it." He spoke the words in a low tone, but by the way the smile dropped from her face and her cheeks flushed under the blue dots, he had no doubt she'd heard.

"What are you going to do with all those canvases?" He nodded at the paint-splattered tiles behind her.

Piper pointed to the silent auction bidding sheet at the end of the table. "We're auctioning them off. Jess and a couple of her students are going to help me finish them off into nice modern art pieces, then the highest bidder will get to choose one first, and we'll go down the line."

Titus stepped to the side as a family came up behind him in line to buy darts and a lady grabbed a pen at the end of the table to add a bid to the silent auction sheet.

"What do you say, Rainbow Brite? Can you take a walk with me?" He reached across the table to tug gently on the end of her color-splattered braid.

Piper exchanged a look with Jess as she helped the family. She nodded. "I'll be fine here for a little bit. Bring me some hot apple cider."

Jess must be in league with his mother. There was no way she didn't know that the apple cider was at his family's booth.

Piper wiped the paint from her hands with a wet wipe, then tossed it in a trash bin under the table. She ducked under a rope and fell in step beside him. "You might want to give me a wide berth."

"I'll take my chances." Those blue freckles made her look like a piece of modern art. "So, I found your gift. It's perfect. And I wanted to thank you again for organizing my trailer. I can't believe you did that. I'm in awe every time I open the door."

"You weren't upset?" She peeked over at him. "I realize I probably crossed a boundary. I should have asked first."

"No. Not at all. Just impressed and grateful."

"If you're not mad, then why did you avoid me all week? You said slow down, but it seems like maybe you really meant stop." There was no anger in her tone. Just a statement of fact. "I'm not interested in forcing myself on you, so . . ."

Direct and to the point. It was one of the things he really liked about her. He rarely had to guess what she was thinking. "I've just been really busy. It has nothing to do with not wanting to see you."

Titus waved and lowered his voice as they passed Zane and Jimmy, the team's water boys, along with Zane's family. Maybe this conversation called for a little more privacy. "I can't stop thinking about you, Piper." He reached over and clasped her hand in his.

She glanced down at their linked hands and raised her brows in question. "This is pretty public if we're taking it slow."

"Yeah, I guess I'm not so good at that." Titus scanned the area, then tugged her through the crowd, across the street until they were hidden away on her back porch. He didn't care what the town or his team thought. "No one gets to choose who I care about. I just need a chance to tell my team how I feel about you. But I want a chance to tell *you* first."

Her eyes widened just a tad. "Oh."

He seemed to have her full attention now.

"It would be smart to be cautious and go slow, but that's not really what I want. You are amazing. I want to be so much more than friends. I want the freedom to kiss you again. I don't want to wait to call you my girlfriend."

That was more than he had intended to spill, but it was too

late to pull it back in now. But maybe a question with a little less pressure was in order. "Will you go on a date with me?"

eleven

Titus's confession muted some of the anxious internal monologue that had been plaguing Piper for days, but the risk of heartbreak still clogged her answer in her throat.

"Come on, Piper, you don't have to commit to a lifetime here, just one date." The emotion in his face seemed to focus into a pleading, vulnerable question mark.

Yes, he was a risk, but that raw vulnerability in his eyes proved he was taking a gamble with his heart too. And if they worked . . . Possibilities washed over her, accelerating her heart rate and sending tingles all the way to her fingertips and toes. Maybe this risk wasn't safe, but it was worth it. "A date. I might be open to that."

His posture relaxed, and he tugged on her hand to draw her closer.

She wove her fingers with his but resisted his tug. "I'm covered in paint."

He groaned and lifted their linked hands to kiss the back of hers. "Later then."

She'd look forward to later. "Maybe we should go get that apple cider for Jess."

"Full disclosure, the apple cider is at my mom's booth. If you don't want to go, I can just bring a couple cups over later."

"I wouldn't mind meeting your mom if you don't mind that I look like a Jackson Pollock painting."

Titus led the way, keeping Piper's hand firmly in his grip. When they arrived, a couple with a baby was at the maple syrup booth talking with the older woman behind the table.

"Thanks, Maggie." The man boosted a little girl who looked just over a year old up higher onto his chest.

"We love your syrup." The wife accepted the brown paper bag the other woman passed across the table. "I'm so glad you have the cinnamon-infused one in stock this time. Pancakes aren't the same without it."

The guy turned and stopped short when he nearly bumped into Piper.

"Sorry!" Piper backed up a step. "I'm a walking wet paint hazard."

He offered her a good-natured grin. "No worries."

Titus shook the guy's hand. "Hey, Jon, Leah. Have you met Piper Caveneau?"

Leah smiled at her warmly. "You're the new teacher starting the tutoring center, right?"

Maybe wandering the festival looking like the aftermath of a paintball tournament wasn't her smartest move. "Yes. The paint is part of my fundraiser today."

Titus rested his hand on Piper's lower back and inclined his head toward her. "This is Jon and Leah Kensington and their daughter . . ."

"Isabella," Leah finished for him when he seemed to be searching for the name.

He graced her with his charismatic smile, then gestured to the woman behind the table. "And this is my mom, Maggie Ford."

"Wonderful to finally meet you." Maggie smiled at her, and Piper could see where Titus got his charisma.

"You too." Piper reached across the table to shake Maggie's offered hand.

"We were heading to your booth next. Leah wants to bid on your paintings." Jon tickled Isabella's tummy as she tried to climb onto his shoulder. "Hey, monkey, this is no time for climbing."

The little girl squealed a laugh and squirmed in his arms, but when he quit tickling, she patted her tummy. "Again."

More than one person had mentioned that the Kensingtons would be good allies to have in her corner for a community project like the tutoring center. Her caution that kept her from contacting them sooner seemed a little silly now. They appeared to be nice, down-to-earth people she could respect. Not at all what she'd come to expect from affluent people, especially at her last school.

"You've got to throw some darts while you're there." Titus leaned toward the little girl peeking at him coyly from Jon's shoulder and offered her a coaxing smile. With a little encouragement, she gave him a huge grin, showing off a row of tiny teeth. Titus pointed at Piper with his thumb. "I'll bet she'd love to see the paint fall on Piper."

"From the looks of it, the fundraiser must be going pretty well." Leah reached out and wiped at a drop of dried paint on Piper's sleeve. "I want to hear about your tutoring center. What goal are you working toward in your fundraising?"

"I want to get the groundwork laid in hopes that the school will adopt the tutoring center and help with the funding in their budget next year. I really don't want to have to charge for tutoring. That would exclude so many of the people I want to help."

"That's a worthy goal." Jon had turned Isabella around so her back was to his chest, and now she babbled and grinned at Titus, and he couldn't seem to wipe the smile off his face.

Man, he was going to make an amazing dad someday. It was definitely getting miles too far ahead of herself to imagine his kids might also be hers, but she couldn't help it.

Focus. This was her pitch to the Kensingtons. She couldn't miss this opportunity. "I'm meeting with the school board at the next meeting, and if they are willing to consider that partnership, they'll probably influence the priorities we need to address. The car wash a couple weeks ago raised enough for the desks and materials I needed to get started, but right now I'm borrowing space in the vacant shop beside Donny's. Since the space is not ideal and my arrangement with Thomas and Janie is just temporary, I'm working toward a permanent location. I applied for some grant money, and I hope between that and the fundraising I'll eventually be able to sign a year lease somewhere."

"What kind of space are you looking for?" The baby dove for Titus, and Jon raised his brows in question. When Titus held out his hands, Jon carefully delivered her into his arms.

Be still her heart. Why did being good with kids make him infinitely more handsome? And he was the hottest guy she'd ever met before he'd charmed the little girl. She could not keep watching him and still have a clear head for this conversation.

She forced her attention back to Jon. Rental space. Right. "I'm not all that picky. I just want a safe space that's easily accessible and free from distractions. Do you have anything available for rent?"

Jon pulled out his billfold and fished out a card for Piper. "Give me a call on Monday. Let's set up a meeting to look at some options."

"Thank you. I will do that." Piper took the card and deposited it into her pocket. The little slip of cardstock could represent a huge step forward, and she was ready for it. She looked over at Titus as he cautiously transferred Isabella to her mother's arms.

He'd suggested putting a title on their relationship, and she was really starting to like the sound of that. Today seemed to be the day for big steps.

A woman Piper didn't recognize approached. "Are you Miss Caveneau?"

Piper turned to the woman. "That's me."

"My name is Martha Palmer. I'm on the school board. I believe you know my son, Drew."

An anchor plunged through Piper's gut, deflating her optimism. She put on her bravest face. "Nice to meet you."

Martha smoothed her slacks and top that were too formal for the occasion but matched her detached demeanor perfectly. "I came because I wanted to see for myself what you are up to. I see you're not even manning your booth yourself."

Piper worked to keep her smile in place. "I'll be back there in a few minutes. I was just taking a break."

Titus's hand rested on her back again, offering reassurance. She wasn't in this alone. He looked ready to say something, but Jon beat him to it.

"Give her a break, Martha. She's networking. We were just talking about some possibilities for her new building," Jon said.

She'd liked Jon before, but his coming to her defense secured her faith in him.

"New building. That sounds like a pretty big expense." Martha's disapproving tone held a note of censure.

"I can't operate a tutoring center without a location. That's why I'm raising funds."

She arched a brow and eyed Piper with a condescending look. "What kind of checks and balances do you have in place for your expenditures? I called your former school, and they said you have a history of mismanaging funds, so I have some concerns about the school board contributing to a mismanaged project."

Piper gaped at her. Mismanaged funds? Had her former school

really been spreading lies about her? No wonder she hadn't been hired by any of the schools she'd applied to last spring and summer. This was a full-on assault on her integrity. Her chest constricted. "What are you talking about? I've never intentionally mismanaged anything."

Titus's jaw clenched, and his hand on her back stiffened.

Martha shrugged. "They said you were in charge of the student council and spent unreported money from a fundraiser."

Piper's heart dropped. Oh no. She suddenly knew exactly what Martha was talking about. Was her former school using her one innocent mistake as an excuse for why they'd fired her? It made sense, since they certainly couldn't advertise the real reason they let her go.

She must have paused too long, because Titus spoke up on her behalf. "I'm sure there is a reasonable explanation. Miss Caveneau is the most honest person I know."

Titus wouldn't be fooled, but the Kensingtons and Titus's mom might not be as easily convinced that she was innocent. Maybe today was not her day after all.

"I did not mismanage those funds." Thank goodness she kept copies of all her paperwork. "I have ledgers and receipts to prove it, and I'm more than happy to show the school board my spreadsheets for the tutoring center as well."

Martha shifted the strap of her purse on her shoulder. "I'm sure it will be an interesting meeting."

When she'd turned on her heel and walked down the sidewalk, Titus wrapped his arm around Piper's waist and pulled her close. "You okay?"

Piper curled into his side and tried to unclench the pressure constricting her chest. "I can't believe the school told her that. I was thrown into supervising student council with no training. The fundraiser was for the prom venue, and I used the money to pay for the venue. I didn't know I was supposed to deposit the money into the student council account first, then request a check to pay the bill. I had the ledger and receipt, so they said it was not a big deal. They never brought it up again."

Maggie leaned across the table and gave Piper's hand a quick squeeze. "I'm on the school board too. We are not all like her. You'll have plenty of others on your side too. We will make sure you have the chance to show your evidence and prove yourself. It'll be okay."

Leah wrinkled her nose. "Martha Palmer lives on the edge of the school district, just off Lake Michigan. She only shows up in town to start drama and flex her influence, but she's not the only one in this town with influence. Don't give up. If you're keeping good ledgers and you're willing to be transparent with your books, you have nothing to worry about."

Nothing except the inquisition she'd face at the school board meeting in two short weeks. She was prepared to give an account for the tutoring center, but now she'd have to unearth her archives she hadn't looked at since before the move and hope all her paperwork was still accounted for.

She'd just lost all the ground she thought she'd gained today. And then some.

Titus had to tell the team that he and Piper were in a relationship, and it had to be today. After a month's worth of training and strategizing, they were back in the Thunder Arena during their Tuesday practice, tackling the course.

Cheers and hollers erupted as Nelson scaled the wall, then turned to watch as Xavier, who he'd been training with, made it up as well. The team's volume grew as the boys tagged the two players who were charged with the Rope Junction next.

In the three days since the festival, he and Piper had spent nearly every waking moment together. This woman who'd turned his world upside down was an enigma—a rare hybrid of hard and soft, fierce but compassionate, serious but witty—and he loved every puzzling facet.

Titus caught the thought and reeled it back. Love? No. It was too soon for love. Wasn't it?

His phone vibrated in his pocket, and he glanced at his watch.

Jeff Dodger

Interview scheduled a week from Saturday. See you then.

Titus dismissed the message. He'd hoped to at least finish the season before he had to think about what the interview might mean.

"This is a whole different team than the one who tried this course a month ago." Seth watched Beau as he aptly swung through the ropes as if he'd been training with Tarzan himself, then looked toward Jay and Owen, who had teamed up for the Bridge of Blades. "It's great to see them working together so well."

Titus nodded. He put the text out of his mind. "I'm so proud of them, but it was a rough road getting here."

"Tell me about it." Nate made a note on the clipboard in his hands. "Life is like that sometimes. But when you see results like this, it's hard to deny that God had a part in it."

Titus hadn't even considered that God might have been involved in repairing the team dynamics, but Titus couldn't take all the credit. He could force all the team-building activities he could think of, but he couldn't change attitudes or hearts. That had happened much more organically. "Maybe you're right."

Jay and Owen completed their obstacles and tagged Jeremy and Wyatt, who launched into the Barrel Roll.

"I finally met Piper at the Fall Festival. I also saw you two walking through the square together." Nate raised his eyebrows in a silent question. "You were looking pretty friendly."

"The boys are holding a grudge against her. They tried to tell me she's off limits. I don't want them to feel betrayed, but I need to tell them that I'm dating her whether they like it or not."

"Being kept in the dark or lied to is what will make them feel betrayed." The look in Seth's eyes said he was speaking from experience. "The way this team has come around, I think you can trust them to warm up to her once they know she's important to you. Just be honest with them."

"I sure hope you're right."

Applause echoed off the gym's warehouse ceilings as Brett crossed the finish line seconds before the time clock displaying a countdown of their goal time buzzed.

Titus, Nate, and Seth threw their arms up and cheered as the team ran to the finish line to celebrate the victory.

When the excitement had calmed, Titus called them over to the sideline. "I'm impressed today, and I have been impressed with the amazing progress this team has made in the last month. I've seen you build your skills, put in impressive effort, and most importantly, I've witnessed your character develop. You are on the way to earning those jerseys, and I can't tell you how proud I am to be your coach. It's an honor."

"Your victory prize is a full year's individual membership to the arena. I hope to see you all back here regularly," Seth added.

The boys grinned and high-fived each other, offering Seth their thanks.

"Before you go, I have to talk to you about one more thing. Many of you have expressed concern about Miss Caveneau, so I thought you deserved to know that I like her and I'm going to start seeing her. Often."

A couple of the boys groaned.

"Come on, Coach. Have you forgotten our conversation about Yoko?" Beau spoke up.

Brett stood up. "Guys, she's not Yoko. No one is arguing that

Miss Caveneau's class isn't hard, but that doesn't make her a bad teacher. I learned more from all the time she took to tutor me than I have from years of other teachers' classes. She made it make sense. And when she couldn't work with me herself, she got other people to help me. That was after I missed or had to reschedule tutoring probably twelve times, but she didn't give up on me. That's the kind of teacher I want in my corner."

Jeremy stepped to Brett's side and crossed his arms over his chest. "She might be tough, but she actually cares about us."

Beau sighed. "But she still cost us at least one win."

"No," Ethan said. "It's not her fault we slacked on our work. We all deserved to fail, and she gave us help and second chances. Our losses are our own fault."

"I still vote no," Beau argued.

"Let's get one thing straight. I am simply telling you as a courtesy because you are my team, and I wanted you to hear about it from me. I am not asking your permission." When the boys exchanged a few annoyed looks, he added, "Unless you all want to have to come to me for permission to ask a girl out. Have the team vote on your dates."

Their eyes all widened and they quickly shook their heads.

"I've got to get home." Brett picked up his bag. No doubt the kid dating his sister wanted to quickly move on from the idea of the coach having a say in who they could date.

Titus's phone chimed in his pocket. "All right, guys, hit the showers."

He pulled his phone out to check the message.

Jeff Dodger

Say, if you get to town early enough, maybe we could grab an early lunch before the interview.

What if Titus did get the job at U of M? Yeah, working with his mentor again would be great, but could he really sacrifice all he'd be leaving behind? He didn't like the idea of a two-and-a-half hour commute to see Piper. If things kept progressing the way he hoped, would Piper eventually be willing to leave her tutoring center behind and follow him?

The first of the players emerged from the locker room in their street clothes, laughing and joking with each other. Jeremy leaned over and shook his wet hair, splattering Wyatt and Xavier with water. Wyatt retaliated by whipping him with the towel he had slung over his shoulder. Xavier held up his phone to capture the friendly wrestling match that followed.

The thought of leaving struck a dissonant chord. His time in Heritage with these boys and getting to know Piper hadn't really felt like biding his time. It felt more like building a life, a life that, except for the tight budget he was still getting used to, he really loved. The dynamics of this team, having his family close, and falling for a hardworking small-town girl . . . He hadn't known this was the life he'd been longing for until he'd experienced it.

But could he afford to throw away an opportunity to build his coaching career?

PIPER COULDN'T HAVE HEARD JON KENSINGton right. Yet the keys he had just dropped in her hand before he left her alone in a vacant storefront just around the corner from her house were evidence of his promise to let her use the property for the tutoring center rent free. When she'd met him three days ago at the festival, she'd dared to hope, but this was more than she could have even dreamed of. Though she still had six weeks before she had to be cleared out of the candy shop, she couldn't wait to start moving in.

This was big. Cam had always been her first call in her big moments, but before she even knew what she was doing, her fingers pulled up Titus's number. Yeah, Titus had quickly become her number one, the person with whom she wanted to share this, and all her big moments. She tapped the call button and propped the phone between her shoulder and ear.

Piper tore down a section of newspaper from the middle of the big storefront window, exposing a view of the south side of the arena across the street. A shaft of light flooded into the room, making the dust particles in the air glow like pixie dust and revealing her and Jon's footprints in the thick coat of dirt and debris blanketing the hardwood floors. It was even dustier than the bakery had been.

Correction, she'd move in as soon as she could get it cleaned up.

"You busy?" Piper asked when Titus answered. Hearing his voice only deepened the ache that her desire to see him had settled in her chest.

Since he'd admitted his feelings at the festival, her better judgment went out the window. Sunday had been heavenly. They'd spent more than twelve hours together, and it was still over too soon. School days, with their whole day of separation for classes and practice, were intolerably long.

"Just leaving the arena. Wanna meet up?" A dinging sound indicated he must be getting into his truck.

She pulled off the rest of the newspaper on the window to let in as much of the waning light as possible. The high ceilings covered in pressed tin tiles and antique hanging light fixtures gave the space character just not found in architecture today. "I'm right around the corner at 314 Richard Street."

"Be there in a minute." His truck's door slammed in the background.

Piper ended the call. Jon said he'd have his assistant turn the electricity, heat, and water on tomorrow, so tonight she'd be limited to the hour or so of fading daylight before the sun sank below the horizon. By the time she loaded up her cleaning supplies, it'd be too late to get any work done.

A text notification chimed, and Piper glanced at her phone.

Cam
____

I haven't heard from you in a few
days. Is everything okay? I've
been going to those meetings you
told me about. I like this group a
lot better than the AA group. Got
a new job too. I started this week.

Piper

I'm good. I've just been busy
with the tutoring center. And I've
been spending a lot of time with
that guy I told you about. I'm glad
you like the meetings. Where's
the new job?

Sure, this place wasn't huge, but there was plenty of space to add a couple of walls and make a couple of private study rooms. She'd keep this front part open for a main conference room where she could host study groups. The building's open layout would give her lots of flexibility. Just a bathroom and a small office on the far end were walled off. She could keep her files and materials in the office.

Cam

Titus Ford? Please tell me it is
Titus Ford. Then invite me over to
dinner to meet him.

Piper

It's Titus but no dinner until I can
be sure you won't be drooling on
your plate.

Cam

I'm not that bad. But I do want
to meet him. Think he'll sign a
hat I have?

Piper

Drooling.

Cam

Fine. But wait, I thought you
didn't like him.

Piper

What can I say? He won me over.

Cam

But he's a football player. You've
sworn for years that you'd never
date another football player.

Piper

Are you trying to talk me into
breaking up with him?

Cam

NO!

Wait, are you dating-dating him?

Piper

Yeah, we're dating.

Although "dating" didn't begin to capture what was happening. Piper was falling for him. Like, head over heels, no going back, all in, free fall. She tried to keep her breathing steady as her heart rate took off at a gallop. He'd be here any minute.

Cam

I was thinking about coming out
to see you in a couple of weeks.
I really should meet him if he's
your boyfriend.

Piper heard the rumble of Titus's truck pulling up outside.

Piper

You won't ask him to
sign anything?

Cam

Fine. Deal.

Piper

I'll ask Jess if you can crash on
the couch. Titus is here. Before I
go, what's your new job?

It's at a weight training gym. Talk
to you later.

Piper dropped her phone in the pocket of her jacket and opened the door as Titus was getting out of his truck at the curb.

"Are we playing hide-and-seek?" He closed the distance between them and gathered her into his arms.

"Yep. I'm just really bad at hiding." She wrapped her arms around his neck and rested her cheek against his chest. They fit together perfectly. She'd spent some time wrapped in his embrace the last few days, but that was all since the kiss in his office at the dance. Moving slow was wise, but also infuriating. What was he waiting for?

"Or I'm really good at seeking. What are we doing here?" He released her and turned to survey the storefront.

Piper struck a pose like a *The Price Is Right* model displaying a new car. "This is the new tutoring center. The Kensington Foundation is letting me use it rent free, and I can even remodel!"

His gaze snapped back to hers. "That's amazing."

"Come see the inside." She grabbed his hand and pulled him through the door. "It needs to be cleaned up, and I'm going to build a couple private study rooms there, and up here I'll have a little lounge area on this side and a conference table there for study groups and stuff. I can't wait to move in."

"You already have it all figured out, huh?" He walked in a big circle around the room, pausing to poke at the walls and stooping to examine an outlet. "I don't want to dampen your enthusiasm at all, but keep in mind that this place is most likely not up to code. You're going to have to have the electrical and plumbing inspected, and you might have to update them before you can start remodeling. Also, these lath and plaster walls are chipping, and I see a few spots that look like water damage. It should all be torn down and replaced with drywall."

Jon had warned her that it needed some work. Maybe she was getting ahead of herself a little bit. So much for moving in. "Well, I have the money from the fundraisers, and I'm hoping to hear back about the grant any day now. How much do you think all that will cost?"

"I used to do construction as my summer job in high school and college, but it's been a few years. I couldn't give you an accurate quote, but I can help you find someone who can. I'll bet some locals would come help if you had a community workday. That will cut down on labor." He squinted at the thermostat.

Piper pulled her jacket tighter around her shoulders. As the excitement faded, the dropping temp seeped through her jacket. He had the right idea. "Jon is going to have the electricity turned back on tomorrow, then I can get the heat on in here. I'd like to get it set up as soon as possible. How long do you think it will take?"

"You're going to have to get the inspection done and find out how much work needs to be done before you get your heart set on a timeline. I'll send you Luke Taylor's number. He's the contractor I used to work with." He pulled out his phone and swiped at the screen. "Actually, you've probably met him. He's your landlord, and he lives a couple doors down from you."

"If I can get him to look at it this week, could I schedule a workday this weekend?" Her phone chimed. She glanced at it. Just Titus's text.

"I'll make you a deal. Come to our game on Friday, and I'll make some calls and try to get a crew to come help on Saturday." He rubbed his hands together, then shoved them into his jacket pockets.

Piper hesitated. Maybe she should be over that betrayal by now, but she couldn't imagine stepping foot in a football stadium without reliving the horrific moment of that awful game.

"This isn't just about not liking football, is it?"

"It sounds dumb, but something happened at a football game when I was a freshman in college . . ." She shivered.

Titus stepped closer and reached out to rub her upper arms. "Come on. My truck is warm."

Piper took a last look around the space in the waning light. Renovations would take time and money, and she didn't have a lot of either. But standing here in the cold worrying about it wasn't going to speed up the process. She sighed and pulled the keys from her pocket and locked the door.

When she turned to the truck, he had the door open for her, and she hopped in. Then he ran around to his side, started the engine, and cranked up the heat.

"Will you tell me about the game?" His voice was gentle, coaxing, but not pushy.

Piper held her chilled fingers up to the vent, soaking in the warmth. The memory of that game weighed down her mood even more. "Every summer when I was growing up, no matter how far apart we lived, we went camping for a week with my mom's best friend, Auntie Beth, and her family. She had a son my age. I had the biggest crush on him, but he never really paid attention to me."

"I already don't like this guy." Titus unzipped his jacket.

Piper cracked a smile. Was he jealous? "Everything was different the summer before my senior year. My family had just moved to the town where they lived, and we started getting together with them more often. Drake and I finally clicked and got involved pretty fast."

"Was he your first boyfriend?" Titus flipped up the armrest dividing the bench of the front seat and shifted his position toward her.

"Yeah, and I thought I was in love." Looking back, she hadn't really known what love was. But now—she stole a glance at Titus— she was beginning to. "We dated all through our senior year of high school and the next summer. We said we would stay together and do the long-distance thing when we went to separate colleges, but it wasn't long before I felt like we were drifting apart."

"Long distance would be tough." He adjusted the heat on the dash.

"A couple months into our freshman year, I decided to surprise him by visiting for the weekend. I got there just in time to watch him play in the game Saturday afternoon."

"I'll bet he loved that." There was a rough edge to Titus's voice.

She looked down at her hands in her lap. "I waited for him by the athletic center exit after the game. When he came out, he had his arm around a girl. She was wearing his jersey and had his number painted on her cheek."

"What a jerk!" Titus put his arm around her. "You deserve better."

She scooted closer to his side and leaned her head on his shoulder. "I felt so stupid. I should have known he'd lost interest. He said he had been planning to break up with me, but he didn't want to do it on the phone, so he was waiting until we saw each other in person. Anyway, I haven't been to a game since."

"I can see why a football field might stir up some bad memories."

Piper straightened and turned on the seat to face Titus. "Yeah, but I've moved on. Maybe it's time to make new memories on the football field."

The building was out of her control, but this was something she could work on. Starting now, she was not going to let her past sabotage her future. It was time to face the football field.

If association was her problem, Titus could help with that. He eyed her next to him on the bench seat of his truck. A good experience at the football field might outweigh the bad memories.

But the last thing he wanted was to trigger her. He'd have to tread carefully.

"I have an idea, but you're going to have to trust me." He shifted the truck into gear.

"Where are we going?" Piper scooted back to her side and buckled her seat belt.

"You'll see." He turned left at the end of the block, went past Piper's house and the town square, then turned right on Teft Road.

Piper settled back into the seat. "You've heard about my ex. What about you? Have you had any bad breakups I should know about?"

Something inside him shuttered at the thought of rehashing this part of his past, but she was finally starting to open up. He couldn't just slam the door she'd tentatively opened. "I've had a few girlfriends, but the only one that was serious and I'd say was a bad breakup was Amber. We dated in college for a few years, but in the end, she chose to believe the bad press instead of trusting me."

"Bad press?"

He stole a glance at her. The scandal had been all over the media for months. How could she have missed it? "Did you really never see it? I thought everyone in the state had me convicted before the facts were even introduced."

"Convicted?" There was a note of concern in her voice.

Great. Now he was making himself out to be a criminal. He didn't need the press to condemn him. He could manage that all on his own. Tension began to knot the muscles across his shoulders as he turned onto Dearing Road. "No. The charges were dropped. But that didn't repair my reputation. I really thought you would have already heard the story in the news."

She reached for his hand. Titus didn't realize until she gently straightened his fingers and weaved them with hers that his hand had even tightened into a fist on the seat beside him. "I'd rather hear your side of the story."

His gaze found hers again, and his shoulders relaxed a little. He took a deep breath and blew it out slowly. He could do this.

"When it was announced that I was a finalist for the Heisman, my teammates took me out to celebrate. After I'd had one too many drinks, I saw a girl who seemed upset that this one guy wouldn't leave her alone. When he grabbed her and started dragging her toward the door, it triggered this memory of my dad pushing my mom around." He shuddered. "I had to do something."

She squeezed his hand, encouraging him on.

"I put myself between them and told him to get lost, but he took a swing at me, and I swung back." His stomach churned and he shifted in his seat. "As soon as the fight started, his friends came to his defense, so my teammates jumped in. It became this big barroom brawl, and the police had to come break it up. When the dust settled, a couple people pointed me out as the one who started the fight, and I was brought up on assault charges."

Piper looked ready to throw down. "Didn't the girl tell them what happened?"

Titus pulled his truck into the athletic center parking lot at the school and parked in the no-parking zone in front of the gate at the stadium entrance.

"She must have run when the fight started because she was nowhere to be found. Eventually, after I was publicly arrested and the media had picked up the story, making me out to be a danger to society, she did come forward and the charges were dropped. But by then, the bad press had destroyed my reputation. It's all about public opinion, and there's no fixing that."

When he'd set out to bring her here, this was not the mood he'd been hoping to set, but they were here now, so he'd better follow through anyway. He hopped out and ran around to her side of the truck and opened the door for her.

Piper took his offered hand and slid out. "For what it's worth, I think you did the right thing defending that girl."

Titus studied her face for a long moment. She couldn't know what that meant to him. He had her trust. For once, someone didn't automatically think the worst of him. "It's worth a lot. Thank you."

Her gaze warmed a moment, then everything shifted as the air between them charged.

Heat coursed through Titus, despite the cold. It would be easy to stop there, to let her believe he was a hero, kiss her, and forget the rest of the story. The truth. He took a deep breath and looked down at the pavement between them for a second. He needed to finish this before he let himself get distracted. He closed the door, then tugged her by the hand to the gate. "That one mistake cost me my shot at the Heisman and the draft."

"So you were trying to do the right thing, and it cost you your future. And instead of being your support, your girlfriend turned her back on you?" Piper's mouth pressed into a hard line and again, she looked ready to jump into a fight on his behalf.

He unlocked the gate and ushered her through. She followed him through the corridor between the bleachers that led to a dusky view of the field at the fifty-yard line behind a railing.

"I can't blame Amber." He gazed out at the field, then wandered down the steps that led to the sidelines.

Maybe it would have been easier if she had seen the bad press. Having to say it out loud was torture. Moment of truth. She deserved to know the risk she took being with him. The worst part was still lodged in his throat. He forced it out. "The guy I hit had three broken ribs and a severe concussion. He was in a coma for three days. I did that."

"There were lots of people in that fight. I doubt you did all of that."

"Maybe not, but it doesn't matter. I let my temper get the best of me, and I was not in control. Amber had seen my temper when I drank before—not against her, but she'd seen it, and I think it scared her. When she came to my apartment to break up with me, I was upset and raised my voice. She flinched. Actually flinched. In that moment, I knew I'd become my father."

Titus couldn't look at her. He didn't want to see her reaction. It couldn't be good.

"You are not your father," she whispered vehemently. When he didn't answer, she spoke again. "Do you still drink?"

"No." The word came out raw. "I never touched it again after that night. Some people can handle it. I can't. Amber's face as she flinched away turned my stomach every time I reached for it. I would never hurt a woman."

"You are not your father. You chose a different path." Her soft footsteps padded down the stairs, and from the top step directly behind him, she wrapped her arms around him and held him fiercely, her head pressed into his shoulder.

"But that man still is in me. My father—"

"Your father was a jerk, and when push came to shove, he made the wrong choice again and again." She reached up and turned his face toward her. "You made a bad choice once and chose a different path. Now you are a man of character and integrity. You are not defined by your mistakes. You know I would never say that lightly."

Titus let her words soak into his parched heart. He turned in her arms, and his hands found her waist beneath her open jacket. He desperately tried to decode the swirl of emotion on her face. He had been open with her. Maybe too open. He'd bared more of his soul today than he'd ever let anyone else see. But he didn't really know how she felt. "I want to be worthy of you. You are not easy to impress. It's a little bit intimidating."

She arched one brow and cocked her head at him. "Do you understand how insanely ludicrous that sounds? Between the two of us, you are the ridiculously attractive football star who could literally have any girl he wanted, and I am the pain-in-the-neck teacher who can't hold a job."

"I think you're holding your job just fine." He dropped his forehead to hers.

She jabbed his side. "But I am a pain in the neck?"

He leaned back and lifted one hand to brush some of her hair from her face. "You are everything I ever wanted."

"Back at you."

"Even after hearing all that?"

"Nothing about that story makes me think less of you. It's just confirmation of why I fell so hard for you. I don't want to scare you away by being too invested too fast, but you have to know I'm all in. I've never felt this way about anyone before, and it's terrifying. I think I . . . I'm falling in love with you."

The tension melted out of him, and he slid his arms around her waist under her jacket. "That is very good news."

He kissed her then, just a gentle, unhurried press of his lips against hers. There was a tender promise in that sweet kiss, an echo of their future together. He broke away just far enough for their gazes to connect. "I brought you out here hoping to change your association with the football field. Dumping my trauma and insecurity all over you is not how I intended to do that. I didn't mean to make it all about me."

"It's not. It's all about us. And that's a pretty powerful association change. I think we just need to make a few more new memories."

His breath hitched, and he pulled her against him with one arm still firmly around her waist and brought the other hand up to cup her cheek. He found her heated gaze again, and the charge between them sent fireworks through Titus's system. His eyes strayed down to her mouth, and he traced the curve of her lower lip with his thumb. The white puffs of their mingled breaths evidenced the cold air, but the fire of her touch warmed him all the way to his fingertips.

He claimed her mouth with an insatiable urgency this time. He deepened the kiss, and she angled her mouth over his, kissing him back with a passion that easily matched his. She pressed into him, and her hands plunged into his hair and fisted handfuls of his curls, holding him to her lips. Not that he was trying to escape. She seemed as eager as he was to eliminate every possible inch of space between them. He crushed her body against his until he couldn't pull her any closer.

She consumed him completely. Her touch, her soft curves pressed into him, her lips indulging on his intoxicated him, but it wasn't only physical. She branded every thought and sensation with an indelible impression, a hollow that would leave a void now if he ever had to live without her.

Finally, the necessity of breath forced Titus to pull back. With no fire alarm to force their parting, he could far too easily get lost in her.

He rested his forehead against hers again as they both panted, clouding a halo around them. Yeah, that was more what he had in mind for changing her association of the football field. But now he had to rein it in.

His desire for her could too easily lead him to take more than he intended, and in the heat of a moment like this, she might too easily offer more than she intended to give. He'd have to be cautious because he did want to live up to her faith in him, and that meant being the man of integrity she believed him to be.

thirteen

PIPER COULDN'T BELIEVE HOW MANY PEOPLE had shown up at the new tutoring storefront to help at the crack of dawn on a Saturday morning. She took in all of the strangers and new friends that filled the building. They had brought everything they needed for the demolition, from mallets and shovels to brooms and dustpans. One guy even brought a wheelbarrow.

She knew many had kids in school, and they were invested for obvious reasons. But others like Mayor Jameson and Chet Anderson were here because they believed in her. In her dream. She glanced at the floor for a moment, pulling back her emotions. She needed to call all of this to order, and it wouldn't help her to look professional to stand up here blubbering.

Titus slid up next to her. "I told you I'd get them here."

"I think I got the better end of this bargain."

"So you didn't hate the game?"

"No, it was fun, and watching you in your element was—I've just never seen you like that. You are amazing with those boys."

"I'm glad." His smile hitched on one side, bringing out the dimple she loved. The memory of their shared kiss—or should she say kisses—on the field Tuesday came rushing back. Not that they ever were too far away, as they daily drove her to distraction.

She glanced at the clipboard in her hand, then at the crowd gathered in clusters around the room chatting, then finally back to Titus. "Could you—"

Before she could finish the thought, his ear-piercing whistle split the area, quieting the space.

"I can't thank you all enough for coming to help today!" Piper gestured to the room with her clipboard. "If we can get this place cleared down to the studs, Luke and his crew can start on updating the wiring. Which is perfect timing, because I just learned the tutoring center won a grant that will help cover an extra phase of the remodeling project!"

Everyone began to clap, but she raised her hands to quiet them. "We already pulled off all the antique trim worth saving so we could reuse it. Any left behind can be torn out." Piper turned toward Luke. Not only had her landlord agreed to take the job last minute, he'd also been volunteering his time this week to get the place ready for the volunteers. "Anything you want to say before we start destroying things?"

Luke rested his large sledgehammer on his shoulder and stepped into the center of the room next to Piper. "Couple of things you should know. First, do your best not to damage the floors. If they can be preserved and refinished, it will save a bundle. Second, I marked the safe places to begin tearing down the walls. We want to avoid damaging any of the plumbing or electric wiring that's hiding in the walls. Now, Piper, I think you should get us started."

Luke pointed to an X he had marked on the wall and handed her the sledgehammer. When he let go of the handle, the weight of it jerked her shoulders. He made it look so light. She lifted the hammer and swung it toward the X. The weight caused it to curve, and the impact was nothing more than a crack in the plaster eight inches from the marked point.

Not the satisfying hammer-through-the-wall experience from HGTV demolitions she'd been hoping for. No one seemed to mind as they all cheered and started smashing the other X's marked throughout the room. Obviously much better at it than she was.

"I know these old walls are stronger than drywall, but that was pitiful." Titus leaned against the cracked wall.

"Well, we can't all bench-press three hundred pounds." She lowered the hammer to the ground, careful not to damage the hardwood floors.

"Come on. Pick it back up. You've got to put that thing through the wall. I'll help."

She sighed and wrestled the hammer back up. Titus positioned himself behind her and reached around her, placing one hand above and one below hers. She didn't really care about putting the hammer through the wall, but if it meant being in his arms, she was glad to try again.

"Move your right hand up a little. There. Now keep it in line with your body instead of swinging out to the side." He guided the hammer up over her right shoulder. "When you swing from this angle, the momentum from the hammer's weight will work with you to give the swing some power."

This time, with his assistance, the hammer crashed through the wall. Piper wasn't strong enough to pull it out.

Titus took over and yanked the thing out, splintering the wood lath and crumbling the plaster. "We make a pretty good team."

They did make a good team. He balanced her out and softened her rough edges. He was a worthy sparring partner, and best of all, he was trustworthy. "I think you might be right."

"What do you say we go out tonight, just the two of us, like a real date?"

"Real date? We've been to Donny's a few times now. Doesn't that count?"

"As much as I love Donny's, I was thinking something more romantic might be nice. I made reservations at a great little steakhouse in Ludington."

Ah, a romantic date. She wouldn't say no to that.

"How fancy is it? Should I wear this?" She struck a pose in her old T-shirt and jeans, already dusty with debris.

"I don't care what you wear." He dropped a kiss on her forehead. "But if the black dress from homecoming made a reappearance at some point, I wouldn't complain."

"Wait! Hold up! Everyone stop!" Luke's voice rang out from across the room.

The racket of destruction tapered off as everyone looked at him.

Piper arched her brow in question as he crossed the room to her purposefully.

"I'm sorry, Piper, but we're going to have to get all these people out of here. While the crew was pulling down the drop ceiling in the bathroom, they discovered the original plaster ceiling. There's a good chance it could contain asbestos. I know the inspector tested the wall plaster and the insulation above the ceiling and they were both clean, but his notes don't say anything about the original plaster above the drop ceiling. I don't think we've disturbed it yet, but it's not safe for volunteers to continue working in here until you have it tested."

Murmurs circulated, and everyone looked at her for an answer. But there was no question. Time to pack up. Piper raised her voice to teacher level. "You heard him. That's it for today. Thank you all so much."

She turned back to Luke as people began filing out. "What do I do if it tests positive?" She had a feeling she wasn't going to like the answer.

"Either hire an asbestos abatement specialist to remove it, or work with the building inspector to make a containment plan."

Piper's heart sank. What if she couldn't afford to make this place safe for kids? "What is that going to cost?"

Luke's expression said it all. Titus rested a reassuring hand on her back, but that didn't stop the figures from spinning through her mind.

Luke glanced up as if mentally measuring, then offered a half shrug. "I can't give you an exact number, but abatement is a pretty big investment. I can give you the number of the company I've used before, and they'd be able to come out and do some testing and give you a quote."

This was a delay she couldn't afford when she needed to be able to show the school board that she could deliver a functional and safe space a week from today. And what if she couldn't even resume the project until she could raise more money from a community that was already tapped out? There was the grant money, but that could take months to arrive.

Luke moved off, herding the last of the volunteers toward the door.

Titus put his arm around her and squeezed. "You okay?"

Piper shook her head and looked up at him. "So much for starting the build-out on Monday. I don't have any wiggle room in my budget, and I only have six weeks before I need to be out of Thomas and Janie's shop. And space is limited. It's cramped for one-on-one tutoring if I have more than myself and even one peer tutor at a time there. I was counting on this place being at least usable in just a couple of weeks. How am I going to make this work?"

Titus leaned down and dropped a kiss on the top of her head. "What do you say we stay in tonight instead of going out? I'll cancel the reservation, and we can just get comfortable and watch a movie or something. There's a great TV room at my mom's place, and she always has comfort food on hand."

How did he know? She hated to spoil the romantic night he had planned for her, but she just wanted to go home, put on her sweats, and eat ice cream. She blew out a slow breath, trying to expel the tension binding her neck and shoulders. "Are you sure?"

"I'll move the reservation to next Saturday instead." He hesitated like maybe he had something else to say but finally shook his head and pressed his lips together. He rubbed her upper arms. "There's nothing we can do about all of this today. Let's go buy junk food, and we can find a comedy on Netflix to take your mind off all of this."

He was right. There was nothing she could do about any of this today. Jess's words about God helping her bring this together floated through her head. Jess believed God could be trusted. This setback seemed like the opposite of help, but if Jess was right, maybe He could still come through for her. It was time to pray, because without a miracle, this tutoring center was back to square one.

Memories of victory washed over Titus as he stepped into the Wolverines' locker room after the interview. The odor of blood, sweat, and tears shed on the field still permeated the space Titus had called home for four years of his life.

The interview this morning had gone better than expected. He'd been invited to stay for the game and meet the team. He hadn't factored this into his timeline for today, but if he could get on the road as soon as the game was over, he should still be able to make it back to pick Piper up for their date.

He walked over to the locker that had been his from his freshman to senior years and ran his hand over the nameplate that had replaced his.

Head Coach Jones came up behind him and patted his shoulder. "I'd bet it's good to be back."

Before Titus could answer, the door burst open, and the first of the players entered.

"Traeger, Nolan," Head Coach Jones waved them over.

Titus recognized their names from the games he'd watched on TV. If he remembered correctly, Traeger was a tight end, and Nolan was a lineman, but without their numbers, Titus didn't know who was who.

Coach dropped his hand on Titus's shoulder. "Let me introduce you to—"

"Titus Ford?" The redhead stood a little slack-jawed before he seemed to recover. "I was always a fan, but Coach has us watch old game tapes, and your ability to read the field was unparalleled."

The other kid seemed to wake up and jumped in. "You totally deserved the Heisman, no matter what anyone says. And what happened at that Chiefs game? Brutal, man."

The coach patted one of them on the shoulder. "Well, he's interviewing for the position coach job. So you might be seeing more of him."

More players filled the room, and Titus turned to greet player after player until he could no longer keep up with names. The volume in the small space grew as stories shifted to typical pregame talk of game day rituals or bragging about their explicit activities from the night before. It was what he remembered from his college days, but something was missing. Maybe he'd just gotten used to the deeper brotherhood in the Panthers' locker room.

When his team had won last night, earning them a place in the playoffs, the parents quickly rallied to plan a celebration today at one of the boys' houses. The boys had begged him to come. Saying no had been torture, especially since he couldn't even tell them why he couldn't go. In truth, he hadn't told anyone about the interview except his mom. He'd meant to tell Piper about it last weekend on the date night he had planned. But after the building setback and her stress all week as she dealt with the asbestos specialists and prepared for the school board meeting, he didn't want to give her anything else to worry about. Not only did this job seem too good to be true and he didn't want anyone getting upset over an unlikely long shot, but even if he got the job, it didn't mean he had to take it.

Jeff Dodger crossed the locker room when he spotted Titus and used Titus's offered hand to pull him into a hug.

"It's a good sign that you're here for the game." His mentor spoke low before releasing Titus.

Yes, it was a good sign . . . if this job was what he wanted.

"I want you to meet our first-string quarterback, Jacob Elliot, but he's not here yet." Dodger looked at his watch. "He's late again."

The annoyance in Dodger's tone was rare from the easygoing coach.

Coach Jones clapped Titus on the back and pointed to a locker down the row with "Elliot" on the nameplate. "He reminds me of you when you first came into the program."

"He hasn't developed as much as you did your first couple of years." The grooves carved into Dodger's forehead and between his brows were deeper than Titus remembered. His eyes, though still bright and sharp, were also hooded with crow's-feet folded into crepe paper skin on the outside corners.

When had his mentor gotten old? Did he know how much he had impacted Titus or how much of Titus's development as a player was due to his genuine, paternal care and patient coaching? The older Titus got, the more he realized how much he owed Jeff Dodger.

"I think I had better go give him a call. He should be here by now." Coach Dodger moved toward the office.

"I really believe that with a little expert coaching, he could do so much better. You'd be the perfect example for him to emulate." Coach Jones tapped Elliot's nameplate.

If he was looking for expert coaching, he already had it with Dodger. But it might be nice to have the opportunity to work one-on-one with a player that had real potential.

Brett surfaced in Titus's mind. Maybe if he was here, he could recommend that U of M recruit him, and Titus would have the chance to work with him again. Getting to know Brett and working with him to draw out that natural talent had been one of the things he had most enjoyed this year. Maybe he'd like this job more than he thought. After all, coaching in Heritage had sure surprised him.

Another player swaggered in the door like his very presence here was a gift they should all be thankful for.

"Ah, there he is." The head coach pointed to the player, who tossed his long hair and sauntered over to another group of players. "Elliot," the coach barked out.

The kid's gaze scanned the room until it landed on his coach. There was no warmth in his eyes. He just appeared bored and annoyed to be summoned. He took his time tying back his hair then finally crossed the locker room toward them. If Titus got the job, this was the guy he would be working with the most.

"He's gotten himself into some trouble that we've had to dig him out of a few times, but he has some raw talent. It just needs to be . . . channeled."

If ever there was a player who demonstrated Piper's invented "entitled athlete syndrome," this was the kid. Her story about her brother's failing to hold a job and failing out of college because everything had been handed to him in high school ran through Titus's head. Clearly this guy had the talent to get him this far, and Titus didn't know anything about his grades or academic capabilities, but his entitled attitude was on full display.

"Elliot, you know we've been looking for a position coach since Coach Dodger announced his retirement."

Elliot huffed. "Good riddance. That useless—"

"Elliot! Show some respect. Clean up your language and your attitude." Coach Jones's voice held a note of warning.

Maybe Titus was overstepping, but he couldn't let that comment go. "Coach Dodger was the best thing that ever happened to me. He's anything but useless."

Coach Jones continued, unfazed by Titus's interruption. "This is Titus Ford. I trust he needs no further introduction. We're looking at him for the job."

Elliot looked Titus over with narrowed eyes swimming with resentment. "Coach says you *were* one of the best. Then you couldn't cut it in the NFL."

"I had an injury."

"So they say." His defiant eyes challenged the notion. "Heard you're coaching a B-level high school out in the sticks."

Every single kid on his team *in the sticks* outranked this jerk in his mind, no matter what his scoring record said.

Come to think of it, what about this kid reminded his coaches of Titus? He sure hoped he'd never behaved this way.

Titus had been looking forward to sitting on the Wolverines' sideline in the Big House once again. But an hour later, he couldn't help wishing he was in the stands with Piper or Brett instead of here, sitting on a bench with this disconnected team that he didn't even want to be a part of. By the time the game ended in victory, Titus was ready to go home to Heritage.

Back in the locker room after the game, Coach Jones gave Titus a firm handshake. "It's been great having you back in the Big House for the day. If you want the job, it's yours. I'll have the office draw up the paperwork and send an offer letter over on Monday. I really hope you'll consider it. We could sure use some of the Ford magic back in the program again."

"Thank you so much for the opportunity, Coach. I will give it some thought." Day one at Heritage hadn't had the same dynamic as they had today either. A team's culture could develop over time with the right leadership. He'd witnessed that firsthand.

Although if Nate was right about God having a hand in it, it may have a lot less to do with Titus than he'd like to think. Still, this job did deserve his consideration, even if it didn't feel like the perfect fit today. After all, God had to have had a hand in connecting him with Jeff Dodger too. The Wolverines' locker room was not out of His reach.

Titus was in his truck and headed home with a full tank of gas by four. He'd still be able to pick Piper up for their date tonight by six thirty if he didn't get delayed. He merged onto US-23 North and tapped the screen of the aftermarket Bluetooth device he'd added to the dash. Why wouldn't it connect to play his Spotify playlist? He reached for his phone in his pocket but came up empty. He tried the other pocket. No luck. He glanced at his watch. No connection. Where had he left it? If he turned around now, he would miss his date with Piper, and there was no guarantee that he would even find it. He'd just have to ask Coach Dodger to keep an eye out and send it if it turned up.

Apparently it would be a long ride home with only his thoughts and the radio that always seemed to be half static. Maybe he needed the time to think anyway. Rain began to sprinkle onto the windshield, and Titus flipped on his wipers.

It would be crazy to turn down this job. Opportunities like this didn't just drop in his lap. And it had been good to see a couple of his former coaches' familiar faces, but something just felt off. Even being in that place where he'd celebrated so much victory and promise was not the same.

The rain picked up to a steady shower, and he turned the wipers from intermittent to constant. The sky ahead darkened by the minute, and he turned on his headlights. He wouldn't be driving out of this anytime soon.

The more he rolled the job over in his mind, the more it didn't sit right. He'd never had a family in his team at U of M. His years there were special because of Coach Dodger, and he wouldn't be sticking around. Sure, he'd made friends with his teammates, but they were much more likely to get him into trouble than to bail him out of it.

But could he really pass up this opportunity?

As he merged onto I-96 West, lightning licked the dark landscape and thunder crashed so loud it rattled his teeth.

Then there was Piper to consider. How would she react if he decided to take the job? They could do long distance, but to what end? Moving to Ann Arbor wouldn't be temporary for him, and she was just getting the tutoring center up and running in Heritage.

He needed to call and find out how the school board meeting went—no phone.

A loud pop from the engine was almost drowned out by the pounding rain, but an instant later, white smoke began streaming out from under the hood of his truck, blocking his view of the interstate and filling his truck with a sickly sweet odor.

This was not good.

He turned on his blinker and eased the truck to the side of the road.

Pouring rain, broken-down truck, and no phone. What a winning combination. And this was bound to be expensive.

This would put a dent in his savings. That money was supposed to be reserved for getting his own place, but even with limited expenses in Heritage, his income wasn't enough to cover these big, unexpected needs. His savings wouldn't last forever. How was he going to make a livable wage to support a family someday if he stayed? Even if he wanted to stay in Heritage, he needed to consider that U of M was offering more than triple his current salary. And that might make the decision for him.

fourteen

PIPER GLANCED AT HER PHONE TO CHECK the time. Almost seven. Titus should have been here by now to pick her up. If he didn't make it soon, they would miss their dinner reservation. They may not be able to push it back on a Saturday night. Maybe she should call the restaurant and find out.

No. She would not micromanage their date. Titus said he had it taken care of, and she trusted him. Instead, she dialed his number and put the phone on speaker as she leaned over the large round mirror on the dining room wall to check her makeup.

Ring.

She'd donned the black dress he'd requested, along with nude heels that went with everything.

Ring.

As much as she hated having to put in contacts, her eyes popped when they weren't hidden behind her glasses, so the discomfort was worth it once in a while.

Ring.

Especially when her eyes were shadowed and lined and mascaraed.

Voicemail picked up. "You've reached Titus Ford. I can't come to the phone right now, but leave me a message and I'll call you back." *Beep.*

"Titus, where are you? I thought you said you were going to pick me up at six thirty. Did I get the time wrong, or was I supposed to meet you there? Call me back. I'm getting worried." She wandered to the living room window and peered out at the empty street.

Piper turned as Jess trotted down the stairs in her sweats and slippers. She looked Piper over. "You look amazing. Titus is going to come undone."

"If he ever gets here." Piper tamped down the anxious gurgle in her gut. He was fine. He was just late. It happened.

"This looks like more than dinner at Donny's. Things must be going well between the two of you." Jess passed through the arch into the kitchen and opened the pantry.

"Yeah, you could say that. I don't know how it happened so quickly, but he's become . . . important." A few stolen moments and quick phone calls throughout the week hadn't been enough.

Something in Piper's voice must have added meaning to the words, because Jess turned from the open pantry with her brows raised. "I've never known you to fall hard and fast. But it almost sounds like you're in love with him."

"I don't know. Maybe. I'm fully aware that I'm getting way ahead of myself, but I can't help it." She hadn't known him that long. Could she really be falling in love with a man she'd only met less than two months ago? Yet somehow he knew her to her fragile core. And he had trusted her with his deepest wounds too. "I really misjudged him when we first met. He's not the entitled athlete I took him for. He's honest and hardworking, kind, thoughtful, and way wiser than I gave him credit for."

Piper looked at the time again. He was also very late.

"Never thought I'd see the day. Did he have something else going on today? I was a little surprised that he wasn't at the school board meeting this morning." Jess returned to searching the pantry.

"I ran into Kristen at JJ's this afternoon, and she'd said the team was out at a player's house celebrating their spot in the playoffs." Piper had been taken off guard too, but she'd never actually asked him to be at the meeting, and he deserved to celebrate with the boys after all he'd done to shape their character and encourage them throughout the season. The way he coached those boys with patience and strength proved what a good father he would be someday.

"Well, it's a shame he missed it. You were amazing." Jess stared absently at the pantry shelves.

"Thanks, but I think the credit goes to his mom. I had way more support on the school board than I thought I would." Maggie had investigated the situation with her former school and defended her even before she presented her evidence. When she was done, Martha Palmer was the only one opposing her. "I think my chances of getting a part-time salary to run the tutoring center are pretty good."

"When will they vote on your proposal?" Finally, Jess closed the pantry door empty-handed and pulled open the fridge instead.

"At the closed meeting next month. The asbestos encasement and wiring wiped out my budget." Piper pulled the dining room curtain back to peek outside again. A big drop of rain splotched a blurry spot onto the window. Another drop, then another pelted the glass. Great. So much for the hour she'd spent curling her hair.

"The dividers the school offered will be faster to set up than building walls anyway, so you'll be able to get the place up and running sooner." Jess closed the fridge and opened the freezer.

"True. The work started on Wednesday, and they're already almost done. But I have to get the walls closed up first. I had to drain my personal savings account to get the drywall. It was delivered yesterday. I can't afford to pay the crew to do it, but Titus has experience. I'll have him help me." She stole a glance at her phone. No calls or messages. Where was he?

Jess pulled a carton of ice cream from the freezer. "If he's going to keep you waiting so long, maybe you need something to hold you over."

An hour later, the ice cream was eaten and dishes washed, but still no word from Titus. Worried became an understatement. Piper took the last dish from Jess and set it in the cupboard. "I'm going to his house. This isn't like him."

"Keep me updated." Jess hung the dishtowel on the oven handle.

"I will." Piper slipped into her coat and grabbed her purse.

When Piper arrived at the well-cared-for one-and-a-half-story cottage nestled in a grove of sugar maples, nothing looked amiss from her visit here last week for their movie night.

She just needed to make sure he was safe. Or if he'd forgotten or discarded her. It seemed unlikely, given the sweet whispers and stolen kisses in the teachers' lounge on Thursday when she'd last seen him, but Drake had been sweet to her too.

She pushed open the car door, marched up the steps to the inviting front porch with potted mums next to the door and eyelet lace curtains in windows glowing with warm light in the dark evening, and knocked on the front door.

A moment later, Titus's mom opened the door, and surprise registered on Maggie's face. "Piper, hello. What are you doing here? I thought you and Titus were going to Ludington for the evening."

"So did I, but he never picked me up, and he hasn't answered his phone all day."

"I wonder if the interview went long. But even if he stayed for the game, he should have been back from Ann Arbor by now."

A cold trickle of dread traveled down Piper's spine. "Interview? I thought he was with the team."

Maggie's face fell. "I assumed he'd told you."

"What interview?" Piper persisted.

She opened the door wide and ushered Piper into the entryway before closing out the chill. "It was for a coaching position at U of M."

He interviewed for a job on the opposite side of the state without telling her about it? Yeah, this relationship was new, but clearly she was more invested in it than he was. The truth fractured the delicate faith she'd placed in him, leaving a raw ache festering deep in her chest. Trust was a fragile promise too easily shattered, and the broken shards always cut deep.

At Maggie's stricken face, Piper took a deep breath to soothe the burning ache. "Have you heard from him at all today?"

She shook her head. "I thought he had just gone straight to pick you up. I left my phone in the kitchen, but I'll call and see if I can get an answer."

Piper followed her through the house as the maple-sweet aroma of something baking increased with each step until they reached a large farmhouse-style kitchen. An hour ago, Piper's empty stomach would have been growling, but she'd lost her appetite.

Maggie picked up her phone and dialed.

When Maggie lifted the phone to her ear, Piper took in the room. Open shelving took the place of upper cabinets and was adorned with eclectic functional pottery and dishes. Butcher-block countertops covered the lower cabinets, and yellow ruffled curtains dressed the window over the vintage ceramic sink. The room was open to the dining room with a rustic table and stairs leading up to another level.

"Voicemail. This is not like him. What could have happened?" Maggie frowned and shook her head, worry carving creases between her brows.

Piper swallowed hard as pressure built in her chest. The thought of losing him hadn't occurred to her. She didn't want to be the kind of person who always jumped to a negative conclusion, and too often, it had been her first instinct. He deserved the benefit of doubt. She needed to reserve judgment, at least until they knew he was safe. "Would you mind if I wait in my car until he gets home? Is it in the way out there?"

"Nonsense. You'll wait in here with me. You'll have to keep me distracted so I don't go crazy with worry. Besides, my cinnamon-maple sticky buns are about to come out of the oven, and if you were waiting for him to take you to dinner, I know you haven't eaten yet."

Piper wouldn't mention the ice cream. Besides, as wonderful as they smelled, she couldn't eat. But she could wait a little while. Surely he would show up or at least call one of them soon.

Piper turned toward the rumble of footsteps running down creaky steps off the dining room, and a moment later, Kristen stumbled through the kitchen door with tears streaming down her cheeks. Piper's heart plummeted. Oh no. What had she heard about Titus? Something must have happened to him.

"What happened?" From Maggie's ragged tone, she must have jumped to the same conclusion.

Kristen ran past Piper into her mother's open arms. "Brett's mom just died."

Kristen's sob broke Piper's heart, but she couldn't suppress the relief that the news hadn't been Titus's tragedy. She couldn't lose him.

She loved him. The thought stole Piper's breath, but it was true. She loved him.

And he was missing.

A little before eleven, Titus finally pulled into his long driveway in the rental car he'd picked up after getting his truck towed to a shop in Howell. The whole process was made exponentially more difficult without his phone. And when he did have the opportunity to use a phone at the repair shop to call Piper, he realized he didn't have anyone's phone number memorized.

He almost went straight to her house, but the cold had settled bone deep, and it had been a long ride home in wet clothes. Besides, his head was pounding with an epic headache. Titus rounded the final bend of the driveway, and his mom's house came into view.

Wait, was that Piper's car? Maybe it was a good thing he'd come straight home. The layer of frost coating her windows proved she'd been here for a while. He parked and made a run for it across the gravel driveway.

When he pushed open the door to the house, his mom rounded the corner from the kitchen with rampant worry in her eyes, and Piper was close on her heels. She looked beautiful and soft in her black dress with her hair in loose curls. Both women's shoulders sagged in relief when they saw him.

"How could you let us worry like that?" Mom swatted his arm. "We called every hospital and police station on your path home. Where have you been?"

Titus shook his head. "Sorry. It's a long story. I lost my phone. My truck broke down. I walked miles through a rainstorm to get help."

He looked past his mom to Piper. The initial relief in her big eyes had shifted to pain and hurt.

If *they* had called every hospital on his path home, that meant Piper knew where he'd been and probably why he'd been there too. That was so not how he wanted her to find out.

Titus sighed and pushed the door closed. He had some explaining to do. He dropped the keys to his rental car into the dish on the console table by the front door.

"I think I'll go up to check on Kristen." Mom turned and headed for the stairway then paused and looked over her shoulder. "Just so you know, Brett's mom passed away a few hours ago."

The news was a gut check. Brett must be devastated. Why hadn't he called—oh, right. No phone. Where would he be now? He'd have to find him and see if there was anything he could do.

When Mom had gone, he met Piper's wounded gaze. First, he would need to do some damage control here. "I'm sorry. I wanted to call."

He led the way to the kitchen.

Piper followed, then paused in the doorway and bit her lip. "How did the interview go?"

"I was going to tell you last week, but with everything else happening, I just didn't want to upset you for nothing." He took a step toward her, but she backed away.

"Honesty is a value I'm not willing to compromise."

He opened the cupboard and pulled out a bottle of Advil. "I didn't lie to you."

He turned back in time to see pain flare in her eyes. That was the wrong thing to say. Trying to justify was not going to help him. He got a glass and filled it with water.

"You gave me hope that we had a future here when you knew there was a chance you were leaving all along." Her voice quivered. "That seems pretty dishonest to me."

"I didn't think I would actually get the job." She had a right to be upset, but she didn't have to turn him into a villain. He'd had enough of that from the media to last a lifetime. He downed a couple of the pills. Couldn't she just understand? "You have to see, this is a chance of a lifetime. It's U of M. Opportunities like this are rare. I had to give it a shot. But taking the interview has no bearing on the way I feel about you."

A tear trailed down her cheek. "This isn't even about the interview."

Not about the interview? "What's it about then?"

She grabbed her purse from the island countertop and headed for the front door. "Relationships require trust."

"You know you can trust me." He abandoned the glass of water on the counter and chased her down the hall.

She pulled her coat from a hook in the entryway and slipped into it. "I trust you to support me, to help me, to defend me, yes, you have proven yourself again and again. But to be transparent with me even if it is uncomfortable? You just showed me I can't. And that is vital to a relationship, especially if we decide to date long-distance."

She pushed through the door.

He followed her out, and the cold blast of night air against his damp clothes sent an icy chill down his spine. "Don't leave. I agree, I should have told you, and I'm sorry. It hasn't happened before, and it won't happen again."

"But it has happened before. You didn't want to be transparent with the boys about our relationship because it would be awkward." She crossed her arms over her chest and hunched her shoulders. "You don't even tell people how your knee is really doing because you don't want pitying looks."

"What?" He couldn't even follow her reasoning with his head throbbing and the cold penetrating into his bones. "Come on, Piper. Don't blow this out of proportion. I've been thinking about you all day. I just wanted to call and talk to you about this."

She sighed and grabbed his arm, moving both of them nearer to the side of the house, out of the wind. "Did you get the job?"

"They offered it to me, but I haven't accepted it yet. I don't know what to do. I don't want to leave you or the team, but this is what I need to do if I want to build a career in coaching. I just don't want to lose you or what I have here." He rubbed his arms with his numb fingers, attempting to still the shudders racking his body.

"This isn't going to work." Her eyes glossed over, and she shook her head.

She'd said his mistakes didn't define him, yet she'd discard him because of one lapse in judgment? Or was it two if she counted the boys? Then what had she said about his knee? Maybe she was just keeping a tally. "If you're walking away over this, then there is nothing more to say. I can't be with someone who gives up on me the moment I don't meet their expectations."

She flinched at the last barb and ducked her head. "Well, I hope you find what you're looking for in Ann Arbor, but no coaching position, no team will ever be enough until you realize that football is not your identity."

"You're leaving?"

The husky, broken voice stopped both of them cold.

Titus turned to find Brett on the steps of the porch, his red-rimmed eyes accusing him of betrayal. Brett shook his head, then turned and ran back to his car, which was still running in the driveway. How had Titus missed that?

"Brett, wait!" How much had the kid heard? As if losing his mom tonight wasn't bad enough. He turned to Piper. "I have to go after him, and I'm not sure there's anything left to say."

Piper nodded but didn't comment. He'd lost her. And maybe that was for the best. He didn't need one more person in his life tracking all the ways he didn't measure up. He turned on his heel and pushed open the door to grab his keys. Brett needed him. He had to focus on that.

Leaving without a phone again was only going to cause more frustration. Keys in hand, he turned and ran for the stairs. "Mom, I need your phone."

She met him at the top of the stairs, phone extended, no questions asked. "Be safe."

By the time he'd reached the country road at the end of the driveway, there was no sign of which way Brett went. He parked the car and did a quick search to find out if he could check his voicemail from his mom's phone. Once he followed the steps, there were nine new voicemails since he'd lost his phone this afternoon.

The first was from Piper, wondering where he was with a hint of worry. Probably the last he'd ever hear that warmth in her voice. He squashed the emotion that tried to roil up in his chest.

He clicked on the next one, from Brett. "Hey, Coach." His voice was thick and heavy, laden with emotion. "My mom just died. The hospice people are here, and we're waiting for the coroner. I just . . . don't want to watch them take her away. My siblings are at the neighbor's, and I could go there too. I just . . . can I come over? Please?"

Titus squeezed his eyes shut and dropped his head back on the headrest. He should have been there for Brett. He'd do anything to go back in time and show up, because that kid needed someone who would show up for him no matter what.

Someone who wouldn't leave.

Brett's devastated words echoed through his mind. *You're leaving?* The failure weighted his soul. He couldn't turn back time. He couldn't fix this.

The next message, from his mom, was much more worried than Piper's earlier message.

Kristen came on next. Instead of worry, she was desperate. "Where are you? What could possibly be more important to you than Brett right now? He needs you! Why would you blow him off?"

She was reading his own internal monologue there. She was right. He was trash. He'd known Brett's mom was barely hanging on. He shouldn't have left.

The next call was from a number he didn't have stored in his phone. "Coach. This is Beau. Me and Jay and Owen and Ethan are at the police station. We were doing something stupid and got arrested." The phone muffled for a moment as he seemed to be speaking to someone else. "Sorry, we were *taken into custody*. But it looks the same to me. Anyway, you're my one phone call. Can you come to the police station and talk to the officer?"

His players got picked up by the police? What were they doing? Maybe if he'd been there, he could have stopped it.

Titus wanted to turn the phone off. This just kept getting worse and worse. But four more messages still blinked in the notifications.

The next message began to play. "Ford, this is Principal Franklin. I'm deeply disappointed in the conduct of your players tonight. Four of your boys were taken into custody for minor consumption, drunk and disorderly, and vandalism of city property."

Were his players actually responsible for all of this? What were they thinking? And here he thought they'd turned the corner.

"We are going to have to be prepared to release a statement to the media. If it's not already obvious, Jay, Ethan, Owen, and Beau are suspended for the remainder of the season."

Titus had begun to believe that maybe God had him here in Heritage for a reason. He thought he was making headway. Maybe even finding the purpose or the path he was meant for. Clearly, he'd been wrong. Whatever it was that God wanted him to do here, he'd failed.

Maybe it was a good thing he had another job lined up. His team deserved better.

Another message from an unknown number began to play.

"Hello. This is Mrs. Schabat. The boy from my neighbor's family, Brett, has been missing since this afternoon after his mom passed away, and his family is real worried. I'm told you are his coach, and I was hoping you and your players might have talked to him. If you know where he is, please call me back right away."

You're leaving? Brett's voice echoed through Titus's aching head again.

Titus dropped his forehead against the steering wheel as pressure from all sides seemed to be closing in on his chest. He'd let everyone down.

fifteen

PIPER SCRUBBED HER FACE CLEAN OF THE makeup and tear trails and glared at her fuzzy reflection in the bathroom mirror.

Titus had accused her of overreacting. And maybe she was. They had only been dating two weeks, so maybe he didn't owe her complete transparency.

But that meant she'd gotten in too deep too fast, and despite his talk of feelings and the future, he wasn't invested like she was.

I didn't lie.

Yeah, well, withholding the truth was just as dishonest. And if he didn't recognize that, it would never be safe to trust him. Being left in the dark hurt just as much as a lie.

It didn't really matter anymore anyway. He was leaving and they were over.

She toweled off her face and slid her glasses in place. It was late, but trying to sleep with her mind racing and her chest aching was a lost cause. She wandered downstairs, flipped on the light, and dropped into one of the stools next to her puzzle table. She'd just started a new one, so the table was covered in scattered, unpaired pieces. She began clearing the platform and organizing the pieces, dividing them by like patterns and colors on the side trays. But try as she might, she couldn't find a single match. This was so not helping calm her racing thoughts or soothe her wounded heart.

She shoved up from the table and went to the kitchen to get a glass of water and took a long drink. Her revised plans for the tutoring center were laid out on the dining room table.

How much had the crew gotten done since she'd last been there on Wednesday?

The whole project had been kind of like one big puzzle she'd been putting together one piece at a time. If she could just go see the progress and envision the finished picture, maybe her heart would feel less shattered. She grabbed her keys and her coat and walked out to her car in her slippers and sweats. She pulled her jacket tighter around her as she slid into the cold driver's seat. Maybe she should have put on warmer clothes. Brrr.

When she turned down Second Street and the headlights illuminated the storefront, Piper's blood ran cold. The door was open. Had the construction crew failed to latch it? Could the wind have blown it open?

As she pulled up to the curb, Piper's pulse ratcheted into high gear. The splintered wood of the doorframe made it clear this had been no wind and no accident.

She pulled out her phone and dialed 911.

"Nine-one-one, what's your address?"

"I'm at 314 Richard Street in Heritage, and there's been a break-in."

"I'm dispatching an officer now." By the time Piper had given them her information, the officers had arrived and cleared the building.

She got out of the car and headed for the entrance, her legs still feeling like jelly.

"Are you Miss Cavanaugh?" One of the officers stopped her by the door.

"I am." Her words were breathy.

"I'm Officer Breckshaw. We've checked the building thoroughly. Whoever did this is gone. If you could walk through and note anything that might be missing. Officer Ray will take your statement so we can file a report."

Piper nodded and stepped over the threshold.

Her breath strangled off. Graffiti in red and black spray paint covered the walls and the hardwood floors she'd hoped to save. One wall read "Leave" in eerie dripping red, and another section called her a name she wouldn't repeat. The new drywall that had just been delivered for the next phase of the project had been violently smashed and broken and scattered around the room.

And in that moment, she was again a little girl coming home from vacation with her family to find their home destroyed. She couldn't breathe. She tried to force her lungs to inflate, but they wouldn't expand.

The tutoring center was destroyed, her fundraising money and savings were gone. Titus was moving away. She clearly wasn't making a difference, and this town didn't even want her here.

Piper took a couple stumbling steps with her lungs screaming for oxygen despite her shallow pants. Lines of spray paint on the beautiful hardwood began to blur.

It was so cold. She couldn't breathe. Her legs sank beneath her, suddenly unable to support her weight. She reached for the wall beside her, but her arm raked down the jagged glass on the edge of the broken window. Pain sliced through her wrist and palm just before everything faded to black.

Titus generally respected an officer of the law who took his oath seriously, but the new deputy in training on the early-morning shift at the Heritage police station tonight wouldn't give him anything.

"I don't care whose coach you are. I cannot disclose any information about minors who we may or may not have in custody." The uniform looked out of place on the skinny kid who didn't look much older than Titus's players.

Titus leaned on the counter, peering over at the new kid. "One of the boys called me as their one phone call. That has to mean something."

The kid cleared his throat. "I *can* tell you that I do not currently have anyone on lockdown."

Titus pushed off the counter and walked in a circle. "Where is Officer Hammond? I want to talk to him."

"He retired last year. And Officer Breckshaw is off duty. He had a long night at a breaking and entering call with a medical emergency. I'm not going to call him and wake him up at five a.m. I'll leave a message for him to call you when he gets in later this afternoon."

"Fine." Titus wouldn't get anywhere with this kid. He returned to his rental car.

After a fruitless search for Brett and a restless attempt to sleep for a few hours, Titus had gone to the police station to see if he could find out what kind of trouble Beau, Owen, Jay, and Ethan had gotten into. Another dead end.

He turned his car back onto the road and a minute later found himself in front of Piper's house. Her car wasn't even there. Where in the world would she be at this hour?

Yeah, he wanted to talk to her, but what would he say? He needed someone who was going to be in his corner no matter what. Someone who didn't give up on him at the first glimpse of trouble. Why couldn't Piper be the one to believe in him? And how had she managed to anchor herself so deeply into his heart in so short a time?

He checked his voicemail again from his mom's phone, but there were no new messages. Where could Brett be?

Maybe Nate would have an idea. He turned his car toward the assistant coach's house. Titus pulled his truck up to the curb. The house was mostly dark, but a single light glowed through a window on the side of the house, and a figure that was too masculine to be Nate's wife moved past the light. Good. He was up. Titus hopped out of his truck and closed the distance to the house, then knocked gently on the front door.

A moment later, Nate opened the door in plaid flannel pants and a T-shirt. His brows drew together, carving a crease between them. "Titus. You look terrible. Come in."

Titus stepped into the warmth of the modest living room. "I'm sorry to barge in so early."

"My door is always open. Is everything okay?" Nate led the way through the dark living room to the kitchen, where the light on the side wall, above the sink, cast a soft glow on a small table with a Bible open next to a steaming mug.

"Brett's missing. And Beau, Owen, Jay, and Ethan got picked up by the police last night. So, nope, everything is not okay."

"I talked to Principal Franklin last night. Never seen him so mad. They were drunk and they were caught trying to move Otis. So much for the playoffs. Tough lesson to learn. What's going on with Brett?"

Titus raked his hand through his hair. "His mom passed away yesterday and now he's missing."

Nate pulled another mug from the cupboard and filled it with coffee. "How long has he been missing?"

"I saw him about eleven last night when he came to find me." Titus ducked his head and swallowed at the rock suddenly lodged in his throat. "I messed everything up."

Nate set the coffee on the table and gestured for Titus to sit.

"Do you remember who you're talking to? I spent a lot of years as a poster child for screwups. But there is life after. Trust me."

"How can you say that? You don't even know what happened." Titus's shoulders slumped as he sank into the chair.

Nate's hand landed on Titus's shoulder. "Maybe not, but I do know that no matter how big it seems, God is bigger."

"Are you talking about the same God who let me shatter my knee to keep me from the NFL? That was nice of Him. Or the one who let me get charged with assault when I was just trying to protect someone? That really helped me too." Yeah, maybe he was a little angry at God. But as the pressure of venting faded, only the sorrow hanging heavy over his heart remained. "He took Brett's mom. He's got it rough, but she was the bright spot in his life."

"She's not the only bright spot. God knew she was fading, so He brought you into Brett's life. Anyone can see the way that kid lights up when you're around." Nate returned to his seat at the other end of the table.

Titus leaned back in the chair and let his head fall back. "And I let him down. I wasn't there when he needed me because I was off trying to get a higher-paying job so I could advance my career. And when he came looking for me, he overheard Piper and me arguing, and now he thinks I'm leaving. That's why he ran."

"Are you leaving?" Nate took a sip from his mug.

"I don't know. It doesn't feel right, but considering everything that has happened in the past twenty-four hours, I might not have the option to stay."

"Were you and Piper arguing about the job?"

Titus let out a heavy sigh. "I didn't tell her about the interview, and now she thinks I can't be trusted."

"Is that true?"

"No." He stared into the black coffee in his mug. "I never want to be dishonest. But I do have a tendency to avoid hard conversations."

"Well, do you love her?"

"Yeah." There was no question about that. The future he'd envisioned before he met her seemed like an empty void now. He didn't even want to think about his life without her.

"Then you'll have to work on that."

"Yeah, I realize that. But I'm afraid she's always going to be waiting for me to mess up. It feels hopeless."

Nate leveled a look at him. "I know what it feels like to be broken and stripped of hope. But the broken pieces of the life you tried to build for yourself are all God needs to rebuild something way better than you could ever hope for. Just keep in mind that God's measure of success isn't money or prestige or fame. Ultimately, all of that is just an empty shell if God isn't in it. But when you're in the center of His will, there is a kind of contentment and satisfaction that you can't get anywhere else."

Something clicked into place. U of M felt off, but these past months in Heritage felt right, in a way he'd never been able to identify. And all this time he'd resented God, but maybe he just couldn't see God working because he was too focused on forcing his own way. "I think you're right. Heritage is where God wants me. But what if I've already destroyed my chance to stay?"

"If God wants you here, and I believe He does, then a few parents and administrators who want someone to blame for their kids' bad behavior aren't going to be able to stand in His way. You didn't buy alcohol for those kids or tell them their behavior was okay." Nate gestured to his arm covered in tattoos, some of which represented his life before Christ. "As a kid who probably would have been getting into trouble with them fifteen years ago, I can assure you, it's not your fault. The school will recognize that, and I know this town will stand behind you."

"Thanks, Nate." A weight lifted from Titus's chest. Maybe God did still have a plan for him, but would Brett forgive him? "I wish I knew where to look for Brett."

"Did you check the football stadium?"

Titus nodded. "Twice. I can't think of any other hobbies he's talked about."

"Has he ever mentioned a place that's important to him? Does his family have a cabin or place they went on vacation or something?"

Titus pictured Brett sitting on his front porch, telling him about how much his mom loved Little Sable Lighthouse. "Yes. I think I might know where to look."

sixteen

IF THE NURSES DIDN'T COME TAKE THIS IV OUT soon, Piper was going to yank it out herself. The emergency room in Ludington was not the place she'd wanted to spend the night. But apparently the cut on her wrist had sliced through an artery. Because she'd lost so much blood, she'd needed a transfusion and fluids.

How in the world was she supposed to get back home from here? Now that the medicine they had given her to calm her down and help her sleep had worn off, she needed to get back to the ruins of the tutoring center, even if it meant she had to walk all the way back to Heritage.

Or maybe she just needed to cut her losses and move on.

It seemed like every time she started to feel like she was making some progress, the rug was pulled out from under her, and she had to start back at square one. Jess had almost had her convinced that God had given her the passion to teach. Maybe He'd even meant for her to start the tutoring center. But if God wanted her to do this, why did He keep letting her fall on her face? Maybe God wasn't any more trustworthy than the people who had let her down over and over again.

At least the remaining four months of the contract would give her some time to make a plan. If only she didn't have to see Titus every day. She couldn't be with him when she'd always wonder if she could really trust him. Story of her life. And he was leaving at the end of his contract anyway.

Maybe she and Cam could find a place to start over. She often gave him a hard time about not having his life together, but here she was in the same boat. Maybe they could get an apartment together.

She grabbed her phone off the side table. Six in the morning might be a little early for Cam, but she dialed his number anyway. The phone was almost dead without getting a charge last night. Hopefully the battery would hold out long enough to talk to him for a few minutes.

"Hey, Pip, guess what I did this week." Cam's upbeat voice was a balm for her wounded heart. He didn't sound groggy at all. He must have already been up.

"I'm not much in the mood for guessing games." She shifted in the uncomfortable hospital bed.

"You sound down. What's going on?" His concern came through in his tone.

"Tell me your thing first. I could use some good news."

"Okay. You know I started a new job at the gym. Well, my new sponsor through Celebrate Recovery, Erik, is a trainer there. He helped me get the job. I've been thinking I'd really like to do what he does, but I'd have to get a degree. He helped me apply to Bay College and wrote me a letter of recommendation asking them to consider admitting me, even though my college GPA was so bad before I dropped out. I had to take a placement test, but Erik helped me study. I just found out they're going to give me a probationary year. I'm going back to college! I start in January."

Piper sucked in a refreshing breath. This was good news. She'd carried a burden of responsibility for Cam's struggles for so long, but he was overcoming . . . now that someone else was helping him. "That's amazing! Why didn't you tell me you were working on this?"

"I just didn't want to get your hopes up. You've always believed in me, and I didn't want to let you down if I failed."

"Even so, I would have been impressed that you tried. But I've never had a moment's doubt that you were capable. I'm so glad you found someone who could help you believe in yourself enough to try. I'm just sorry you always felt like you couldn't measure up to my expectations." Ironic how Cam got his life together just as hers fell apart. "I think the Heritage tutoring center needs someone like Erik in charge."

"Uh oh. Not going so well?"

"I think I've done enough damage here. As soon as Mrs. MacDonald comes back from maternity leave, I need to move on."

"What happened?"

"Some of the kids I was trying to help vandalized the new center. There's graffiti all over the walls calling me names and telling me to leave. They smashed up the brand-new drywall and destroyed the hardwood floors."

"Oh, Piper, that's horrible. I'm so sorry. Is Titus there with you? I don't think you should be alone."

"Titus and I broke up."

Thinking of him reopened the wounds his flippant betrayal had sliced into her chest. *I didn't lie.*

"When? Piper, why didn't you call me?"

"We just broke up late last night, right before I found the center destroyed. Then I guess I passed out and cut myself on some broken glass from the window. Thankfully, the cops were there. They found me and I woke up on a stretcher. An ambulance took me to the ER. I just needed a transfusion and some stitches, but they drugged me. I just woke up."

"Piper! That's the kind of information you lead with! You're in the hospital? Have you called Mom and Dad? I can get in the car right now and be there by lunchtime."

"No, Cam. You driving six and a half hours won't change anything. I'm fine. I'll be released any minute." Hopefully. Or she'd be releasing herself. "And you just got a new job. You aren't going to miss work for me."

"Okay, but if you need me, I'll work it out. When you start job hunting, you should check out schools up here in the Upper Peninsula."

"After being driven away from schools two years in a row, I don't know if I even belong in this profession. I don't know what I'm going to do now."

"Are you kidding me? You are the best teacher and tutor I know."

"That's why it took someone else coming alongside you to make you believe in yourself."

"That was not because you were a bad teacher. It's because I was a bad student. I wasn't interested in learning. I've always had to learn the hard way. God had to change my heart, but I never would have tried again without your voice in my head telling me I could do anything I set my mind on."

Since when did Cam talk about God? "I haven't known you to be vocal about faith. What prompted your change of heart?"

"My first meeting, it was like God was talking straight to me. I've been so hopeless for so long, and now . . . I don't know how to describe it. I was living in the dark, and now the lights are on and I have purpose. I can see a world of possibilities."

Cam's encounter with God must have been powerful to instantly transform his attitude and outlook. Good for Cam, but Piper couldn't help feeling like she'd been left behind.

The curtain swished to the side, and Jess walked in with a steaming Styrofoam cup in each hand. "Thought you might like some coffee."

Gratitude and relief washed over Piper. Jess had come to pick her up. One less thing to worry about.

"Cam, I'm going to have to call you back later. Jess just came in." Piper ended the call.

Jess winced. "Sorry. I didn't realize you were on the phone."

"No problem. It was just Cam. I can talk to him anytime."

Jess handed her a cup. "I've been in the waiting room all night, but they wouldn't let me in until you were awake."

Piper wrapped her hands around the warm Styrofoam and inhaled the coffee-scented steam. She'd been worrying and Jess had been here all along. "Sorry you had to sit out there all night."

Jess pulled the chair close to the bed and grabbed Piper's hand. "You have nothing to apologize for. I just wish I could have been in here with you. I'm so sorry about the tutoring center. Officer Breckshaw called me down there when you passed out and sliced open your wrist last night. I followed the ambulance here. Do you remember what happened?"

"It's completely destroyed." The image of the graffiti and crumbled drywall pressed the air from her lungs once again.

"I meant your wrist. How did you cut it? You could have died. It's a good thing the police were there to stop the bleeding and call an ambulance right away!" Jess nodded at Piper's left wrist, wrapped in a thick layer of gauze.

"It's a little fuzzy. I think I fell into the broken window."

"Did you trip?" Jess searched her eyes.

"I think I was having a panic attack or something. I couldn't breathe and I felt like I was about to pass out, so I reached for the wall but put my arm through the broken window instead."

Jess sighed and squeezed her hand. "How long will this set back the opening? Have you talked to the insurance company?"

Insurance, yes, she needed to call them. "I don't know if I will open. Maybe I can find someone else to run it."

Jess blinked at her. "What? Why? Are you leaving?"

"Not right away. I'll finish out my contract at the school."

"What about Titus?"

"It's over." A vice tightened around Piper's chest.

"Over?" Jess leaned forward in her chair, studying Piper's face. "What happened?"

"He got a coaching job with the U of M football team. He's leaving."

"Maybe you could do long distance."

"We've been talking about our future together, and the whole time he's had this interview scheduled, and he didn't even tell me about it. I can't do the long-distance thing again, especially since I can't trust him."

"Did *he* want to break up?"

"Not at first, but then he said he couldn't be with someone who would always think the worst of him."

"Sounds like both of you are protecting yourselves, but you two are good together. I know trust is hard for you, but if you're expecting perfection, you're looking on the wrong side of heaven." Jess's gentle tone didn't soften the truth of her words. "Everyone will eventually fail to measure up, so any relationship is going to require a little grace." Piper's high standards had sabotaged too many of her relationships. She'd lost friends over this, and she hadn't spoken to her parents in too long. She owed them a phone call. Titus felt like she was too quick to give up on him, and maybe she had been. But it was too late now. "He's leaving and he doesn't want me anymore."

"I doubt that's true, so don't write him off just yet. But even if it is really over, that doesn't mean you have to leave too. The kids need you. This town needs the tutoring center. You have done such a wonderful job of making it happen." Jess set her coffee down on the bedside table and rested her hand on Piper's arm.

"Maybe the town does need it, but they don't need me. The writing was literally on the wall." The expletives in graffiti on the walls marked her heart as well. "Me being here just makes the place a target."

"This is not your fault." Jess leveled a firm look at Piper.

"Maybe not directly, but it's definitely because of me. How can I guarantee the tutoring center will be a safe place for students when there are people in this town who are so eager for me to leave that they would destroy what I'm trying to build?"

"I know that's hard, but you have to trust God to protect you and the kids."

"Trust God? He didn't stop this from happening." He didn't protect her at her last job or save her from heartbreak with Drake or Titus. He hadn't even protected her house from her biological father or made her parents tell her the truth. "Trusting God hasn't worked out so well for me in the past."

"We can't always understand why God sometimes allows hard things, but they don't mean that God's forgotten about you or that He can't be trusted. There's a bigger picture here, just like with your puzzle. God sees the finished picture all those shattered pieces will form. He knows how they're going to come together."

Piper couldn't see how all this brokenness could ever come together. "It sure doesn't seem that way."

"I know, but that's where faith comes in. The Bible is full of people who went through hard things."

"If God is so powerful and loves people so much, you'd think He could spare us from stuff like that." Piper sipped the coffee that warmed her fingers through the Styrofoam cup.

Jess nodded. "He could have spared Joseph when he was rejected by his brothers, sold into slavery, and imprisoned. He could have saved Esther before she was taken from her family and forced into marriage to a ruthless king."

"Could have, but didn't." Piper was starting to sound like a petulant child, even to her own ears. Maybe she needed to take a breath and open her heart to what Jess was trying to say.

"Yes, but those terrible circumstances led them to positions where they were used by God to save whole nations. If He'd spared them that pain, or if they had chosen to reject Him because of it, Israel's history would have been a short story, because God's chosen people would've been wiped out."

Piper hadn't thought about it like that before. Could her pain actually have a purpose?

"God could have spared Jesus from suffering. He was beaten and taunted and crucified. But if God had spared Him, it would have deprived the whole world of hope. You've got to have faith that God isn't finished with your picture yet but that it's coming together."

Believing that God had been working to bring the pieces together for Joseph and Esther was one thing, but trusting that He was doing that now for her was a different matter. She'd need some evidence that He was still at work before she'd be ready to make that call.

A nurse pulled back the curtain. "How are we feeling this morning?"

"Ready to go." Piper extended her arm with the IV. "Can you please take this out?"

"I'll go tell the doctor to get your paperwork ready, then I'll come get that taken care of for you."

Piper longed to believe the idea that God cared and was working to put the broken pieces together, but faith required trust, and she wasn't sure she could trust Him.

God, please let Brett be here.

Titus plodded through the sand leading to Little Sable Lighthouse and scanned the area again. Brett had to be here. There. A tennis-shoe-clad footprint by the lighthouse. He'd recognize those size fourteens anywhere.

Relief flooded Titus. He pulled out his mom's phone and sent a quick text to Kristen, letting her know he'd found Brett. He didn't have anyone else's number, so hopefully she'd spread the word.

He walked around to the other side of the lighthouse to find Brett leaning his back against the tall red-brick structure. Titus dropped down next to him.

Brett's gaze never left the horizon. "How'd you find me?"

"You told me your mom used to bring you here." Titus leaned back against the chilly brick. How long had Brett been sitting out here? It was so cold.

"She's really gone." His whisper was ragged.

Titus dropped his arm over Brett's shoulders. "I'm so sorry I wasn't there."

"You're leaving too."

"No. I'm not. Miss Caveneau and I were arguing about an offer that I had not accepted yet. It didn't take me long to realize that I'm already where I'm supposed to be right now. I'm not going anywhere."

Brett nodded and his chin quivered. "When I was twelve, Mom took me to a U of M football game, and we saw you play. I was in awe, but she told me that I could be just as good as you if I worked hard, put my heart into the game, and played for the glory of God. Before she died, she told me that she knew my dad wouldn't encourage me to live my dreams, so she'd prayed every day for me to meet you and for you to encourage me to dream big. You got injured about the time she was first diagnosed. She said when she saw it, she knew God was bringing you home for me."

God had spent the last four years redirecting him until he finally gave in and came home? Was it all because of a mother's prayer? Or was that His plan all along and she'd had the intuition to pray for what was already God's will? It didn't matter.

Brett was worth it.

Piper was worth it.

There was no doubt that he was in the center of God's will. Maybe God never intended Titus for professional football. Maybe it was Brett who would fulfill that destiny. "I'm glad He did. And I will be here to make sure you keep dreaming big, because I know God has big things in store for you. Your mom knew it too."

Brett peered out at the water for several minutes. "My grandparents want my dad to move to Ludington by them so they can help with the kids."

"Is he considering it?" Titus tented his legs and massaged his knee. The cold sand intensified the ache.

Brett shrugged. "He doesn't tell me anything. But if he does move, I don't want to go."

"I doubt he'll make a decision about that right now, but when the time comes, you'll have to be open with him about what you want and make sure to ask him respectfully to consider your wishes. Until then, pray about it. God's looking out for you. If it's His will for you to stay, He will work it out."

Brett looked down at his hands in his lap. "It doesn't feel like God is looking out for me."

Titus gripped Brett's shoulder. "I get that. I've spent a lot of years mad at God. You don't have to have it all figured out right now. There are a lot of worried people waiting for you to come home. Are you ready to head back?"

"Guess I'd better go call my dad. I left my phone in the car." Brett got to his feet.

Titus got up too. He still had a lot of wrongs to make right. He needed to talk to Piper. And he needed to find out what kind of trouble the boys had gotten into. This would all be so much easier if he had his phone. He'd have to go home and see if he could get his service transferred onto an old phone or something.

As he got into his car, his mom's phone rang, and Kristen's picture appeared on the screen. He answered and started the car. "Hey."

"You found him?" She sounded exhausted.

"Yeah. We're just leaving Little Sable, headed back to Heritage. Can you let his family know?"

"I called them as soon as I got your text. Miss Caveneau's roommate, Devin, was there. She told me that Miss Caveneau almost died last night. Did you hear anything about that?"

No. His blood ran cold. "What do you mean she almost died? What are you talking about?"

"The tutoring center was vandalized. Devin said it was completely destroyed. I guess when Miss Caveneau saw it, she passed out and fell into some broken glass and got cut pretty bad."

"Where is she now? Is she okay?" Titus's pulse pounded so loud in his ears he had to strain to hear his sister through the phone's speaker. He'd never told her he loved her. He needed to find her, to apologize, to tell her how he felt.

"She was in the hospital in Ludington all night, but Miss Gable told Devin she was about to get released."

"So she's okay now?"

"I think so. She got lots of stitches and a blood transfusion."

His lungs finally allowed him to take a full breath.

If the tutoring center had been destroyed, Piper had to be devastated. Knowing Piper, she'd want to go straight from the hospital to fixing the center. That part he could help with, and maybe it would prove that both he and this town cared about her too.

"Kristen, I need your help."

seventeen

PIPER WASN'T SURE IF SHE BELIEVED THAT God was putting the pieces together for her, but the fact that Jess and Devin were convinced did give her pause. Maybe she *should* stay in Heritage.

The late-morning light glinted off frosted rooftops as Jess slowed the car entering Heritage city limits. It had taken more than two hours for the doctor to finally release her from the hospital, and now, another forty minutes later, she just needed to get to the tutoring center.

How would she ever afford to rebuild? Maybe insurance would cover some of it, but she had no reserves left to make up the difference. Maybe that's where faith came in.

"Can you take me straight to the tutoring center? My car is there, and I want to see how bad it is in the light." Piper picked at the plastic hospital bracelet on her wrist.

"Are you sure? It was a pretty intense night. The doctor said to take it easy. Maybe you should just rest today. We can get help to tackle it tomorrow." Jess turned the car onto their road.

She didn't need rest. She needed to do something. "You're the one who sat up all night. Just drop me off, then you should go home to sleep."

"I'm not going to leave you alone there. I did get a little sleep. I'll be okay." She bypassed their house then turned right at the end of the square onto Richard Street at the end of the block.

Otis had moved to the corner of the square facing toward the tutoring center as if he was watching over it.

As soon as they turned the corner, Piper saw Titus standing on the sidewalk in front of the center.

The raw spots deep in her chest weighed heavy on her, warring with her heart's buoyancy at the sight of him.

A couple of his players came out of the storefront's broken door-frame, carrying a large chunk of drywall. Titus directed them to a massive pile that had already accumulated on the sidewalk.

Piper leaned forward and peered through the car's windshield. "Are they cleaning up the mess?"

"Piper, this town cares about you. Titus cares about you. God cares about you. Why does it surprise you that people would pitch in?"

"It just seemed like everything was falling apart. I couldn't even figure out how to put the pieces back together." Maybe God did know better than she did. Cam had trusted God, and it had made all the difference for him.

"You don't have to do that alone. You just have to trust God and the people He's put in your life." Jess slowed the car and pulled up to the curb.

That was harder said than done. Trusting God completely might take some time. But Jess was right. Relationships required grace. She couldn't expect people to be perfect. She couldn't put that burden on Titus. She loved him, so if she wanted to keep a tally, she'd mark the good, not the bad. Today she'd mark that he was here, pitching in to help her put her broken pieces back together.

"Maybe you're right." Piper pushed open the door and got out of the car.

When Titus spotted her, he ran over and gripped her upper arms to hold her at arm's length.

Barefaced, in her rumpled sweats, slippers, and glasses . . . again. Not exactly the polished look she liked to present.

His searching gaze scrutinized every inch of her as if he were taking inventory. "Are you okay? By the time I heard you were in the hospital, you were already being released."

"I'm fine." She lifted her bandaged wrist. "Just some stitches."

"I know how important honesty is to you, and I'm sorry I didn't tell you about the interview. If you'll give me another chance, I will not make the mistake of keeping things from you again. And just so you know, I'm not going to take the job. I know now exactly where I'm supposed to be."

Yeah, he was worth a little grace. Heaven knew she needed a little grace herself sometimes. "I shouldn't have put unrealistic expectations on you. It's scary caring so much about you, and I was afraid you didn't feel the same, but that's no excuse."

He pulled her to his chest and wrapped her in his arms.

"Well, let me clear that up for you right now. I love you, Piper." He whispered the words against her hair above her ear.

She leaned in and wrapped her arms around his waist. His words settled into the wounded places of her heart like a soothing balm. "I love you too."

He leaned down and kissed her gently, then reluctantly let her go. "Have I told you how cute you are in your glasses?"

She rolled her eyes. "Oh, please."

"I love how you seem to relax when you put them on." He touched the hinge that attached the arm to the frame.

"Well, I'm sure you'll be seeing more of them." She smiled up at him. She glanced at the storefront. "Have you heard if the police have any idea who might have done this?"

"No arrests have been made yet, but while we were clearing the drywall, one of the boys uncovered a Rolex with a broken clasp. We called Officer Breckshaw, and he took the watch into evidence. The back was engraved, so I think he has a pretty good idea where to start looking."

Piper didn't want to jump to conclusions, but Drew, the kid who'd tried to intimidate Kristen into writing his paper, flashed through Piper's mind. She'd seen a nice watch on his wrist.

"There are more people inside who'll be glad to see you're home. Come on." He took her hand and led her toward the door.

Jess hopped out of the car. Clearly she'd been giving them a moment of privacy.

"She's here!" someone called out from inside the tutoring center.

Cheers exploded from the doorway and window that had been cleared of broken glass. Her heart warmed again. Piper stepped into the building to find dozens of people scrubbing walls, sanding the floor, loading debris into a wheelbarrow, and sweeping away dust.

Her vision swam with happy tears. "I can't thank you all enough."

Aaron abandoned the wheelbarrow and jogged up to her. "Miss Caveneau, you are the only teacher who has ever believed in me."

"You're the first teacher to ever tell me I could do better than a C," Owen said. "I hated having to go to the tutoring center to redo that paper, but when I brought home the paper with an A at the top, it was the first time my dad had smiled in weeks." Piper had seen the pallor of a hangover on Cam enough to recognize it on Owen a mile away, but despite his dark circles and pale lips, his voice rang with truth.

Jay, Beau, and Ethan nodded their agreement, but they looked just as bad. There must be a story there. They wouldn't be putting in hard labor the morning after by choice.

"We've never had a teacher who cared as much about us as you."

Kristen propped her broom against the wall and came over to give her a hug. "We're so glad you're here."

"Yeah, even if your class is the hardest class I've ever taken." Jay dropped his sponge back into his bucket and tried to grin at her, but with his eyes squinting against the light, it looked more like a grimace.

"That means the world to me. Thank you."

These were the people God had put into her life. And they cared enough to help her put the pieces back together when she was too broken to see the big picture. Maybe He was trustworthy after all.

Fans lined the stands in the second game of the state tournament, and the Heritage Panthers trailed by two with fifty seconds on the clock in the fourth quarter.

They could still pull out a win. Maybe.

"You know what to do." Titus sent the offensive line onto the field in their crisp, clean new jerseys and took a deep breath.

Titus spotted Piper and her brother, Cam, sitting with Kristen and his mom. Wait, was that Jeff Dodger sitting in the stands next to his mom? They were looking pretty friendly too. He didn't hate it.

Titus shifted his clipboard to his other hand and refocused on the field as Noah hiked the ball to Brett.

Without Jay, Owen, Ethan, and Beau, who cheered from the bench in plain clothes, the team's chances of winning state were pretty slim. Titus had asked Officer Breckshaw to waive the hefty fine they earned for messing with Otis in exchange for their community service helping clean up the vandalism at the tutoring center. Despite their hangovers, they had agreed to escape the five-thousand-dollar fine, but seeing the damage and the effect it had on Piper had been good for them. They had even volunteered to help with the rebuild. The Rolex watch found at the scene belonged to Drew Palmer, and he and a friend of his had been charged with vandalism and destruction of property.

Wyatt plowed through the Raiders' line, and Titus bit his cheek as the wide receiver ran for the pass.

On the bench, Owen yelled and cheered with both hands thrown in the air as Wyatt dodged a linebacker, narrowly avoiding a block.

Titus held his breath as Brett let the pass fly, but just before the spiral reached Wyatt, the Raiders' cornerback leaped up and tipped the ball off course, and it sailed past Wyatt's outstretched fingers.

Sixty-four yards to the end zone with thirty-seven seconds on the clock. That win was less likely by the second.

It seemed the whole town of Heritage had made the trek to the Eastern Michigan University stadium for the game. There was Jon Kensington and his family. A few weeks ago, he'd offered Titus a lease on one of the houses his company owned that needed some work. He'd proposed an exchange of reduced rent for labor to fix the place up. Titus had moved in last week.

On the field, Brett turned to Titus for the play. Maybe they just needed to try something different. Or maybe something crazy. Titus signed the signal for a hurry-up offense. "Reverse 73."

Brett stared at him a minute, then shrugged and yelled to the players on the field, passing along the play. When the line was set, Brett looked over at Titus again. He couldn't really see his expression in the helmet, but the extra look seemed to indicate he wasn't sure about this play, but he was trusting Titus anyway.

Hopefully it would pay off. Every single one of those boys would have to remember what they were supposed to do, and even then, this play was a long shot.

Noah lifted the ball for the snap, but instead of hiking it, he stood and handed it over his shoulder to Brett. Everyone else held their positions. Brett stood and cocked his head to the side as if he was confused, then, holding the ball loosely in one hand, he walked casually through the defensive line.

The Raiders' line didn't seem to grasp what was happening as Brett walked past them. A few of them stood and looked to see what Brett was looking at. Brett made it several steps past the line then tucked the ball into his side and took off like a shot. Yes! It had actually worked!

As soon as the Raiders registered what was happening, chaos ensued. They were running into each other in their scramble to get after Brett.

Titus's heart was in his throat as Brett's speed picked up and a Raiders' linebacker dove for the tackle and missed. Titus had just hoped to get the ball close enough to kick a field goal, but maybe Brett could take this thing all the way.

The fans were on their feet along with everyone on the sidelines. Brett made it all the way past the thirty-yard line before one of the Raiders finally caught up with him and took him down.

Titus couldn't take a breath until Brett was back on his feet. "Get the kickoff team in there."

A minute later, Nelson's kick sent the ball between the goal posts just as the time clicked to zero. It was a miracle! Titus dropped the clipboard and thrust his fists in the air. They had pulled it off!

As soon as the game was called, half the town of Heritage flooded the field to celebrate the victory with the team. They'd made the top four. And earned the new jerseys Coach Hutchens had promised them.

Piper ran ahead of his family and threw her arms around his neck. "Congratulations!"

As Titus pressed a kiss to her forehead, Brett's dad extended his hand to Titus, and he released Piper to shake it. "Good to see you, Walter. I'm so glad you were able to make it to the game. You must be so proud of Brett."

Walter nodded. "I didn't give him enough credit. He really is something special. That's why I have something I'd like to talk to you about. Sorry to bring it up today, but Brett said you wouldn't mind. I've been offered a job in Ludington, and I've decided to move there so my parents can help me take care of the kids. It's really important to Brett to be able to finish high school in Heritage. I know it's a lot to ask, but I was wondering if you would serve as his emergency contact and legal guardian. I'm not sure which of his friends will take him in or if he'll have to move from place to place, but he's pretty determined to stay."

"I'd really like Brett to stay as well, and I'm happy to serve as his legal guardian. I've actually just moved into a house with a couple of extra bedrooms. It's not in great shape, but I'm working on fixing it up. If you're comfortable with him staying with me, I think it might be good for him to have that consistency."

"You really think you're up to having a teenage houseguest for the next year and a half?" The hesitantly hopeful look in his eyes showed how much he'd come to trust Titus with his son.

"Absolutely." Titus shot a smile at Brett. "The room is free. He can move in anytime."

"All right, we'll have to work out some sort of compensation for rent and food and other expenses."

"I'd be glad to take Brett's help on my renovation in exchange for rent and basic groceries." Titus turned to Brett. "Are you up for that?"

Brett's eyes reflected deep gratefulness when he smiled and nodded. "Yeah, I think I can handle that."

Titus gave Brett's shoulder a pat, then turned back to Walter. "Great. You can work out with Brett what he'll need for his personal and school expenses, but you don't have to add anything for me."

Piper extended her hand to Walter. "I'm Piper Caveneau. I'm Brett's substitute English teacher, and I also run the tutoring center."

He shook her hand. "Nice to meet you."

"She's also my girlfriend, so Brett will be seeing a lot of her." Titus wrapped his arm around her waist again and sent her a questioning glance.

She nodded, then looked back at Brett's dad. "He'll have lots of people watching out for him." Piper shifted her gaze to Brett. "If you ever need help with homework or college applications or anything, you know where to find me."

Brett nodded. "Thanks, Miss Caveneau."

As Walter and Brett moved off, a woman in a bright-pink business suit shoved a microphone in his face. Titus stiffened. He hated reporters.

"Coach Ford, congratulations on your victory. The Raiders are a tough team to beat, especially with starters sitting out, but the Panthers seem to be unstoppable this season."

He turned to the camera but kept his arm firmly around Piper. "This team has adapted this season to work well together and be flexible. I think that shows how all our boys have developed as players this year."

"This season hasn't been smooth sailing for you, though. Early in the season, you had fights breaking out between players, ineligibility issues, and some of your best players were just disqualified from the playoffs. But despite so many challenges, your record is impressive, so your nomination for Coach of the Year is no surprise."

Titus's brows shot up. What was she talking about? "I haven't heard anything about this."

Piper snaked her arm around his middle and gave him a squeeze.

"Well, I just happen to have the nomination essay right here. It was submitted by a number of players and a faculty representative named Miss Caveneau."

Titus glanced down at Piper, and her eyes glowed with pride.

The reporter lifted a paper in her hand, then began to read.

"'The Panthers football program and Heritage High School proudly nominate Titus Ford for Coach of the Year. Not only did Coach Ford and his coaching staff train up an inexperienced team to break a seven-year losing streak, he also set an example of how to become a man of character. He's helped his players learn from their mistakes so they can grow into responsible young men. Because of his leadership, these boys have improved amazingly as players, become better teammates, better students, and better men with brighter futures. An uneventful season isn't what proves an effective leader, but success throughout a turbulent one does. He isn't just a football coach. He's a mentor and an excellent example of what these boys could grow up to become.'"

Titus opened his mouth to speak but couldn't find the words.

Piper smiled up at him. "I think I speak for the whole town of Heritage when I say we all believe he deserves that award, but Coach Ford will care far more about the players around his bonfire pit in the backyard than he will about an award on his mantel."

"An award like that could mean big things for your coaching career. Any plans to move up?"

Titus didn't hesitate. "No. I'm exactly where I'm supposed to be."

As the reporter moved off, Titus hugged Piper to his side. "Coach of the Year, huh? I can't believe you did that."

"It wasn't just me. I may have mentioned it to a few of your players, but they decided on their own to follow through. They had a good start on the essay before they brought it to me for help." Piper pushed up on her tiptoes to kiss his jaw. "Besides, it's easy to brag on the man I love."

Titus flashed his dimples. "I'm glad to hear that because, with you, I'm playing for keeps."

Bonus Epilogue

Thank you for reading *Playing for Keeps*. We hope you loved the story. Find out what happens next with our Bonus Epilogue, a special gift, available only to our newsletter subscribers.

This Bonus Epilogue will not be released on any retailer platform, so scan our QR code to get your free gift. You acknowledge you are becoming a Sunrise Publishing, Andrea Michelle Wood, and Tari Faris subscriber. Unsubscribe from any of the newsletters at any time.

READ ON FOR MORE FROM THE
Home to Heritage
SERIES

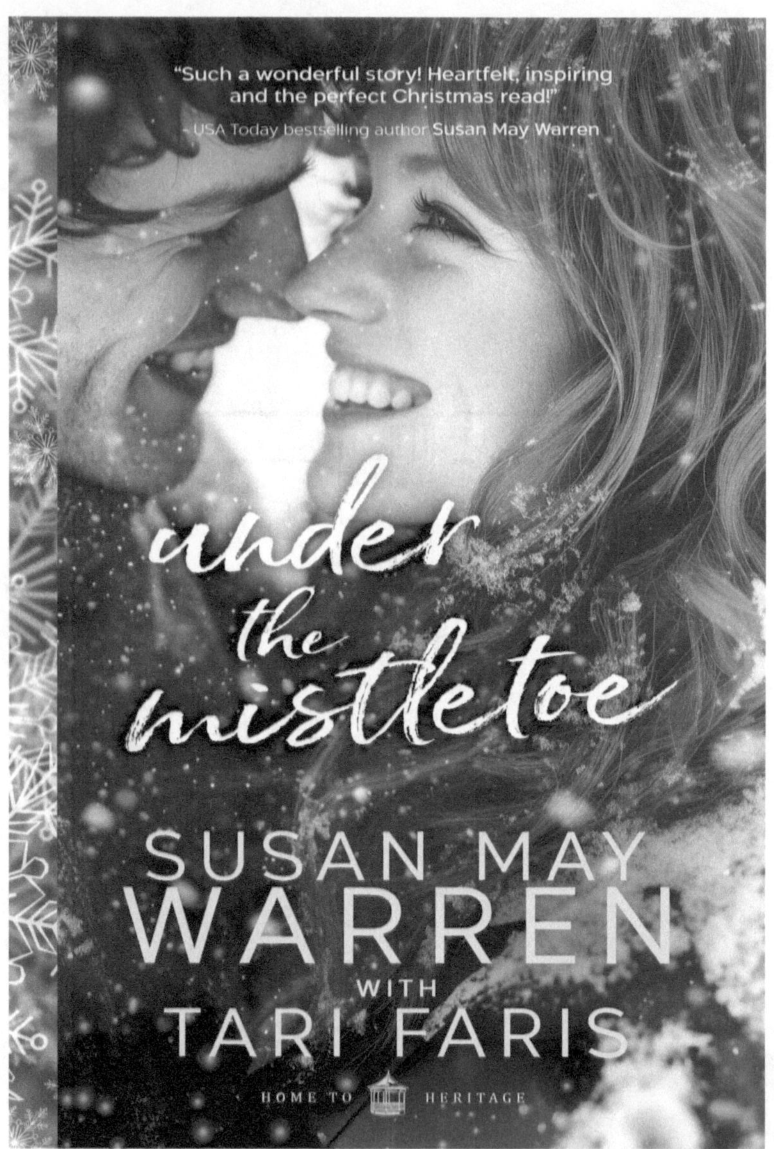

Sometimes the best Christmas gifts come wrapped in second chances...

Social worker Devin Hendrickson pours her heart into running Heritage's foster care support program, organizing magical Christmas events for families while trying to ignore her own abandoned heart. When her program faces shutdown, she'll need a Christmas miracle - and maybe the help of the one man who once broke her heart.

Logan Kingsley, the bestselling author behind the pseudonym Victor Holt, hides away in his cabin fighting writer's block and his forbidden feelings for Devin. But when three foster siblings capture his heart, he realizes he might be ready for more than just writing happy endings.

As Devin races to save her program and Logan struggles to finish his book, they discover they need each other—at least for the season. With three children's futures hanging in the balance, they must decide if they're brave enough to risk their hearts again. If they fail, it's not just Logan's career or Devin's program at stake - it's the chance at the family they never knew they wanted.

Can a Christmas-loving community coordinator and a reclusive author learn to trust in love again? Or will past hurts and present fears keep them from building the family they both desperately want?

"Under the Mistletoe" delivers all the cozy small-town Christmas romance feels with a heart-warming story about chosen family, second chances, and the courage to fight for love. Fans of foster family dynamics, secret identity reveals, and Christmas community events will fall in love with Heritage and its enchanting cast of characters.

This sweet contemporary Christmas romance features childhood crushes, secret bestselling authors, Christmas charity events, found family dynamics, and enough holiday magic to make you believe in second chances.

I T WAS A THANKSGIVING MIRACLE. DEVIN HENdrixson's parents were actually going to carve out time for her—at a restaurant, no less—because nothing said American family holiday like filet mignon. As soon as her mom sent the address of the restaurant, Devin was more than happy to drive two hours on snowy roads to make it happen. At least she could count on an hour of uninterrupted quality time with them, and that was more than she'd had in six months.

Devin paced the length of her living room, her phone clutched in her hand. At this rate she'd wear right through the plush gray area rug and at least the topcoat of the dark cherry floors. She needed something to distract her, but both of her roommates, Jess and Piper, had each gone to spend Thanksgiving with their families. Jess had even taken her French bulldog, Pearl, with her, so the place was quiet. Too quiet.

Devin dropped on the couch by the window and opened her text messages. Still nothing from her mom, but the one her boss at LIFE had sent last night taunted her. She tapped it and read it over once more, as if there was some small chance it might have changed overnight.

MaryLynn
The meeting with the board didn't go as well as I'd hoped. Let's talk soon. And pray.

Devin sank back into the couch and closed her eyes. Pray? Pray for what? That the board of the small nonprofit would approve the new budget she'd sent over? Pray that she still had a job? Those were very different prayers.

Devin
Can you elaborate?

She'd sent that response last night, but it still sat unanswered. What did she expect? It was Thanksgiving, and most people spent the day with people.

The phone rang in her hand, and she jolted upright. But it was Jess's face that appeared on the screen, not her mom's. Devin accepted the call. "Hey, Jess, how is Grandma Evans?"

"Spicy as ever. You'd never guess she's pushing ninety-five." There was laughter in the background that became muffled as if her cousin had escaped into a bedroom. "I'm calling to make sure you saw the weather."

Devin eyed the Heritage town square across the street out the big front window. The sun was bright off the fresh snow that had fallen last night, creating a Christmas wonderland. She'd been surprised a few weeks ago when the town put up Christmas decorations so early before Thanksgiving, but now she could see why. "We got about ten inches last night, but the sun is out now."

The thirty-foot Christmas tree just south of the gazebo was covered with thick snow, creating different-colored glow patches where the Christmas lights struggled to shine through. Even Otis, the mysterious seven-foot brass hippo that mysteriously moved around town, had drifts up to his ears, leaving just a bit of his back evident in the snow.

"It's supposed to start up again." Jess's worry didn't seem to match what Devin was seeing outside. "Maybe you shouldn't go."

Ah. That's what this was really about. "Jess—"

"I just hate the idea of you sitting alone in that nice restaurant on Thanksgiving. I wish you'd come to GG's here in Indiana with me. We are cousins, after all."

"Second cousins once removed and on the other side of the family."

"I don't care if she isn't your great-grandmother. She's known you since you were born and would love to see you."

"And I would love to see her. But I haven't seen my parents in six months."

Jess huffed. "How are the illustrious Drs. Hendrixson? Have the two eccentric scientists cured cancer yet?"

"Their work is in type-one diabetes, not cancer—and if they'd cured it, you'd know. I know I'm not close with my folks like you are with yours, but I take what I can get." Devin swallowed down a lump as she picked at the threads of the couch. When someone's life work was to cure a disease that affected more than three million children in the United States alone, everything else came second—even their only child. "Besides, GG is six hours from here, and you know I have the pinewood derby race tomorrow and I can't miss that."

"Maybe I should've stayed home."

"Would you stop worrying about me?" Her phone buzzed with an incoming text.

<u>Mom</u>

About to leave. See you in about two hours.

Then there was a location link to the restaurant.

She sent back a thumbs-up.

"That's my mom now." Devin stood and grabbed her teal winter coat and pulled it on. "I need to go."

If her parents were really going to follow through this time, she wasn't going to be late.

Devin ended the call and stepped out onto the wide, covered porch of the Victorian rental house as she tapped the link. According to Apple Maps, Benton Harbor was two hours and five minutes south of Heritage.

She paused at the top of her porch steps.

The town square was even more beautiful from here. From the silver bells on the light to the garland and red ribbon trimming along the old one-room schoolhouse and gazebo, Heritage appeared Hallmark Christmas–movie worthy. It really was the perfect little town. And maybe that was why, when she'd had the opportunity to move here, she'd jumped on it.

Not for the decorations, but because she'd spent her entire childhood wanting to climb inside her TV and have a beautiful family Christmas. She had to figure out how to convince the board this place was worth the investment.

"Devin!"

Devin hurried down the few steps and then squatted down as her neighbor Roman ran toward her full steam along the freshly shoveled sidewalk. His red coat was unzipped, one mitten in place, and a blue hat was pulled down so far that only a hint of his red hair peeked out. She caught him mid-run and struggled to keep her balance as she scooped up the four-year-old in her arms.

His green eyes lit up and his smile stretched full across his freckled face. He was missing one eye-tooth because of a playground incident, not Mother Nature.

"Happy Turkey Day!" He wiggled his finger below his chin. "Gobble, gobble."

"And Happy Turkey Day to you!" She mimicked his gobbler motion. "Where is everyone else?"

"They're slow." He pointed to where Luke walked toward them down the sidewalk, Roman's missing mitten in hand. Luke was just over six feet and had a head of dark hair with a bit of wild curl to it. The guy looked so much like his half brother Liam, her friend from college, that even after six months of living two houses away, she still did a mental double take every time she saw him.

Liam and his fraternal twin brother Logan were off living their best life and rarely checked in with the friend group or their family, from what she gathered—which was crazy. She'd give anything for a family like this.

Although, she wasn't sure what she'd do if the twins did visit more. She and Liam were still friends. Logan and her? She wasn't so sure. Then again, she'd never really seen him as a friend. And after their last encounter, he definitely didn't see her as one.

Roman slid to the ground and claimed his mitten from Luke. "We're gonna go watch the parade at my grandma and grandpa's house."

Devin's ears snagged on the use of *grandma* and *grandpa*, and her eyes darted to Luke's.

He nodded in confirmation. "It's official. Or it will be after the court date in January."

"Yup. I'm a Taylor." Roman jumped with the words, a smile stretching across his face again. Even at just four years old, after two years in the foster care system, he got it. People who wanted you around were not to be taken for granted.

She pushed down the building pressure in her chest and concentrated on Roman again. "You'll have to tell me tomorrow about your favorite balloon from the parade."

The screen door squeaked open and smacked shut again as six-year-old Joseph and ten-year-old Asher exited their house and started walking toward them. Joseph was practically a clone of his father, and Asher was a spitting image of his uncle Thomas with his strawberry-blond hair and wide grin, even though he too was adopted about a year ago.

"You should come with us." Roman grabbed her hand and tugged it. "My grandma makes great pies. She lives on Carter Road. You know where that is?"

"I do. But you can't invite me to someone else's house." She bopped him on the nose as the other two boys joined them.

"Grandma says there is always room at the table for one more. Right, Dad?" Roman smiled up at Luke. "She calls it table math."

"I told her that table math doesn't math," Asher interjected. "If there's always room for one more, that could never end."

"I think that was her point." Luke ruffled his hair. "You are definitely welcome, but you look like you're on your way out."

And for the smallest fraction of a second she wanted to deny it. Agree to join them. Because as much as she wanted to see her parents, it wouldn't be this. There would be no warmth, few smiles, and definitely no conversations about parades or pies. They would talk about work and how she had the opportunity to do more with her life, then hang out with kids.

She shoved away the thoughts because they may not be perfect, but her parents were all she had. "I'm meeting my parents in Benton Harbor."

"Is that where you's from?" Roman worked unsuccessfully at his zipper.

"Nope." She squatted down and helped him with his coat. "I grew up in Chicago. But they have to work tomorrow and so do I, so we're meeting halfway for dinner."

"You don't work tomorrow. We have the race." Roman's face twisted in confusion.

"That *is* her work, dodo head." Joseph nudged Roman's shoulder.

"No name-calling." Hannah walked up, carrying a casserole dish and joined them, with her long dark hair flowing over her shoulders. She was followed by their oldest, Jimmy, who was carrying a Tupperware container of cookies. At fourteen, he was the typical quiet teen boy, but his chin lifted in greeting.

"I have one more thing I need to grab." Hannah handed the foil-covered dish in her hands to Luke. "But if you don't get back too late, Devin, you should join us for pie and games."

"Maybe." But she wouldn't. As much as they said she was welcome, and as much as she longed for a family like this, she had no need to impose on others. *Asking for help when you are capable of doing it yourself is selfish.* Her mother had drilled that into her all her life. Maybe this wasn't asking for help, but the same principle applied. Take care of your own needs.

Hannah's easy smile turned down at the edges as they made eye contact. She walked back to Devin and laid her hands on Devin's shoulders. "I used to try and do it all alone. It doesn't work. I learned you are never alone in Heritage. Even when you want to be. Remember that. Consider us your extended family. It's what we consider you."

Something gripped Devin in the chest, and she struggled to swallow. This was what she wanted, but it wasn't her reality, no matter what Hannah said. Her reality was detached parents who, if she didn't hurry, would be waiting for her at the restaurant. And not patiently. She pulled out her keys as she stepped back. "I've got to go."

"Just promise if you need anything, you'll let us know." Hannah pinned her with her gaze.

Devin nodded as she climbed into her car. *Consider us your extended family.* Could it be that simple? She started the engine and headed south on Henderson Road.

She waved to the Taylor family as they divided between their minivan and Luke's truck. What would a traditional Thanksgiving be like? A family where everyone was welcome and no one was made to feel like an inconvenience?

She needed to stop feeling sorry for herself. After all, she hadn't had a rough childhood. Working with kids in foster care and those who had gone through adoption had taught her it could've been worse. So much worse. She'd always had everything she needed. Everything but people. Actually, Karen, her nanny, had been very present until she'd been let go when Devin turned twelve. She laughed to avoid the tears forming. How sad was it that her emotional rock was the memory of a nanny she hadn't seen in over fourteen years?

As she wound her way through the town toward Heritage Street that would lead to the US 31, the Victorian homes slowly gave way to the larger properties and farmhouses set back from the road.

Her phone rang through her radio, and Devin accepted the call. "MaryLynn?"

"Hey, Devin. I know it's Thanksgiving, but do you have a moment?"

"I'll be driving for the next two hours. What's up?" Her heart gave a small poke as she passed the green Carter Road sign on her right.

"I was going to call you for a meeting on Monday, but I don't want you freaking about my last text until then." A deep sigh accompanied her words, and Devin would put money on the fact her friend had removed her glasses and was rubbing her eyes like she normally did when she was stressed. That wasn't good. "We had an end-of-the-year budget meeting last week, and we need to make cuts."

Cuts? As in cutting a few events, or as in eliminating her job? "But we just started this program. It takes time to—"

"I know. I told them. But giving has been down this year, and right now, yours has the highest spending with the lowest return."

"What can I do to change their minds?" Devin adjusted the

heat as the chill of the car settled in her toes. The road had been cleared, but occasional clumps of snow broke free from the trees and littered the path.

"I don't know. But we'll try to save it, trust me. I have to go. Let's talk more tomorrow. And don't worry about it, enjoy Thanksgiving." The line went dead.

Not worry about it? She had basically said the program here was as good as dead. But it wasn't her own job she was worried about. MaryLynn had told her before that if the program failed, they would move her position back to Detroit. But where did that leave all the kids she worked with? Their little faces flashed through her mind. The last thing they needed was one more person walking out of their lives.

The phone rang through the car with another incoming call, and she glanced at the screen. Mom. A pit landed in her stomach. Devin tapped the screen and accepted the call. "Hey, Mom, what's up?"

"We have amazing news." The tone said it all. There was only one thing her parents got this excited about, and it wasn't seeing their only child. "We were headed out the door when one of your dad's samples showed up positive. Can you believe it?"

Strangely, she could. It would still be positive tomorrow, but they wouldn't want to waste a minute. She flipped on her blinker and turned into the Marathon gas station just before the on-ramp to US 31.

"I was hoping to catch you before you left, but it sounds like you're already on your way." The disappointment in her mom's tone was a gut punch. They'd still agree to meet her, but they wouldn't be happy about it, and they'd be distracted the whole time. She couldn't hold back the tears that sprang to the corners of her eyes.

"I've not gotten far." She kept her voice steady. The Marathon station was dark, but a few of the pumps were open. She needed gas, but two cars were filling up, and she was fairly certain that was

Mrs. Smith at last pump. The last thing she needed right now was someone asking her what was wrong and breaking into tears while she talked to her parents. "I can turn around."

"Oh, great. We do want to see you, but this is actually very important." The story of her life.

"No worries." Devin turned away from the pumps and chose a remote parking spot away from the other cars. It hadn't been cleared of the six inches of snow that had fallen in the night, but it would give her more privacy. She was about to stop when her front wheels dropped down off what must have been the edge of the asphalt. Grinding from the scraping of the undercarriage filled the car. Oops. She shifted into park. "Happy Thanksgiving, Mom. I'll see you soon. Love you."

"Christmas for sure. There's no way we'll miss that." Her mom's voice had softened but shifted back to its practical tone. "After all, they close the lab that day."

Of course they did. Because that was the only reason her parents would guarantee taking time off to see her. That was the only way their daughter wouldn't be seen as an interruption to things that were actually important.

She ended the call and drew a steadying breath. So much for Thanksgiving dinner. So much for her parents showing up this time. Another lump formed in her throat. She had to convince the board this program was worth it. She refused to abandon the kids who had just begun to trust her, because showing up mattered.

When the last car drove away from the pump, she shoved her car into reverse and pressed the gas. But the car only rocked as the whir of spinning tires filled the air. She tried again, slower, but this time the car didn't even rock.

She popped open the door and stepped out into the frigid air. Her breath escaped in white clouds as she squatted by the front wheel and brushed away the snow to get a better look. The tire had dropped off the edge all right, and it was down about six inches on solid ice. She wasn't going anywhere.

Great.

Not only was she not getting that family Thanksgiving, but now she'd have to pull someone from their family time to help her.

He didn't have time for a big family dinner today, but Logan Kingsley couldn't very well drive the two hours south to his parents' house today only to download his manuscript from his editor and *not* stay for Thanksgiving.

Logan secured the lock on the cabin door, then wound his way down the porch steps to the driveway. The dark wood cabin built into a hill had the main entrance on the second floor off a large wooden deck. It wasn't fancy. A few bedrooms and a main area that served as living room, dining room, and kitchen, but he didn't need more.

He'd gotten this place at a steal a couple years ago and had planned on making it just a writing cabin, but after last year, the break away from everything had been good. Life was easier with fewer people in it. Dogs were much more loyal anyway.

He reached the bottom of the steps and scanned the snow drifts in the surrounding dense woods. No sign of Cal. He lifted his fingers to his mouth and released a piercing whistle into the air, then waited.

He needed to start editing his manuscript today, but with no internet at his remote cabin, his options were limited. He'd just have to make it a short visit because he had a gut feeling his latest book would be no small amount of work.

His first three novels in his epic fantasy series hadn't been easy, but they had been a story inside of him bursting to be told. They'd taken untold hours of tedious rewriting to hammer into a final form, but the stories themselves had been a passion. Book four? Not so much. Every scene, every chapter, every bit had been a fight to get his characters to perform.

But he'd done it, and now with his editor's insights, he would make it better. What was the old saying? *Books aren't written— they're rewritten.* He was ready to get rewriting.

Logan swung open the rear door to his 2023 Bronco, then flipped up the rear window as the jingle of a collar reached him just before Cal bound toward him. His labradoodle was so matted in snow that Logan could barely see the dark brown of his fur. But with the way his pup's tongue hung out of his mouth, Logan couldn't begrudge him having the time of his life.

"Dude, you are a mess." Logan stopped Cal and brushed him off the best he could. "Good thing I love you. Want to go for a ride?"

Cal's whole backside wiggled, and the moment Logan patted the side of the Bronco, Cal leapt in, circled the back three times, and then landed with a flop on the blanket that had become a permanent fixture on the floor. With the back seat down, the dog had plenty of space to make his own, and he definitely hadn't been shy about doing so.

Logan secured the back, then walked around to the driver's door and got in. He was glad he took the time last week to put up the fluorescent road markers to line the driveway. Once off his property, navigating the trees would be a lot trickier now that the winding dirt path had been erased by the eight to ten inches they'd gotten last night. Logan started the engine and put it into four-wheel drive. His tires struggled to find purchase on the uphill slope, but once he locked the differential, he made steady progress out to the main road. He'd have to pull out his plow attachment soon, but he could handle this.

He reached the main road in a matter of minutes. It had been long cleared, and the surface was even dry from the sun. He un-locked the axle and put it back into two-wheel drive before turning south. The roads were pretty quiet, no doubt because most people were already with their families, elbow deep in pumpkin pie. He passed a familiar bend in the road. Nothing about it looked any different from the rest of the forest, but it was the unseen boundary of civilization and cell service. He reached for his phone but set it back down. He'd enjoy the peace a little longer.

He could just drive to the local diner only thirty minutes away to download the file. But who knew if they were open on Thanksgiving or if their internet was even working? It seemed to go down every other week. Besides, he hadn't been to his parents' in two months and even then, it had been a drive-by. For the most part, his family visited him under the guise of weekend vacations, but he was pretty confident they were only making sure he didn't turn into a full-on hermit.

Almost two hours down the road, he couldn't put it off any longer. He powered on his phone and connected it to the CarPlay app. Let the never-ending notification chimes begin. His remote cabin had definitely helped him make his last few deadlines, but living without communication had its drawbacks. He'd checked into satellite Wi-Fi, but the trees surrounding his cabin blocked any hope of that.

When the notifications stopped, he glanced at the icons on the display in his car. Six new voicemails, zero emails, and over three hundred texts. Awesome. That wasn't too bad for being over three weeks since he'd last checked in.

He pressed the phone icon to play his voicemail.

"Logan, this is Sandy." Good, he was hoping to hear from his editor at Palmer & Jones Publishing. "I plan to have your manuscript back in your inbox the day before Thanksgiving. I don't need to remind you that this is a tight turnaround. After your two extensions, we need you to make this your top priority."

He glanced at the email icon again. Zero. Strange. He checked the date of the voicemail. Sandy had left that nearly two weeks ago. He pressed play on the next message.

"Hey, Logan, this is Mark." His agent's deep voice came over the line. He turned up the volume. "I have some exciting news. Give me a call when you're back in service."

About the missing manuscript or something else? He checked the time. Almost eleven. But with it being Thanksgiving Day, he'd wait until this evening. He pressed delete and waited for the next message.

"Lo-gan!" Liam's familiar voice echoed through the car. "You are missing it! Switzerland is amazing! You should be here." That was pretty much how Liam started every phone call. But the adventure life was for his twin. Logan preferred the quiet cabin. "Anyway, I got a new gig offering paragliding tours here. It's sweet cash, and every trip down is awesome. Well, almost every one. Yesterday, the lady I took down screamed the entire time. In the end she said she had fun, but I'm pretty sure I'm deaf in my left ear now."

There was a muffling sound, then Liam came back. "I gotta go, but tell everyone Happy Turkey Day, and I'll try to call Mom later, but the time difference makes it tricky. Love you, bro."

The line ended, and Logan deleted the voicemail.

The next three were spam and he deleted them. No more from his editor. Strange. Had she sent it to the wrong email? He tapped on the display screen of his Bronco and called his brother Luke.

Luke answered on the second ring. "Hey, you're in service." His voice lowered as he seemed to be making his way to somewhere more private. "Does that mean you're coming to dinner after all?"

"I'm about five minutes from the Heritage exit. Mom and Dad still have no idea?"

"I think Dad suspects, but not Mom. She'll be thrilled. Hold on."

Hannah's distant voice carried through the line as she talked to Luke in the background, her voice a little distressed.

"Everything okay?"

"A friend of ours car is stuck at the Marathon just off US 31, and I need to go get her. Wait. You're right there. Can you grab her as you go by?"

"Her?" Logan shook his head even though Luke couldn't see him. "You really think a woman wants to get into a car with a strange man even if you say you know me?"

"Actually, you know her. It's your friend Devin from college."

Everything went cold for a moment before heat coursed through him as a pair of big blue eyes framed by light-auburn hair flashed in his mind. No doubt she still had the smattering of freckles that had driven him to distraction in more than one of his college classes. "Devin Hendrixson?"

Like he needed to clarify. There had only ever been one Devin in his life. In so many ways.

What was she doing in Heritage? Last he knew, she was living in Detroit. No doubt visiting her cousin Jess, who was from Heritage, but then, why couldn't Jess pick her up? Maybe the roads were worse off the main road.

Luke's voice broke into the silence again. "This is perfect, she's—"

"You seriously can't be asking me to do that." Logan knew his voice sounded frantic, but if anyone should get it, it'd be Luke. "Don't you remember our conversation last New Year's about the Christmas party Liam and I threw?"

"Was that the one at your parents' old house in Chicago?"

"Yes, Liam wanted a final hurrah with our friends there before the moving trucks came. There was a girl . . . there was a mistletoe . . ."

Luke didn't even know the whole story, but he knew enough to understand this was a bad idea.

"Wait, that was Devin?" The humor in Luke's tone didn't offer the sympathy Logan was hoping for. "I don't remember Liam ever dating Devin."

"It was short-lived, but he definitely showed up with her as his date to the Christmas party and then stuck pretty close to her all night." The memory of Liam walking in with her hand in his, leaning down to whisper in her ear, touching the small of her back . . . He shoved the image away. He was over it.

"It's been almost a year. I bet she's forgotten. I mean, you've put it in the past. I'm sure she has too." Luke was right. She probably hadn't thought of Logan once since that night. "Unless you *haven't* put it in the past."

"I have."

"I mean, if you're still in love with—"

"I'm not." And he wasn't. Not anymore. He shared a lot with his twin, but never girls. So he'd buried that crush, and he'd never felt more free. At least, that was what he kept telling himself.

"Then consider this an opportunity to apologize." Luke wasn't letting this go, and if Logan fought this any longer, his family would get suspicious.

"Fine. I'll be there in about two minutes." He ended the call, then checked his reflection in the mirror. His gray beanie covered his mop of dark hair in desperate need of a haircut, but he was about a week overdue for shaving. Not the best first impression after almost a year.

Shoot! He was doing it already. Not ten seconds with Devin back in his life and he was falling down the rabbit hole.

As if sensing his mood, Cal stood and nosed Logan's shoulder over the seat. Logan reached back and patted his head. "We're almost there. But I do fear, buddy, that leaving the house today was a bad idea."

Because the last thing Logan needed was to spend the next year getting over Devin all over again.

Acknowlegdements

Huge thank you to my editor and friend, Tari Faris, Susan May Warren and the whole Sunrise team who worked to make this story the best it could be. Working with Tari and Susie was a dream fifteen years in the making and I'm so grateful they took a chance on me.

Thank you also to my friends and family who were such a huge support to me through this process. Thanks especially to my parents and daughters who are my biggest fans now and always.

About the Author

Andrea Michelle Wood hails from South Dakota where she works as an interior designer. She loves being the mom of four beautiful daughters. Andrea finished her first story nearly 30 years ago and has been writing ever since. In addition to reading and writing, her hobbies include playing in the mud on the pottery wheel, baking sourdough bread and goodies, and spoiling her French bulldogs.

Find her at andreamichellewood.com/author-page.

About the Author

Tari Faris is the author of Restoring Heritage Series and Home to Heritage Series. A member of American Christian Fiction Writers and My Book Therapy, is the projects manager for My Book Therapy, and special projects manager at Sunrise publishing. She was awarded Mentor of the Year from ACFW in 2023 and awarded the Genesis in 2017. She has an MDiv from Asbury Theological Seminary and lives in the Phoenix, Arizona, area with her husband and their three children. Although she lives in the Southwest now, she lived in a small town in Michigan for 25 years.

Learn more at TariFaris.com.

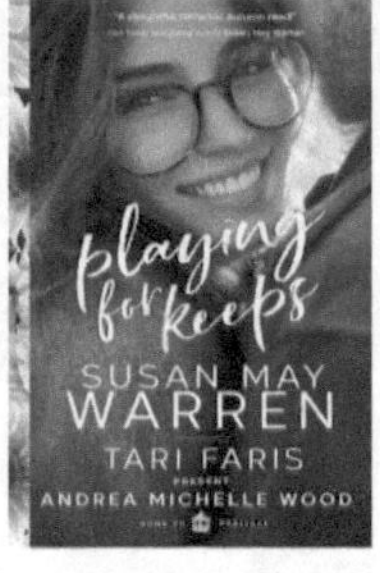
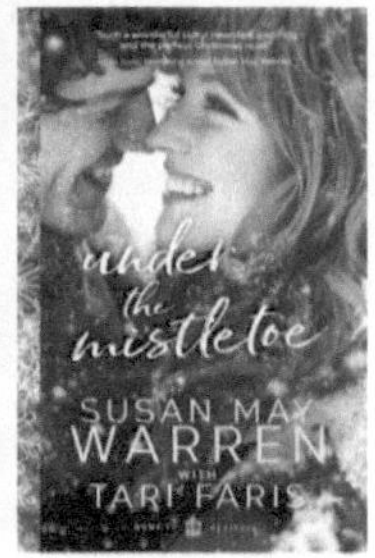

SUSAN MAY WARREN and **TARI FARIS**

with **Mandy Boerma** and **Andrea Michelle Wood**

We solve the problem of what to read next.

Available on Amazon

Restoring Heritage

Created by New York Times bestselling author

RACHEL HAUCK

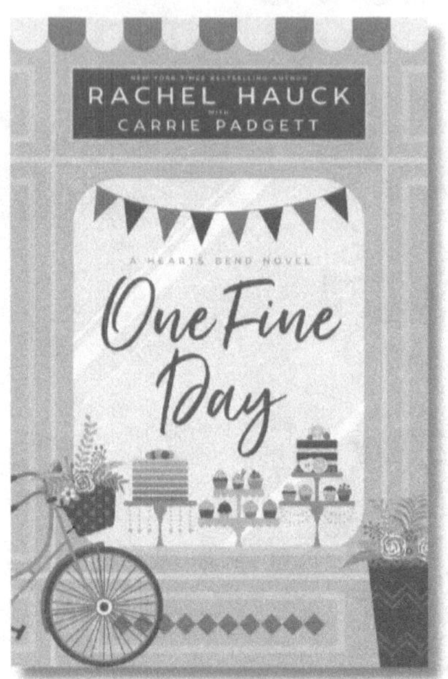

Escape to

Hearts Bend

for sweet stories of romance, faith, and happy endings.

We solve the problem of what to read next.   Available on Amazon

YOU MAY ALSO LIKE...

When a blizzard strikes Deep Haven and Megan is overrun with catastrophes, it takes a former Ranger to step in and help. But the more he comes to her rescue, the sooner she'll move out... Come home to Deep Haven in this magical tale about the one who got away... and came back.

Still the One **by Susan May Warren and Rachel D. Russell**

Working together to keep Fox Bakery from going under, Robin and Sammy find that something more than friendship is simmering between them. But will Robin follow her old dreams back to the glamor of Paris, or will she discover how sweet it is to be loved in Deep Haven?

How Sweet It Is **by Andrea Christenson**

Dani Sullivan is determined to revive Jonathon Island's fading charm and reunite her fractured family. Her plan? Reopen the Grand Sullivan Hotel. But without the funds to restore the hotel, Dani's forced to accept help from Liam Stone—a big-city hotel developer whose sleek, modern vision is everything she's trying to avoid.

Meet Me at The Grand by Lindsay Harrel

We solve the problem of what to read next.   Available on Amazon

**WHERE EVERY STORY IS A FRIEND,
AND EVERY CHAPTER IS A NEW JOURNEY...**

Subscribe to our newsletter for a free book, the latest news, weekly giveaways, exclusive author interviews, and more!

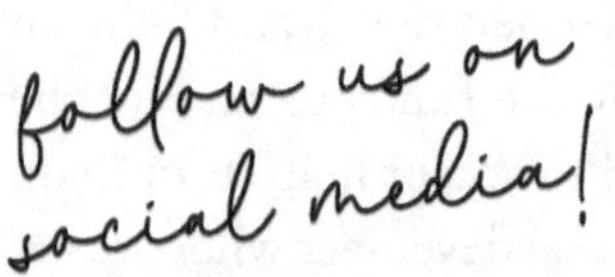

Shop paperbacks, ebooks, audiobooks, and more at
SUNRISEPUBLISHING.MYSHOPIFY.COM

www.ingramcontent.com/pod-product-compliance
Lightning Source LLC
Chambersburg PA
CBHW021043310726
48969CB00006B/1780